The YEAR I DIDN'T EAT

Samuel Pollen

 **YELLOW JACKET**

* CONTENT WARNING *

This is a book about eating disorders.

Please read and share carefully.

YELLOW JACKET

An imprint of Bonnier Publishing USA
251 Park Avenue South, New York, NY 10010
Copyright © 2019 by Samuel Pollen
All rights reserved, including the right
of reproduction in whole or in part in any form.
Yellow Jacket is an imprint of Bonnier Publishing USA, and
associated colophon is a trademark of Bonnier Publishing USA.
Interior design by Eileen Savage.
Manufactured in the United States of America
First Edition

10 9 8 7 6 5 4 3 2 1

Library of Congress Cataloging-in-Publication Data is available upon request.
ISBN 978-1-4998-0808-7
yellowjacketreads.com
bonnierpublishingusa.com

For Mum and Dad,
who put up with a lot

December 24

Dear Ana,

I'm kind of new to this, so I don't really know what to write. I guess I should start at the beginning. I'm Max. I turn fifteen next August. And right now, you're pretty much the only person I can actually talk to.

Mum and Dad say they want to help. But I know that if I told them how I was really feeling, they'd pack me straight off to the loony bin.

Same with Lindsay, my psychologist. Whenever I tell her stuff, it ends up coming back to bite me, because she makes me do stuff I really don't want to do. The other day, we were talking about exercise, and she suddenly told me I'm not allowed to run anymore. Like, at all. Who knows what rule she's going to make up next.

I have two friends at school, Ram and Stu, and I have no idea why they put up with me. I hardly ever hang out with them now. When I do, I snap at them all the time. I don't want to tell them about what's happening, because they'll either run a mile or start treating me like some special case. I'm not sure which would be worse.

Oh, and there's Robin. Don't tell him I said this, but my brother's actually pretty cool. Sometimes.

1

He doesn't treat me like a special case, like Mum and Dad and Lindsay do, even though he knows all about you. He just gets on with it. He pretends you're not even there.

I wish I could do that.

Even so, there's loads of things I can't really talk to him about. Because, uh, he's my brother. "Hey, Robin, is it true that chili speeds up your metabolism? And will any girls ever want to go near a freak like me?" There's no way I'm going to ask him any of that stuff.

I look it up online sometimes. Okay, a lot of the time. All the time. But I pretty much always regret it. There's loads of people out there talking about you, Ana. And for some reason, most of them think you're the best thing since sliced bread. Bad choice of phrase. But you know what I mean.

If we ignore the internet weirdos, there are six people in my life: Mum, Dad, Lindsay, Ram, Stu, and Robin. That's everyone I've got. Who would you talk to?

That's why you're winning. That's why I'm writing this. Because there's no one else left. There are eight billion people on this planet, and somehow, the only person I can actually talk to is you.

It's 12:32 a.m now. So, um, Happy Christmas!

Tomorrow's going to be super-hard. Like, the

2

hardest day of my life so far. Breakfast will be okay, because it'll just be me, Robin, Mum, and Dad, and they already know what I'm like. They won't mind when I say no to coffee and croissants and the juice with bits in it they've bought specially. They won't mind when I only eat one slice of toast, with the thinnest smear of low-fat spread.

Well, they will mind. But they won't say anything.

But then, everyone else will arrive. Auntie Jess, Uncle Rich, James, Louise, and Gran. And they've not seen me like this.

They don't know what I'm like now.

1

I stay under the covers as long as I can. Last year, I raced down the stairs, hunting for my stocking, yelling at Mum and Dad to get up. Like any normal kid.

There's a soft knock on my door. "WHAT?" I shout, and then immediately feel bad. Getting angry over nothing is my specialty these days.

My mum opens it a crack. "Happy Christmas, love," she says. "Do you want to come down?"

"In a bit," I tell her.

"It's eight o'clock," she says.

"I know." I point at my wrist. My watch is on the smallest hole now, and still hangs loose. It looks weird, like one of those tags they put on birds' legs to study their migration patterns. I'm proud and ashamed of it at the same time.

Mum comes into the room properly and sits down

on my desk chair. She perches on the edge of it and sits really upright, like she wants to make the smallest possible impression on the room. I hate the way my parents are around me now. Like they're on eggshells. Like they're waiting for me to snap.

"Are you feeling all right about today, sweetheart? You talked it through with Lindsay?"

It's tiring. I'm tired all the time. Some days, I go to bed at 7:00 p.m. "It'll be fine," I tell her, turning over in bed so I'm facing the wall. "I'll be fine."

"I'll drag your brother out of bed soon. Or I'll try at least. Your father's picking Gran up right before lunch. I'm not sure about your auntie. She said she'd call before they left."

"Okay," I say to the wall.

I hear her get up, but she doesn't leave the room. I can feel her eyes on me. I pull the cover right up around my neck because I hate the thought of anyone looking at my body. Even my mum.

"Listen, love," she says. "If it's too much, just tell me, and we'll sort it out. Okay?"

I don't say anything.

"Come down when you're ready. I love you."

I wait for the door to click shut before getting up.

Even though I'm not exactly looking forward to today, I'm still excited for my presents. Well, some of them. I've asked Mum and Dad for some new binoculars and a book on the birds of Borneo and the new *Zelda*. Auntie Jess has probably got me some clothes that won't fit. And Gran always gets me, Robin, and Dad the same thing: one each of those little round cheeses in a wax shell. I'll give mine to Dad this year, I guess.

But it's Robin's present I'm really excited about. Robin is super into woodworking, and he always makes my present himself. Last year, he made me the nest box that now hangs from the apple tree at the end of our garden. It's still empty, but I'm hoping a nuthatch or something will use it next spring. The year before, Robin made me a whistle that sounds just like a little owl. He told me he thought I'd have a hoot with it. My brother makes *a lot* of terrible jokes.

I look out across the garden. The squirrel's at the feeder, which is definitely supposed to be squirrel-proof, and I can hear some wood pigeons in the trees at the back. I like this time of day. It's quiet, and I haven't had to think about food yet. Usually, this is when I take Sultan, our red setter, for a walk. But not today.

I pull on some clothes and head downstairs.

"Happy Christmas, Max," my dad says, without looking up from his crossword, as I walk into the living room. He's sitting in his armchair, under a mound of newspapers. The tree blinks behind him.

"Happy Christmas," I say, heading straight past him toward the kitchen.

I help Mum lay the table. It probably sounds weird, given everything, but I like helping with meals. It makes me feel like I'm in control.

Once the plates and cutlery are sorted, I make toast. We always have Hovis Soft White Medium, so I know exactly how many calories are in a slice. I put one slice in the toaster; everyone else is having croissants. The smell of them kills me.

Robin comes down a few minutes later and punches me on the arm. "Hey, Happy Christmas," he says, tearing a strip off one of the croissants Mum's just taken out of the oven. "Mmm."

"At the table, please," Mum says, whisking the tray away.

~

Breakfast is fine, I guess. There are no major incidents.

I have my toast with a smear of spread and some water. No one tries to offer me anything else. Robin, on the other hand, demolishes a bowl of Cheerios and four croissants. We all wait politely for him to finish.

"We're going to feed you at lunchtime, too, you know," says Dad.

"Turkey takes ages," Robin explains. "And Mum's only just put it in."

"Do you not want to open your presents?" Mum asks.

"Of course," says Robin. "Presents are very important. But if I'm hungry, I won't be able to give them my full attention."

In Christmas movies, kids tear the wrapping paper off the presents, scrunch it up, and toss it on the floor. Not so in the Howarth household. Dad insists on us reusing wrapping paper. So when we open presents, we carefully peel off the tape, then fold up each sheet. Dad's like this with everything. We have a huge rain barrel in the garden and solar panels on the roof. We haven't bought a shopping bag in my lifetime. We are the only family I know that puts pieces of aluminum foil through the dishwasher.

Seriously.

My presents are exactly what I asked for: *Zelda*; *The Birds of Borneo* (14th edition); and a pair of Nikon 8x42s, to replace my Helios 10x32s, which have started to go misty. I jump up and go to the patio window to try the binoculars out. I watch the squirrel burying the nuts he's nabbed from the feeder.

"Thanks, Mum," I say, leaning in for a hug.

I feel Mum flinch. Hugs have gotten more awkward lately. My parents don't like feeling my ribs through two layers of clothes.

Robin's presents are mainly tools. I have no idea what most of them are; one looks like a mini–cheese grater. He seems happy enough.

I thought a lot about what to get my parents. I've put them through crazy amounts of stuff this year, so I wanted whatever it was to be special. But there's no gift that says, *Sorry I had a screaming fit when I found out you'd bought semi-skimmed milk by accident.* Or, if there is, I couldn't find it. In the end, I settled on pretty normal stuff: some new gardening gloves for Dad and a leather-bound copy of *Vanity Fair*, Mum's favorite book. It turns out they were good choices: After she opens hers, Mum won't stop going on about how thoughtful I am.

Robin, as usual, has outdone me. He's made a vertical planter for the front garden out of reclaimed scaffolding and bought a load of herbs to go in it, thus making Mum, Dad, Planet Earth, and himself happy in one go. God, he's annoying sometimes.

Even so, I decide to give him his present. Robin's other hobby, when he's not making things out of wood, is mountain biking. He goes out to the Forest of Dean or the Peaks most weekends. So I've got him a pair of cycling gloves.

"Thanks, bro," he says. "Although I'm disappointed you didn't get gloves for Mum, too." It hadn't occurred to me that I'd bought gloves for two-thirds of my family. He picks up *Vanity Fair.* "Maybe she can make some out of the cover?"

I punch him on the arm.

He laughs, then says, "Your turn." He reaches way under the tree and pulls out a rectangular present, eight inches long, six wide, four deep, wrapped in colorful paper. When I look closer, I realize the paper's a world map: The top side is mostly the Democratic Republic of Congo. A year or two ago, I was really, really into maps. There are still tons of them up in my bedroom.

I carefully detach the tape and peel back the paper. Inside is a smooth wooden box. At first, I think it's another nest box. But there's no hole. I turn it over. It looks exactly the same on the other side.

"Thanks, Robin," I say. "Um, what is it?"

He winks. "I'll show you after dinner." I go to ask him something else, but he raises a finger to his lips. "Trust me, little bro."

I hate it when he calls me that.

~

The first thing my auntie says to me when she walks through the door is, "You're looking skinny, Max!"

Skinny. When you're like me, you kind of want to hear that word, and you kind of don't. On the one hand, your whole life revolves around getting thinner, and while you can interpret almost any other description (*happy, tired, hungry*) as code for fat, *skinny* is pretty unambiguous. On the other, the fact that someone's noticed you're skinny means they're looking at you. At your body. Out of the eight billion bodies they could be looking at, they've chosen yours.

Which is the worst feeling.

And it's not like it means much coming from Auntie Jess, either. My auntie is the kind of person who tells forty-year-old men that they're *growing lads*. I'm not trying to be mean, but she and Uncle Rich both have the body shape of a Christmas pudding.

So I just nod.

She looks me up and down. Uncle Rich and James and Louise come through the door behind her and stand next to her, to join the judging panel. I want to die. But then Robin comes and saves me.

"And look, it's our very own Joseph of Nazareth!" Auntie squeals.

I've been standing there like a lemon for thirty seconds, but when Robin barrels into the hallway, he immediately goes in for a hug. I'm sure he used to be super-awkward, too. But to see him now, you'd never believe it. He shakes Uncle Rich's hand and then crouches down and hugs my cousins. If he wasn't wearing pajamas, you'd probably think he was a politician or something.

Auntie Jess is my mum's sister, but they couldn't be less alike. Mum is tall and thin and elegant; Auntie Jess looks like a hobbit, hairy feet included.

I'm fourteen, and I'm already taller than her. Mum has straight, dark hair, whereas Auntie Jess has these amazing mouse-brown curls that stick out in every direction. Mum's laugh is a sort of quiet wheeze. Auntie Jess sounds like a kookaburra.

One thing they have in common is that they're both competing for the title of World's Nicest Person. Right now, it's a toss-up to see who'll win. Mum's on the school management committee, and the treasurer of a charity that looks after old racehorses. Auntie Jess works at a soup kitchen every Friday night. Mum puts up with me, but Auntie Jess puts up with Uncle Rich. Competition continues.

No one likes my uncle. Like, at all. He's one of those people who, if you weren't around when they became part of your family, you can't understand how people let it happen. He always talks over Auntie Jess, even though he has absolutely nothing to say. He smells really bad. And his only hobby seems to be sitting in front of the TV in his boxers.

My cousins are pretty normal, considering. James is nine and likes dolls much more than he likes the remote control cars Uncle Rich keeps buying him. Louise just turned seven. She's totally obsessed with painting. Still lifes, animals, portraits—she'll paint just about anything, all day long. She asks us to model for her all the time, but you've got to have a lot of patience: She expects you to sit there for hours. She takes a serious, Elizabethan approach to portraiture.

Robin's now dangling Louise upside down by her ankles, while James tickles her stomach. She's screaming her head off. My auntie and uncle are arguing about something they've left in the car, or possibly at home. Sultan shuffles into the hall and barks disapprovingly. Sultan is the same age as me—fourteen—and generally doesn't get up anymore unless he's definitely going to get a walk or some food out of it. There's too much going on, and I can feel my heart racing. I slink off to my bedroom.

December 25
Dear Ana,

Lindsay gave me two bits of advice for getting
through today:
    Make a food plan, and stick to it.
    Whenever things get too much, take a break.
    Apparently, if I follow these two simple steps, I
can keep you in your box. She said the big mistake
people make is thinking they can take a day off. They
kid themselves that they can ignore you for a day
and it will all be fine. That's when things go wrong.
    (My opinion? No one like me has ever thought
this. It's family and friends who think stupid stuff
like this. I know I'm stuck with you, 24/7, whether I
like it or not.)
    Me and Lindsay wrote the plan out together, a
month ago. Then we had a special meeting with Mum
and Dad to take them through it. Mum had to leave
work early to come. That's right: I literally dragged
my mum out of work to discuss how many roast
potatoes she should serve me on Christmas Day.
    The answer is three, by the way. AKA, the bare
minimum that looks normal. Christmas dinner is
just a normal dinner. Today is just a normal day. No
big deal.

Why do I get the feeling you don't see it like that?

I'm currently following Lindsay's second piece of advice, i.e., avoiding my family. They're downstairs right now, sitting around eating a box of chocolates, because apparently on Christmas Day you have to graze continuously like a cow. A cow who likes chocolate. Did I mention we're eating Christmas dinner in an hour?

In brighter news, Robin's got me a good present. At least, I <u>think</u> it's a good present. I haven't exactly worked out what it is yet. It kind of looks like the box Uncle Rich keeps his cigars in. But that makes zero sense.

Hey, at least it's distracting me from everything else.

2

According to Lindsay, there are three stages. Stage one is, you want to eat less than your body wants you to. Stage one is simple. You start to lose weight. You feel better for a little while. Then you feel terrible.

Stage two is wanting to eat less than other people want you to. People start to notice you've lost weight and try to make you eat more. Some people spend their whole lives in stage two, fighting people's expectations. Some people die in stage two. When you're like me, there's nothing more important than what people think of you. In my opinion, this is the worst part of the whole thing. Not the disease itself, but the distance it puts between you and everyone else.

If you can make it through that, you get to stage three: the light at the end of the tunnel. Sort of. Stage three is, you're okay with eating anything, as long as you're in control. You're in recovery. The bad news is, stage three can be permanent. You never stop needing to be in control.

But there's more bad news. Because it's way, way easier to slide down than it is to climb up. It's like a game of Snakes and Ladders where there are no ladders. However high you climb, you're always one wrong move away from being right back at square one.

All it takes is a little bit of pressure. One moment that you've not prepared for. One situation that you don't know how to deal with.

Like Christmas dinner, for instance.

~

I spot it immediately: the blue tub with a spoon in it. Suddenly I'm on a roller coaster, plummeting toward the ground.

"Mum," I mumble.

Mum turns around, sees my face, connects the dots.

"It helps them crisp up, love," Mum says. "I do it every year."

This year isn't every year, I want to tell her. *How can you not see that?*

"You're not measuring," I say.

It sounds really childish. Petty. She's putting some lard on the potatoes and she's not measuring. So what? But that's the biggest thing about being the way I am: Other people don't get the rules.

"I've used less than four ounces," Mum says confidently, trying to avoid a scene. This is what we agreed on: four ounces of fat for the potatoes, total. This is the number I based my whole plan for the day on.

But she wasn't measuring. She can't know how much she's used, and it looks like *a lot*. So, I say the thing I don't want to say, the thing I know will upset her, because I can't not say it. "I'll just have two."

"Max, love," Mum says, massaging her temples.

"It's not a big deal," I say quickly. This is one of my mantras: *It's not a big deal*. I'm not sure who I'm trying to convince. "Honestly. I'll just have two."

Mum sighs and goes back to tossing the potatoes in the pan.

At one o'clock, Dad returns from fetching Gran, who promptly distributes her cheeses. Then Mum tells us to go sit at the table, because dinner's almost ready.

The dining room looks great. Mum takes entertaining pretty seriously—I think it's a sibling rivalry thing—and it's clear the moment you look at the table. We've each got a Christmas cracker, and a holly-print napkin folded into a bishop's hat. And, of course, there's the centerpiece. It's a Howarth family classic: a papier-mâché sleigh, two feet long, pulled by a grand total of thirteen reindeer. Everyone who has Christmas dinner with us has to make a reindeer. Mine, which I made when I was five, is an empty toilet-paper roll with pipe-cleaner legs.

I glance across at Mum. She seemed really stressed this morning, but now, she's beaming. Mum's one of those people who seems to live entirely for her family. I don't mean she doesn't work; Mum's a lawyer, and she does longer hours than Dad, who works for the county council. I mean, socially, Mum doesn't do much other than hang out with us. She never goes to the pub with her friends like Dad does, and she's not in any clubs or societies or anything. Which means the way things are at home pretty much determines how happy she is. Lately, she hasn't been happy at all.

We all tell her how great the table looks, then take our seats. I'm between Gran and Robin. I asked

Mum not to put me next to Auntie Jess or my cousins because I was worried they'd quiz me on why I wasn't eating more.

"Christmas crackers!" Louise squeaks.

I pull my cracker with Gran. I look at her wrist, and I can't decide whose is thinner, hers or mine. Gran lives on her own, and 90 percent of the time, she eats these microwave meals she gets delivered—nice ones, that come with little cards telling you about the farmers who grow the ingredients, or where they catch the fish, or whatever. Each card also has the number of calories in the dish printed on it. I think about this a lot: how much easier it would be if someone did all the counting for me. If I never had a choice.

Mum and Robin start bringing out food. Soon, the table is heaving with plates of stuffing, potatoes, carrots, parsnips, sprouts, gravy, bread sauce, cranberry sauce, and a huge turkey. I feel sick just looking at it all.

Mum's already made up my plate in the kitchen. She puts it down in front of me while everyone else is helping themselves. For one sweet moment, I think no one's noticed. But then Gran says, "Is that all you're having, Max?"

Shit.

I can feel my cheeks burning. I'm trying to avoid looking anyone in the eye, but it's kind of tricky when everyone around the table is looking at you. I stare at my reindeer.

Robin tuts loudly. "No wonder, the way you were going at those croissants this morning, Max."

I look up at him. He winks.

Sometimes, my brother is the coolest person ever.

"What a shame," Gran mutters. I'm pretty convinced she's about to start lecturing me about how *Your mum's gone to all this effort.* But she doesn't say anything else.

Thank God.

That's when I look down at my plate and realize Mum's given me three potatoes. My stomach lurches again, for the second time in thirty seconds. I've not even taken one bite yet, and Christmas dinner is already a disaster.

I mentally recalibrate. Today's really important to Mum. I'll eat the potato and lop some calories off tea. No big deal.

Uncle Rich is talking about his new car, a hybrid. This is the third Christmas in a row he's talked about it. The year before last, he took us through what a good idea electric cars are in general. Last year, he had a short list and was seriously considering a purchase. Now we get the full review.

Robin, who's about as interested in cars as I am in woodwork, pipes up. "You must need a really long extension cord."

My uncle laughs in that way that also gets across how little he appreciates being interrupted. Like when a Bond villain laughs at one of Bond's jokes.

"Hey, Louise," says my dad, seizing the opportunity to change the topic. "Do you remember which reindeer is yours?"

Louise nods, like this is the stupidest question in the whole world, and points at the reindeer at the front of the pack, which is covered from snout to heel in pink glitter. "He's called Mr. Sparkles," she says, shaking her head as if she bitterly regrets this decision.

"He's a pretty great reindeer," says Robin. "James, which is yours again?"

James points at another reindeer, with sequins arranged all over it like scales. It's like a disco ball in reindeer form. This is actually James's second reindeer: A couple of years ago, he decided his first one wasn't up to scratch.

"What's he called?" asks Robin.

"Eric," says James.

Robin laughs. "I guess Mr. Sparkles was taken."

I can't eat it. I'm staring at the last potato on my plate, and I can't move, and I don't know what to do. If I leave it, I know someone will say something. Gran, probably, or Auntie Jess. I've *got* to eat it. But eating one stupid potato suddenly feels like the hardest thing in the world. Like climbing K2 or running a hundred miles in one go.

Everyone's still talking—I don't think they've noticed anything's wrong—but inside my head, there's just electricity. A screaming wall of static between my brain and the rest of the world. That's something a lot of people don't get: Anorexia hurts. Only it's a kind of pain you can't really describe. Believe me, I've tried. It's like trying to explain color to someone who's never seen color before.

But it hurts. Right now, it hurts so much I want to scream.

I hear Louise saying something. It sounds far away. "Is Max okay?"

I realize I have my head in my hands. I don't look

up, but I can feel everyone looking at me.

"Max?" Mum says.

"He's not finished his dinner," says Auntie Jess. "Are you feeling all right, Max?"

"He only had a couple of potatoes!" says Gran, amazed.

"He's probably saving room for dessert," Robin says. "My brother sure loves Christmas pudding."

I know he's trying to cover for me—again—but even the idea of this horrifies me. The idea of eating *more*. And now it feels like I don't have another option. I'll have to eat Christmas pudding, and I'll have to eat loads. A bumper portion. I looked at the packet again yesterday. Our Christmas pudding is two pounds, and it's supposed to feed eight. I can tell you how many calories are in each portion, how many grams of sugar and fat. I don't try to memorize these numbers, but they stick to my brain, like gum to a pavement.

It's an effort to look up at everyone. "That's right," I say, with a weak smile. I don't know what else to say.

There are eight of us around the table. Mum hates Christmas pudding, so that's seven. And Gran eats like a bird, and Louise is only seven years old. Which means I'll get a sixth, maybe more. This meal will be the most calories I've eaten in one go in months.

You can't do it. No way. Don't be disgusting.

We had a plan. I was going to say I didn't like Christmas pudding, and Mum was going to give me a meringue nest and six strawberries. But now the plan won't work. It's not just my head that hurts anymore. It's everything. My nerves are on fire. My limbs feel like custard.

Mum and Robin are clearing away plates. Uncle Rich is talking about his car again, about how quiet the engine is. For once, I'm grateful. I want him to carry on talking about his dumb car forever.

When Mum brings out the pudding, everyone coos. I look up. Blue and pink flames lick at the sides of the dish. Dad makes some lame joke about not wasting the alcohol.

Mum glances at me when she starts serving. It's a look that says, *Please hold it together, Max.* She starts across the table, with Louise. "Ladies first," she says. Louise beams. "How much do you want, love?"

"Loads!"

Maybe it will be okay, if everyone has a big portion. But when I look at Louise's bowl, I see Mum has given her barely anything.

Mum works her way around the table. When she gets to me, she dishes out about the same amount as Louise had. *I can do this*, I tell myself.

But then Uncle Rich says, "C'mon, Rebecca. Give him a proper portion."

"I'm fine, thanks," I say quickly.

"It's Christmas Day!" says Auntie Jess. "It's only one day." She winks at me.

Mum gives me an apologetic look, then digs in again and adds a little more to my bowl. "There you go, love," she says.

It didn't seem like she added a lot, but somehow, it grows in front of me. It's a mountain. It looks like at least half of the pudding. In my head, I calculate exactly how many calories that would be.

Look at it. God, it's disgusting. How could anyone eat that much food?

I can't do it. I can't face it. I'm not strong enough.

"I'm sorry, Mum," I say, looking up at her for as long as I can bear. I can feel the tears coming. That rippling feeling behind my eyes.

"For what, love?" says Mum.

For spoiling Christmas. For not giving you even one day of rest. For everything.

I pull back my chair and run.

~

It was stupid. I know it was. It seemed like I didn't have another option, but there's always another option. I could've pretended I was ill. I mean cold-sweats-and-puking ill, not ill-in-the-head ill. Auntie Jess *asked* me if I was ill, for God's sake. Why didn't I just say yes?

I'm running toward the woods. We live on the edge of a big patch of woodland called Shepples Common. I go there a lot, more since I've been ill. It's where I run, or used to run. Where I walk Sultan and watch birds.

My hiding place.

Once I hit the trees, I slow down and catch my breath. Now I *actually* feel ill. I guess running for ten minutes right after you've eaten a roast dinner isn't the smartest idea.

You could make yourself sick.

The thought leaps into my head from nowhere. As Lindsay's very fond of telling me, anorexia is different for everyone. Technically, there are like five different types of eating disorders, and they all have different symptoms. Anorexics starve themselves; bulimics binge and make themselves sick, or take laxatives to get the food out of their body. And so on. But the boundaries are pretty fluid. For example, lots of anorexics make themselves sick occasionally.

I've never done it, though. I'm too scared. I can't stop picturing myself ripping my throat open or choking to death on my own hand or something else equally horrible. I'm not much of a binger, either. I've never gobbled a whole pack of doughnuts or a family-size pizza. The furthest I'll go is licking the knife after I've cut something, to get a few extra crumbs, and then hating myself for it. I'm the most controlling, the most neurotic sort of anorexic: the restrictor. Everything is about numbers, rules, routines. It's not the kind of eating disorder you read about in the papers. It's boring. Anorexia, slow and steady.

And then, before I know it, before I can think myself out of it, I'm crouched down next to a tree, with my fingers down my throat. If I'm going to be like this, I want to do it right. I want to be the textbook anorexic. The one everyone wants me to be.

I gag and immediately remove my fingers. I'm too scared. I cough, spit, slump down on the mud and leaf mulch. My throat stings, and I feel a hot lump forming, like I'm about to cry.

You can't even do anorexia right. What kind of anorexic can't make themselves sick?

I call her Ana. Her, it: the monster inside me. The voice inside my head.

Imaginative name, right?

It doesn't actually feel like someone else. It feels like me. They're my thoughts, my feelings. But Lindsay says it's good to *externalize the disease*. So, I'm doing my best. That's why I write my diary and address it to her: to remind myself that my disease isn't me. I haven't told Lindsay about that, though. It's too embarrassing. Like the kind of thing a kid would do.

At the moment, she's in my head 24/7. When I stand in a mirror and turn to my side, she tells me,

Your belly sticks out.

When I'm about to eat a cereal bar, she says,

Better check the calories.

even though I've already checked them a hundred times. Even though I could recite them in my sleep.

She asks questions all the time, too.

Do you really need to eat that?

Is Robin avoiding you?

Is that girl across the street staring at you?

I try to ignore her. But she never shuts up for long.

And right now, she's really mad at me.

I start to cry.

Don't be so pathetic. You're acting like a whiny little girl.

"Max? Are you there?"

Robin. Over the years, my brother has spent as much time in these woods as I have. I haven't exactly chosen the greatest hiding place. I look around. This bit of the woods is mostly birch: light and airy. Spread out. Anorexics are good at avoiding people—but right now, I've got nowhere to hide.

I stand up and walk toward my brother. Did he hear me retching? Will he say anything if he did?

"Hey," I say.

"Hey. You all right?"

I wipe my mouth with my sleeve. "I'm fine."

"You scared us, you know."

"I'm sorry."

Robin shrugs, like he doesn't know whether to accept my apology or not. "At least you gave me an excuse not to listen to Uncle Rich anymore." He grins. "Come on, I've got something to show you."

I figured Robin would be on strict orders to bring me straight home, but if he is, he ignores them. We walk deeper into the Common, then loop back around toward home. We cross the peat bogs and end up at Deanwater: a big, peanut-shaped artificial lake. As usual, it's teeming with ducks, geese, coots, and moorhens. At the narrowest part, a heron stands on a stump and surveys his terrain. I wish I had my new binoculars with me.

We sit down on a bench and look out across the water. There's a sour taste in my mouth: I guess a bit of bile came up when I was retching. I swallow. My throat feels raw.

Robin reaches into his pocket and pulls out a pack of chewing gum, offers it to me. "It'll take the taste away."

A bolt of ice shoots down my spine. So he did hear me.

"No thanks," I mumble.

"It's sugar-free," Robin says.

"I know," I say. "It's not that." I look down, embarrassed. We both know it is not that. I'm suspicious of anything that has flavor—coffee, gum, Diet Coke—even when I know, rationally, there are no calories in it.

"Suit yourself. Hey," he says. He reaches into his coat again and pulls out my wooden box. "Any guesses yet?" he says.

"Why did you . . . ," I begin, but I let myself trail off. You learn not to ask why when you're talking to Robin. I still have no idea what the box is, so I just shake my head.

"Feel under the bench," he says. I must look confused, because he adds, "Trust me." That seems to be Robin's catchphrase today.

I don't really want to feel under the bench, because if school's anything to go by, it'll be covered in old gum, or worse. But reluctantly, I do as my brother says. I start in the middle, sliding my hands toward my end. It feels like the underside of a bench: wooden slats covered in a powdery layer of lichen and mold. Cold, wet metal. On the plus side, there's no chewing gum.

Then, right before I get to the end, there's a bump: Something or other juts out below the bench. I'm so surprised, I actually jump.

Robin smiles, like he was waiting for this reaction. "Take a look," he says.

I have to pretty much lie on the ground to see under the bench. In a puddle. I'm plotting ways to pay Robin back when I realize what I'm looking at: a box the same shape as mine, only a bit smaller, and made out of black plastic.

"Robin," I say. "Did you steal my present from a park bench?"

He laughs. "Pass it over here, then," he says.

I pull the box off the bench. It comes away more easily than I thought it would. I turn it over and look at the four little magnets in the corners. "What is it?" I say, getting up and passing the box to Robin.

He looks at me, grinning like an idiot. "That's what I want you to tell me."

December 27

Dear Ana,

congratulations, you ruined Christmas.

Okay, so I was expecting you to screw it up one
way or another. But you really outdid yourself. Now
Auntie Jess and Uncle Rich and Gran and James and
Louise are all in on the secret: Max is a psycho.
And you know what the worst part is? They were
all super-nice about it afterward. I guess Mum
must have said something. Come to think of it, she
definitely said something, because Auntie Jess didn't
offer me any chocolates all afternoon, which has
literally never happened before.

It's a week until school starts again, and at this
point, I'm almost looking forward to it. If Ram
and Stu actually still want to talk to me, maybe
it won't be so bad. At home, you kind of hang over
everything. Don't let this go to your head Ana, but
. . . even when we're not talking about you, we're
thinking about you. Mum and Dad tiptoe around
me, like at any moment, I'm going to tear them a
new one.

But at school, it's totally different. Don't get
me wrong: I'm still pretty sure that, if you asked
anyone, they'd confirm that I was a 100 percent

certified freak. But most of the time, people don't even notice me. I'm invisible—like the world's worst superhero. Max, The Disappearing Man.

Hmm. I guess that works in more ways than one.

3

"*So, did you* have a good Christmas?"

I see Lindsay once a fortnight, at the hospital. There's a separate building for outpatient appointments, and the room we meet in feels more like my mum's office than a doctor's surgery. I guess that's deliberate. Some anorexics are weirdly proud of all the times they've been hospitalized, all the drugs they've been given, all the psychologists they've seen. In my experience, eating disorder forums are mostly full of people boasting about how ill they are. So yeah: sending us to the most boring, non-medical office building in the world makes total sense.

I'm sitting in a plastic chair that was probably made for a ten-year-old. I'm sitting very upright, with my hands clasped together in my lap. I keep swallowing, because I don't know what to say. The roof is made of those gray-white tiles you get in offices, to hide all the cables. I count in one direction, then another, and multiply to get a total.

Anorexia is definitely good for your mental math.

We sit in silence for what feels like ages. It's probably like a minute. My sense of time is completely screwed.

"Max?" Lindsay says eventually.

I look at her. I'm not trying to be rude, but what does she want from me? *It was horrible. I ruined Christmas for my whole family.*

"It was fine," I say.

"Any good presents?"

For a moment, I consider telling her about Robin's present. But I don't know what I would say. I still haven't figured out what it is myself yet. "I got some new binoculars," I tell her.

"Oh, brilliant!" She beams at me, like me getting a new pair of binoculars has made her week. I can't help but smile. I think 75 percent of Lindsay's treatment technique is just to smile at people until they feel better. She kind of reminds me of Auntie Jess. "And how was the day itself?"

I gulp. "It was fine," I say again.

"Are you sure?"

"It was . . ." I breathe in, out, close my eyes. I don't really want to talk about it, but it's not like I have anything else to bring up. How do you change the topic when your whole life revolves around one thing? "Dinner didn't go as planned," I say. I pull my feet up onto the chair and hug my knees. I feel like a four-year-old.

"I'm sorry to hear that, Max. Tell me what happened."

So I do. I figure I might as well do something to pass the time. I tell her about the plan, and the roast potato, and the Christmas pudding. I tell her how I stormed off. I leave out the part about trying to make myself sick.

Lindsay listens to me, making notes as I talk. She doesn't say anything until at least thirty seconds after I've finished speaking. I think this is something they teach you to do when you train to be a psychologist: wait until the tap's run completely dry.

Eventually, she says that the plan was *very smart*, and that there will *always be setbacks*. Which is exactly what I expected her to say. And it's nice. Having a cheerleader is nice. But I don't see how it helps. I feel better—but I know that it'll only last about thirty seconds.

She's getting fatter, I swear. Are you really going to take advice from someone that weak?

That's another thing about Ana. She doesn't only try to bring you down: She has a pop at everyone around you, too. And you end up feeling bad, because her thoughts are your thoughts. You can't help it. It's all happening inside your head.

Shut up, Ana.

I only started seeing Lindsay in October. She hasn't given me a diet plan or anything yet. Apparently, she wants to observe me for a while first, to figure out what will work best.

The only thing that's changed so far is the running. As in, me not being allowed to. According to Lindsay, this isn't about calories—or at least, it isn't *just* about calories. My bones are now so weak they might break, plus there's a chance I'll have a seizure or a heart attack. It's amazing how many different ways Ana tries to kill you at once.

We talk some more about how things are at home,

and at school, though because of the Christmas holidays, I've barely been to school since my last appointment.

"You've been keeping your food diary up to date?" Lindsay asks me.

"Yes," I reply.

As part of my treatment, Lindsay's asked me to keep a journal of everything I eat. This is pretty easy, because I was already keeping one for myself. When I gave her my first two weeks' records, with all of the calories totals already added up, she was delighted.

She scans my food journal, nodding approvingly, as if it's healthy for a fourteen-year-old boy to eat this little . . .

"Okay," she says. "For the next two weeks, I'd like you to eat one Mars bar a day, on top of your normal meals. Or a Snickers or something if you prefer. As long as it's this size." She reaches into her desk drawer and pulls out a Mars bar. She obviously sees my look of terror because she adds, "Just give it a try."

She hands it to me. I take it from her like it's a nuclear bomb.

I can't believe she said it like that, as though asking

me to eat a whole extra chocolate bar every single day is nothing.

As soon as I leave the outpatient building, I take the Mars bar out of my pocket and look at the nutritional information. I stare at it for a moment, amazed there can be so many calories in something so small. It's like it's a neutron star, or a black hole. A calorie TARDIS.

I find today's page in my journal, and write in:

2:00 p.m. Mars bar x 1

I throw the Mars bar in the bin. I hate wasting food, but I don't have another option. Then I run toward the parking lot to meet Dad.

January 1

Dear Ana,

I finally figured out what it is.

Okay, I didn't. Robin told me. After I'd made about a million stupid guesses—some kind of beehive, a binocular box, a USB hard drive—Robin told me that my present is called a geocache. Geo as in "earth," cache as in "place where you hide stuff." He showed me how the lid slides off, and how there's a logbook and pen inside. Most people use an app to find them, but you can use any kind of GPS.

Apparently, there are thousands of geocaches, all over the world, in parks and city centers and world Heritage sites. Anyone can start one. Some of them are tiny, as small as a penny. Some of them are ten times the size of mine.

When you look up a cache online, there are GPS coordinates, and a name, and some kind of riddle that hints at its exact location. Robin showed me the listing for the one under the bench. The cache was called Lake View. The description was, "This bench has a secret!" He said that it was a pretty dumb one.

We left a message in the logbook together: "TFTC. Merry Christmas!" TFTC means Thanks for the cache. It's, like, the default thing to write in people's logbooks, apparently. That was yesterday. Today, I took Sultan out for a walk to find one of the other two caches that are on the Common. This one is by the entrance to the golf course, and the clue is "Score a birdie." It took me a while to find it: an empty nest box on the side of the clubhouse with a little film pod tucked inside. I made sure no one was looking, and took out the film pod. Inside was a pencil stub and a neat little scroll of paper. I unrolled the paper. There were dozens of messages, dating back to 2016. I found the last one—from four days ago—and wrote, "01/01/18 TFTC. Happy New Year! Canorus04," below it. Canorus04 is my username. Canorus is the species name of the common cuckoo, which is my favorite bird.

According to Robin, part of the fun of geocaching is that you have no idea who looks after each one, or who else is searching for them. He said, "You feel like a spy." So now, Ana, I'm not just invisible: I'm an invisible spy. If I could get rid of you, I could actually have some fun with all these superpowers.

4

It's the first day back at school, and I'm standing in the playground, trying to explain to Ram why I don't want to trade half of his cheese sandwich for half of my ham sandwich.

"But it's *ham*," he pleads.

Ram is actually called Ehtiram, but no one calls him that except his mum. His parents are divorced, and he lives with his mum, who doesn't let him eat pork. But his dad gives him bacon for breakfast every other weekend. The rest of the time, he's on the look-out for extra pork products to supplement his diet. I used to be his go-to.

"Sorry," I tell him. And I am sorry. I don't want to be a weirdo. I want to switch sandwiches with my best friend, if that's what he's into. I don't want it to be a big deal.

"It's the same size," Ram says. Then he adds, "You stingy bastard."

Stuart, our other best friend, snorts.

"I know," I say to Ram.

"Fine," he says, in a voice that makes it seem very not-fine. He tears the corner off one half-sandwich. "I'll give you extra."

"It's not about that . . . ," I start to say.

"Do you want me to starve? Is that it?" asks Ram.

I flinch at that word: *starve.*

"No, Ram, I don't want you to starve," I tell him.

"She's looking at us," Stu says. We both give him funny looks, like, *What are you on about?* He nods beyond us. We turn and look.

It's the new girl, the one who just joined this term. Evie or Evvy or something like that. People hardly ever join our school partway through the year. It only happens when something big has happened—like with Shinji, who came last spring after the earthquake in Kobe. I wonder what happened to Evie. Or Evvy.

She's standing across the yard, staring at us, like she doesn't give two hoots if we notice. I guess she doesn't really have anyone to hang out with yet. But even so: why would anyone pick *us*?

"What was her name again?" I ask.

"Elvis," says Stu confidently. "I think."

"Ignore her," says Ram, with a wave of his hand, like he's swatting away a fly. He's given up on bartering with me and is now munching his cheese sandwich. He doesn't look like he's enjoying it very much. "She's weird. Hey, have you guys got to the bit where—"

The second he starts speaking, Stu raises a hand to silence him. "No spoilers. My nan was at our house all Christmas, so I've barely had any time to play yet."

Zelda. We all got it for Christmas. Every time we get a new game, Ram is desperate to talk about it, and Stu is desperate not to.

"You're no fun," Ram mutters. He turns to me, catches me looking at Evie/Evvy/Elvis, and sighs. "Oh, for God's sake. See you later, losers." He slings his rucksack onto his shoulder and stomps off toward the music building.

~

After lunch it's PE, aka the worst two hours of my week, unless we're doing cross-country, which is the only sport I'm not terrible at. (Cross-country is technically running, but Lindsay doesn't mind me doing it, as long as I'm with other people who'll take me to the hospital if I trip over and break a leg or whatever.) Unfortunately, we only do cross-country when the fields are too wet to use, and today, it's clear and dry. And bloody freezing.

I hate getting changed. Our changing room is basically a corridor with a bench on either side. People run up and down the middle, flicking one another with towels, and shouting, *Get your willy out!* repeatedly, and sometimes going up behind people and pulling their boxers down. It's also freezing, even when it's not that cold outside. One of the side effects of being anorexic is that you're cold *all the time.* Stripping down to your boxers in an unheated, concrete-floored PE building in January doesn't help with that particular problem.

Stu's in the same class as me. While I try to put my PE kit on under my clothes, he tells me about his Christmas.

"It was rubbish. My nan wanted to play Scrabble in the morning, and then we went for a walk. I didn't get to open my presents till three p.m."

"What did you get?" I ask, sliding my jersey under my shirt.

"A Raspberry Pi. *Zelda. FIFA.* That new Stephen King book I wanted." He sits down on the bench and shrugs philosophically. He's not even started getting changed. "Not a bad haul."

Stu's a certified geek but gets a pass because he also happens to be really good at football. He's a striker for the school and the county. Last year, he had a Discworld-themed birthday party, and pretty much the whole football team dressed up as wizards and elves. It was hilarious.

It gets darker all of a sudden, and we hear a booming voice from the end of the corridor: "Mr. Swindells, will you be joining us on the field today?" I look up. Mr. Stott is silhouetted in the doorway, blotting out the sun like a supervillain.

Mr. Stott is like a cross between a beer barrel and a military general. He cares about two things—football and rugby—and anyone who doesn't share at least one of these interests is in big trouble.

Luckily, Stu does. "Yes, sir," he mumbles meekly, pulling his shirt and sweater off in one go.

"Anyone who isn't outside in two minutes gets detention," Mr. Stott says. He turns and marches out. Step, two, three, four.

I've got my jersey on. All I need to do now is take off my trousers and put on my shorts. I take a deep breath, but before I can start, Darren taps me on the shoulder.

"Gonna show us your dick, Max?" he asks, laughing as if this were the funniest thing anyone has ever said in the history of humanity. Darren bugs me and not because he's a bully. He's thin. Like, crazy thin. He's one of those kids who eats pies continuously and somehow still looks like a rake. He's also the only person in my year faster than me at cross-country.

When he asks if I'm going to show him my dick, I'm supposed to turn around, so someone— probably—can come up behind me and pull my boxers down. Instead, I carefully sit down on the bench before replying. "I'm all right, Darren," I say. "Cheers, though."

"Knob," Darren says, with an irritated sniff. He stomps off.

When most of the group have gone outside, I

whip my trousers off and put my shorts on as fast as I can. Okay, so no one wants their whole class to see their junk, I don't want it on a whole different level. Anorexia slows down puberty. Your pubic hair stops growing, and everything sort of . . . pauses. I don't know if it'll happen to me, but I'm scared. I stand in the mirror sometimes and look at my dick and balls. They look small. But everyone thinks that, right? I don't exactly have anything to compare them with.

My dick is probably the only bit of my anatomy that I want to be bigger.

Stu and I are the last ones to leave the changing rooms. He elbows me as we walk outside. "Nicely played with Darren, mate."

I grin. "Thanks."

We're playing rugby today. I mean, everyone else is. As well as running, Lindsay has decided contact sports are probably a bad idea for someone whose bones are like twigs. So my parents wrote to the school, asking if I could be excused from tackling—which, if you've never played rugby, is kind of a major part of the game. I'm allowed to do the drills and warm-ups, but that's it. It's like they're trying to make me look like the biggest freak possible.

This happened right before Christmas. Today's the first time it's come up. So far, Mr. Stott hasn't said anything. Maybe no one told him, or maybe he forgot. I'm certainly not going to mention it. *Oh, by the way, Mr. Stott, not sure if anyone told you, but due to my being a massive freak, I can't play rugby anymore. Sorry. Here, look. I've got a note.*

On balance, I'd rather risk breaking all my bones.

We start with a warm-up jog, which is fine. Then we do a passing drill. Everyone runs down the field in a line, passing the ball and then running around to the other side. I'm so nervous, I drop the ball literally every time someone passes it to me. On my last go, I catch it, but then forget to pass it on, and run around the back with the ball in hand. The other boys in my group are almost in tears. "Nice job, idiot," Shinji says when we reach the end of the field.

"Sorry," I mumble.

"You're apologizing for me insulting you?" he says.

I don't say anything.

Shinji spits on the ground. "Pathetic."

Shinji is Darren's best friend. He's pretty much the opposite of Darren physically: He's sort of like a younger, more muscular version of Mr. Stott. His legs are the size of tree trunks. In Stu's opinion, Shinji's not actually any good at rugby, but he's so strong he makes the first team anyway.

After the drill, Mr. Stott calls us over to work out teams for the game. One thing I like about him is that he doesn't let people pick their own teams. Instead, he divides everyone up himself, so people like me don't have to go through the humiliation of being picked last, week after week.

We head slowly toward him, chatting and joking and messing around, until he booms, "Hurry up!" at which point we run. When we arrive, he looks at us and shakes his head. "That took far too long. Everyone sprint to the posts and back. Except you, Mr. Howarth."

I gulp.

The rest of my class run off down the rest of the field while I shuffle toward Mr. Stott like a shy zombie. I can already feel my hands getting clammy.

He looks me up and down. "No contact, is that right?"

I look down at the grass. "Yes, sir."

I'm expecting him to call me a sissy or something.

"He did?"

"Yeah. He made it sound like you're running for the county or something."

I shrug. "Who can say?"

Maybe Mr. Stott isn't so bad after all.

January 7

Dear Ana,

I have about a million questions floating around in my head. But the biggest one is, why?

Why me? Why now? Why not last year or next year?

If you break your leg, it's because you fell off your bike. If you get pneumonia, it's because you inhaled some pneumococcal bacteria. But figuring out why you decided to climb into my head isn't so easy.

Maybe it doesn't matter. You're here. It's happened. Some angry god grabbed a bolt of lightning and tossed it to earth, and it happened to hit me.

But that can't be right, can it? There's got to be a reason. And I really, really, really want to know what it is.

Near our house there's this big National Trust property called Ashford Park. We used to go every year or two when me and Robin were younger. In front of the main house, there's this giant hedge maze, which is pretty much the main reason anyone goes. The first time I went in on my own—I must have been, like, seven—it took me as long to get back out as it did to get to the center, because I didn't memorize the route as I went. But the next year, I'd figured out it was probably a good idea to think about what I was doing, so I could retrace my steps.

If you know how you got somewhere, you know how to get out, right? Why should anorexia be any different?

The only problem? I have NO IDEA how I got here. I don't have a single clue how you managed to climb into my head. Which means I'm totally lost.

5

Mum comes home super-pissed. *She's spitting feathers again* is how Dad puts it, once Mum's out of earshot. Apparently, the other partners have scheduled a get-together for the night of the school management committee meeting without telling her. This kind of stuff happens a lot. Mum's the only female partner at her firm, and a lot of them like to make her life difficult. Dad pours her a very large glass of wine.

Dad's cooking dinner tonight. During the week, he does most of the cooking because he always gets home hours before Mum does. We're having chicken Kiev, boiled potatoes—which I'll skip—and peas. It may not sound like an anorexic's ideal meal, but from a counting perspective, it's easy.

I love things that come in a box with calorie numbers on the back.

In the meantime, I do my chemistry homework. And because the universe hates me, it's all about calories. *A calorie (symbol: cal) is the energy required to raise the temperature of 1 g of water by 1°C at a pressure of 1 atmosphere,* my textbook tells me. *A kilocalorie (symbol: kcal or Cal), also known as a food calorie, is the energy required to raise the temperature of 1kg of water by 1°C at a pressure of 1 atmosphere. When people talk about the number of "calories" in food, they're almost always talking about kilocalories.*

I already know this bit. When I first learned what a (food) calorie was, it blew my mind. Anything that can be divided by a thousand must be pretty big, right? I started getting annoyed by the missing *kilo* whenever people talked about calories on TV. Like they were lying to me, trying to make me fat.

But there's something else that's bugging me. I go into the kitchen to find Dad.

"How was your day?" Dad says, before I can say anything. He's standing over the stove, fiddling with the heat on the potatoes.

"Okay."

He turns around and looks hard at me. My parents give me a lot of these kinds of looks now. I'm-asking-a-serious-question-and-I-want-you-to-take-it-seriously looks. "PE is going okay?"

"Yeah," I say. I don't say, *PE is now the best part of my week because I get to go running on my own.*

"Good. Do you want to weigh the peas?"

"It's okay," I say. "I'll weigh mine after they're cooked."

"Fair enough," he says.

"Dad, are the—"

"Oh, bugger," Dad says, swiveling back to the stove. The potatoes are boiling over, there's a shallow pool of starchy water around the burners. Dad picks up the pan, pours a little water out in the sink, and turns the heat down. "That's better," he says. "Don't cry over spilt milk and all that. You got homework to do?"

"Yep," I say. "I've got a question."

My dad never gets upset about anything. (Well except, like, recycling.) I'd say he was pretty relaxed about the potatoes, but he would've been the same even if the water had spilled over his shoes, too. Or if I told him I wasn't doing homework anymore and was giving up school to join the circus.

"Shoot," he says, pointing at me with what can only be described as finger guns.

I cringe. "Um, *anyway* . . . Calories measure the energy it takes to heat up water, right?"

"So I'm told," he says, going over to the freezer to look for peas. "Though before we go any further, I'd like to point out that I last studied chemistry when John Major was prime minister."

"Yeah. But you know everything," I tell him. "Does that mean, if you heat up a meal, it's more calorific?"

Dad opens the freezer, fishes around for the peas. He pulls them out, turns to me, and frowns. "Humans can't absorb heat energy, Max."

"No, but we're endotherms, right? We use energy heating up our bodies."

He raises one eyebrow. "I suppose that's true."

"So if I eat something hot, I have to use less energy keeping myself warm."

"Maybe, but it's a tiny amount of energy."

"Is it?"

"Well, let's see." One of the things I like about my dad is that he doesn't treat me like a kid. We can have normal, adult conversations. He puts the peas down on the side and picks up his mug. "Say you have a cup of tea, two hundred fifty milliliters, give or take. It's, what, eighty degrees Celsius when you drink it? That's sixty above room temperature. So you've added sixty times two hundred fifty calories. What does that work out as?"

I think for a minute. "Fifteen thousand."

"And that's calories. So fifteen kilocalories."

At least Dad appreciates the difference. "Yes," I say.

"That's assuming you drink it all in one go, when it's at eighty degrees. I reckon ten calories is probably more realistic."

"Probably," I agree.

"That's less than one percent of your daily calories. And the body generates lots of excess heat anyway. I doubt it makes any measurable difference at all, come to think of it."

"Okay."

Dad puts a hand on my shoulder. The hand of doubt. "Max, this isn't going to become a thing, is it?"

I flinch slightly. I try not to, but I can't help it. "No," I tell him.

He nods slowly. "Glad to hear it." He doesn't exactly look convinced.

I can't stop thinking about it. Not the tea bit, because I don't really drink tea anyway. Not even the hot food bit, because I figure, like Dad says, unless you're outside on a freezing day, it probably doesn't make much difference. But say you drank a liter of ice-cold water when you were already cold. Your body would have to work extra hard to heat you back up, wouldn't it? You could cheat yourself into burning calories faster.

Robin steps through the door just as Dad is dishing out. Good timing. As soon as we sit down, he starts telling us about his day. Robin's now eight months into his apprenticeship, and he's starting to learn what he calls the *good stuff*. Today, apparently, was all about the different types of dovetail joints.

"I'm not sure I knew there were different types of dovetail joints," says Dad.

I'm thinking, *I'm not sure I care.*

"Oh yeah," says Robin, "There are loads." He leaps up, goes over to the sideboard, and picks up a pencil and paper. "You've got your basic dovetail, like this"— he starts sketching—"which you'd use for an ordinary drawer. But if you don't want people to see the end grain, you can do this . . ."

I look across at Mum. She seems really quiet tonight. Like, more so than normal. Maybe she's still cross about the meeting, but she normally gets over stuff like that pretty quickly. After all, she's kind of used to it. This feels different. Right now, she's staring into space, and occasionally eating a forkful of something. Okay, so I'm not exactly in a position to criticize other people's eating habits. But it's like she doesn't even care. I can't even get my head around anyone not caring about the food in front of them.

After sketching five different types of dovetail joints, Robin puts down his pencil, satisfied, and resumes shoveling food into his mouth. "How was your day, anyway?" he says to Dad, through a mouthful of boiled potatoes.

"I was scouting sites for the new recycling center," Dad says. "It was a barrel of laughs, as always."

Dad has been scouting sites for the new recycling center for three years. About a year ago, he thought he'd found the perfect place, out near the bypass. But the rich families who live in Woodgrove Park—half a mile away—kicked up a fuss.

"That other site was perfect," says Robin. "Great access, isolated, no environmental issues. Those posh idiots."

"Robin," Dad says in a warning tone. "I wouldn't want it near my house, either. It's easy to criticize."

As well as never ever getting cross, Dad is annoyingly reasonable. In my experience, most people are hypocrites about at least one thing. For example, Robin lectures us all about forest conservation, but also eats beef, which is the biggest cause of deforestation worldwide. Stu freaks out about spoilers but will happily tell us the plot of a book he's read without asking.

But Dad isn't like that. Even if you do catch him doing something hypocritical, he won't get defensive about it. He'll say, "Good point," and change his behavior. Once, when I was eleven and a total smartass, I told him that it wasn't fair for him to get at us for leaving lights on as he always leaves his phone charger plugged in. He's turned it off at the wall ever since.

You may think this is a good quality in a dad, but I disagree. It's like living with a monk or the pope or Barack Obama. There's nothing you can really complain about, and you just end up feeling guilty the whole time.

"Max, have you sorted your you-know-what yet?" Robin asks me.

I shake my head. "No. But I've decided where it's going. I'm going to put it up on Saturday."

"What's all this?" Dad cocks an eyebrow.

"Nothing you need to worry about," says Robin.

"Fair enough," Dad says.

See? He takes whatever you say at face value. I'm sure parents aren't supposed to be like that.

"Right, who wants dessert?"

Robin nods. I shake my head. And Mum doesn't even respond.

January 10
Dear Ana,

According to, like, every single website I've looked
at, I shouldn't even call myself an "anorexic."
Instead, I'm supposed to say that I'm a "person with
anorexia," because I'm still a person. Having you
inside my head doesn't stop me from being me.

I guess I agree with that—but the whole argument
seems kind of dumb to me. If I call Dad a county
council worker, I'm not saying he's not also my dad
and a man and a member of Bolford Choir. My opinion
is, right now, I kind of have bigger fish to fry. So
to speak.

Plus, even if I wanted to stop thinking about
myself as an anorexic, I'm not sure you'd let me,
would you?

"No one wants to hang out with an anorexic."

"Proper anorexics can make themselves sick, you
know."

"Who cares what some sad little anorexic thinks?"

When I've got you in my ear 24/7 saying stuff like
that, I don't exactly have much choice.

I finally chose a spot for my cache. I'm actually
pretty proud of it. According to Robin, a good cache
is one that's "hidden in plain sight." It's not much

fun if your cache is in some random place, like in one of a hundred identical fence posts, or if people have to wade through a tunnel to get to it.

So, want to guess where I'm putting mine?

There's this massive oak tree on the west side of the Common. It's amazing. Dad told me once that he reckons it's over 250 years old. It's got these huge branches that spread out in every direction, kind of like if you peel string cheese right down to the bottom. Some of them are only a few inches off the ground, which means it's pretty awesome for climbing, and I reckon it would be a pretty awesome place to hide a cache, too. If you climb up three branches, there's this little hollow in the trunk from where they cut off a branch or something and you can't see it from the ground.

Perfect, right?

I tried to put it there today, but it didn't go well. I had Sultan with me, and when you have Sultan with you, people always want to stop and talk. This woman who works with Dad basically gave my goofy mutt a full body massage while I just stood there, answering her dumb questions.

"How's school?"

"It's fine."

"Oh, you like that, don't you, Sultan? Yes, you do!"

By the time she finished, it was too dark to go into the woods.

But it's okay: I can do it tomorrow instead. It turns out, when you don't hang out with anyone—or, you know, eat—you end up with a lot of spare time.

6

I'm bored out of my mind.

Generally, I really like biology, even if the human bits make me, um, faint. Sometimes. Occasionally. (Apparently, being an anorexic isn't enough: Max Howarth has a whole separate, extra way to make himself a social outcast. Whenever someone starts talking about anatomy or disease or bodily functions, all my blood goes to my feet, and I collapse. Trust me, it makes me seem *super*-cool.) But I like *nonhuman* biology. I want to do a zoology degree, then become an ornithologist.

I just have to, you know, make sure I survive that long.

Today is a review class, which is easily the most annoying thing ever. For example, Mr. Edwards, our teacher, has just told Gopal that his answer to a question about enzymes wasn't right, because he said they get *deformed* at high temperatures, not *denatured*. His exact words were, "That's correct, but you need to say it differently to get the marks."

That's why I'm bored out of my mind.

I'm doodling in my notebook, but I don't even realize I'm doodling until Ram leans over and says, "Hey, that's pretty good."

I instinctively cover the page, like he caught me looking at porn or something, and scowl at Ram. He looks surprised, which I guess isn't surprising. It's not like he was actually doing anything unreasonable. My face drops, and my cheeks start to burn.

I move my hand to inspect my drawing. It's the oak tree on the Common. Swirls of ballpoint twist out from the trunk. Now that I look at it, it's kind of creepy, like a tree in a horror movie.

I want to say sorry to Ram but I don't know how, so I carry on doodling. I start filling in the hollow halfway up the trunk. I scribble over and over, until the page is saturated with ink and starts to tear. It's kind of therapeutic.

I still haven't come up with a good clue, and it's starting to bug me.

Or maybe he'll just plain refuse my parent's request and give me a speech about how I've got to toughen up.

But instead, he puts a hand on my shoulder. "Everything all right?"

"Uh . . . yes, sir. Thank you."

"You happy to run while we play? You'll freeze to death otherwise."

I look at him in disbelief. This is a bit like someone asking a pig whether, instead of being made into sausages, they'd like to play in mud for a while. "Yes, sir."

"Off you go, then. Stick to the normal cross-country route."

I guess Mr. Stott didn't get the memo about me running on my own. I'm not going to correct him.

I spend the rest of the lesson running. I do three loops of the whole school: along the little stream at the far edge of the fields, around the music building, through the woods where we do pond dipping for biology sometimes. It's the best PE lesson I've had in months.

Stu comes over to me as we go back inside. "What was that all about? Stott told us you're on some special training program."

"Sorry," Ram murmurs.

Wait a second. *He's* apologizing to *me* because I lost my temper with him over nothing? It makes me feel about ten times worse than I already did.

Mr. Edwards is talking about evolution now. "Lamarck's theory was popular for a long time," he says. "What's the key problem with his version of evolution?"

I've got some salt-and-vinegar chips in my bag that I was supposed to have for lunch. I was actually going to eat them today. Maybe. But I decide I should give them to Ram to say sorry. I pull them out, keeping them hidden under the bench so Mr. Edwards can't see. "Here," I whisper. "Present."

Ram looks at me like I'm offering him a Porsche. He stares at my hand.

"Take them," I hiss. "Before . . ." I nod toward Mr. Edwards.

"Are you sure?" Ram says.

"Max, is everything okay over there?"

I freeze, like a chicken who's been spotted by a T. rex. Mr. Edwards sidles toward us.

"Everything's fine, sir," I mumble.

"Good, good. I'd ask you to share those around,

but we all know it's dangerous to eat in the laboratory."

"Yes, sir," I say. I'm thinking, *He must have bat ears.* (Fun fact: Bats can change the shape of their ears to hear better. Sort of like having a built-in ear trumpet.)

"So instead, I'll look after them until the end of class," Mr. Edwards continues. He holds out his hand. I give him the chips. "Thank you. Now, can you explain to everyone how a kidney nephron works?"

I swallow. "Um . . . the blood gets pumped into the Bowman's capsule, which forces everything out of it."

"Good." Mr. Edwards nods, in that way teachers do when they're slightly annoyed that you've given them the right answer, because they know you weren't listening properly. "Then what?"

"Then the liquid travels along the convoluted tubule. And anything we need is absorbed back into the blood at the loop of Henle."

Ram gives me a look, like, *How do you know all this stuff?* Trust an anorexic to know everything there is to know about the human body. Even if that knowledge makes him faint sometimes. Right now, for instance, I'm pretty nervous because everyone's looking at me, and my body's gone into a fight-or-flight response. My sympathetic nervous system is going haywire, the pituitary gland, at the base of my brain, is pumping out a hormone called ACTH, and my adrenal glands are releasing cortisol and epinephrine. These things are working together to speed up my heart, release sugar into my blood, increase the blood flow to my muscles. There's a hollowed-out feeling in my stomach, because all the blood's been diverted elsewhere.

Of course, if Mr. Edwards makes me go into any more detail, things will change. Fast. My vagus nerve will dilate my blood vessels and slow down my heart until there isn't enough oxygen going to my brain. Then, *BAM!* I'll black out and fall over: my body's way of getting blood back into my head. Fainting may be super-annoying, but it's pretty clever. Well done, evolution.

"And what is that process called?" Mr. Edwards asks.

"Um . . ."

I know the bad stuff, too. The stuff that keeps me awake at night, about how anorexia is slowly ruining my body. I don't eat enough meat, which means I'm short on iron. That's why I sometimes can't breathe properly. I have to wear gloves at this time of year, even on warm days, because my circulation is so rubbish.

And I'm not going to grow a beard anytime soon—unlike Ram, whose chin is already fuzzy—because of the whole puberty-slowing-down shebang.

But the thing that scares me most? My kidneys. My kidneys don't work quite as well as the ones in our textbook, the ones I'm currently telling the whole class about. My ion balance is screwed up, so they get a little more damaged every day. According to Dr. Singh, they're okay for now, but kidney failure kills hundreds of anorexics every year.

The thing is, knowing stuff only helps if you can do something with that knowledge. Otherwise it just sits there, like some kind of mental bowling ball you have to carry with you everywhere you go. Making you feel like fainting and throwing up and crying, all at the same time.

Sometimes, I feel like I know too much. About calories. About kidneys. About all kinds of stuff. I need, like, a lobotomy or something, so I can carry on living my life, without all these thoughts getting in the way.

"Selective reabsorption," I say eventually, trying not to think about what the words mean.

"Correct," Mr. Edwards says. "All of you, please make sure you use that phrase. *Selective reabsorption.*

And what's the main thing that's reabsorbed in the loop of Henle, Max?"

My head's starting to go fuzzy. The edges of my vision go dark, like someone's applied a photo filter directly to my eyes. I just want it to be over. But this time, I don't know the answer. "Sugar?"

I'm pretty sure I see Mr. Edwards smirk, like, *Finally, I caught you out.* "Actually, glucose is almost all reabsorbed in the proximal convoluted tubule."

"Yeah, *idiot,*" whispers someone across the room. I think it's Darren, but I'm not sure. I hear a few stifled giggles.

"*Thank you,*" says Mr. Edwards, in a warning voice.

"Oh. Ions?" I say.

Mr. Edwards smiles. "Yes, ions. And with them goes . . ."

"Water."

"Exactly. Thank you, Max." He turns and loops toward the back of the class, raising his voice. "Water is sixty percent of your body weight, folks. The renal medulla is *hypertonic* to the fluid in the nephron. Who can tell me what that means, and why it's important?"

He walks on, looking for someone else to pick on. I can't believe I made it through that without fainting.

I try to tune him out, now I don't have to listen. But something he said sticks in my mind. Sixty percent of your body weight is water. Sixty percent of *me* is water: ordinary, comes-out-of-the-tap water. I mean, I guess it makes sense. Cells are basically tiny water balloons, and we're made up of thirty-five trillion of them. So are other animals. So are plants. If you are a plant, you survive on water, sunlight, and air, and basically nothing else. It sounds a lot easier— like an even-better version of Gran's nursing home.

But 60 percent seems nuts.

I feel a tug on my sleeve.

Sorry, Ram mouths to me.

I shake my head: *Don't worry about it.* He looks relieved. *Jesus,* I think. Are my friends scared of me too now? Did he think I was going to flip out at him?

I take another look at the doodle in front of me. The hollow sort of looks like a mouth. I don't have a better idea, so I write underneath it, in block capitals: THE MOUTH IN THE SKY. Then below that: *How does a tree eat?*

Okay, so it's not the greatest riddle ever. But it's something. I'll put the cache online this weekend; all I have to do is add the info and hit the button.

There's this weird twisted feeling in my stomach, and suddenly I clock what it is: I'm nervous. Maybe it's just leftover nerves from being quizzed in front of the whole class. Maybe it's a kind of oh-god-I'm-going-to-faint hangover. But it feels different.

January 18
Dear Ana,

waiting for stuff sucks. I put my cache online five days ago, and so far, no one's visited. I've been to check it like eight times already. I keep imagining something's gone wrong, like maybe a muggle—that's what you call someone who doesn't know what geocaching is—has found it, and decided it must be a bomb or a drug stash or something, and reported it to the police. Or a squirrel's knocked it out of the tree.

But each time I go back, it's still there.

I asked Robin about it. He shrugged and told me sometimes it takes a while to show up in everyone's app, and also, it's not like there are that many people in Bolford out searching for geocaches in the middle of January. "It was 2°C yesterday Max, for crying out loud," he said. I guess he has a point.

Hey, at least when I'm worrying about my geocache, I'm not worrying about food. I've finally found a way to shut you up.

Talking about weird girls who won't leave me alone . . . I swear Evie (yes, I finally found out what her name is) is crazy. Yesterday me, Stu, and Ram were on our way to music, and she ran up behind us and was like, "Hey, guys! Time for music!" To be absolutely clear: This is the first time she's ever spoken to us. None of us had a clue what to say. Eventually, Stu asked her if she played any instruments, which I reckon was pretty nice of him. She said no. That was it. We let her walk to class with us, but she didn't say anything else. And she went and sat on her own. Now that I think about it, I feel kind of bad we didn't ask her to sit with us. But there's not exactly a lot I can do about it now.

7

At Deanwater High, there's a zero-tolerance approach to mobile phones. If a teacher sees you using one or even just holding one, they confiscate it and you have to go to the assistant principal at the end of the day to get it back. No excuses. If it happens twice, they keep it for a week. Every parent has to sign an agreement saying they're fine with this policy before their kid gets a place at the school. It's a big deal: Our principal does interviews with national newspapers where she talks about the *menace of distraction*. She's kind of a phone-hating celebrity.

Anyway, the main outcome is that every toilet cubicle in school is occupied throughout break time and lunchtime because everyone goes in there to check their phones. Like, it would be a real problem if you actually needed to use a sit-down toilet. I don't know what the girls do.

Who knew that trying to stop 1,200 11–16 year-olds from using their phones wouldn't work?

I sprint out of history as soon as the bell goes and reach the nearest toilets before anyone else (which is a pretty big achievement, actually—there are at least five classrooms that are closer). I close the door, pull out my phone, and open up the listing for my cache.

And guess what? Nothing. Nada. Zilch.

I do have a text from Ram, though.

Where did you zoom off to? LOL. Meet us in the usual place. I need your help!

I've met Ram and Stu in the usual place for three years, since we first came to Deanwater High, so I'm not exactly sure what else he was expecting me to do.

When I get there, he beams. "Max! So glad you could make it."

I turn to Stu. "Why's he being weird?"

Stu frowns. "No idea. It's making me pretty nervous actually."

Ram shakes his head. "Fellas, there's no need to be nervous. I want to pick your brains."

"About what?" Stu asks.

"My birthday, of course."

I look at Stu. He raises an eyebrow.

"Your birthday's in May," I tell him.

"Exactly," he says enthusiastically. "We have plenty of time to figure it out."

"Figure what out?"

"My dad says I can do whatever I want this year. It's going to be, like, the biggest social event of the year. So, what do we want to do? Oh, you're both invited by the way."

"This would've been a pretty awkward conversation if we weren't, frankly," says Stu.

Ram ignores him. "So, what do you reckon?"

I'm about to suggest he has his party at the zoo because that's definitely where I'd have a birthday party, if I ever actually had one: My birthday's in August, so no one's ever around.

But before I can say anything, Ram's off again. I think he's already forgotten that he asked a question. "At first, I thought Laser Quest, but then I thought, maybe we're too old for Laser Quest."

Stu strokes his chin. "Is anyone ever truly too old for Laser Quest?"

"We might be," says Ram, deadpan. "Keep up, Stu."

Stu gives me another look.

"How about the zoo?" I say.

Ram snorts at this, which I guess means no.

"Bowling?" Stu offers.

Ram scowls. "Everyone goes bowling, Stu. I've been bowling like twenty times in the last year."

"It's almost as if bowling is fun," mutters Stu.

I haven't, I think. I can't remember the last time I went bowling. I can't tell if Ram's exaggerating, or if there are all these parties I don't get invited to. Parties I don't even know about.

Probably. Who'd want you at a party?

Yeah, okay, Ana. You may have a point there.

The bell goes for third period, which today is PSHE—Personal, Social, Health, and Economic education—aka the lesson where we all have to pretend we've never heard of condoms.

"You two are about as useless as an inflatable dart-board," Ram concludes.

"Glad to help," says Stu brightly.

"Anyway, keep thinking about it. I want to brief Dad at the weekend."

"Brief?" Stu says. "You're not a spy, Ram."

"That's exactly what a spy would want you to think," Ram says, touching his index finger to his head, like, *Think about that for a moment.* Then he groans. "Oh, look who's back."

You guessed it.

"Um, hi," Evie says. "So, what's PSHE?"

"Personal, Social, Health, and Economic education," we all chant in unison, like the world's worst barbershop quartet. Barbershop trio, I guess.

"O-kay," Evie says, like we're insane. She wrinkles her nose. "And what the hell is that?"

"Basically, they tell us stuff we already know about how sex works. The videos are good, though."

Evie grins. "Cool."

She *is* kind of pretty. Her hair is chocolate-brown, and her bangs hang right down over her eyes. It must be kind of annoying, but it looks cool. And she has about 18,000 freckles on each cheek.

There's an awkward pause where no one really knows what to do. Then Ram picks up his rucksack and blurts, "See you there."

I see a little flicker in Evie's face.

"You can come with us if you want," I say. I don't

actually look at her when I say it. I just stare at my feet.

She frowns at me. "*As if.* See you later, dickheads." Then she marches off across the courtyard.

~

Robin's already there when I get home from school. He's normally at work till six, but apparently some delivery got rescheduled or something, so he could clock off early.

"I'm taking Sultan out," he announces as soon as I walk through the door. "Wanna come?"

"Yep. Just . . . give me a sec," I say. I stumble into the kitchen.

Um, confession time: I didn't eat lunch. Our PSHE class ran over because they had this guest speaker, who was a nurse from a sexual health clinic in Manchester, and he got stuck in traffic. By the time I got out, there were massive queues to even get into the toilets, and I really wanted to check my phone. Maybe if I was less of a wimp, I'd subtly check my phone wherever I was. But I'm not. And anyway, I kind of like having an excuse to be on my own.

Unsurprisingly, no one had visited in the two hours since I'd last checked.

By the time I got out, there was only, like, five minutes of lunch left. So I skipped it.

Now I'm feeling pretty woozy. My arms are actual custard, and my stomach feels like it's being vacuumed from the inside. I should eat something— but the thought of eating now scares me. I feel like I could eat twenty cheeseburgers. What if I start eating and can't stop myself?

Better not risk it. The hunger will go away soon. You're not that weak, are you?

One thing you learn when you're anorexic is that hunger doesn't go in one direction. It peaks and it dips; you can be ravenous one moment and then, an hour later, you barely feel like eating.

And if you ride the wave, you can get away with eating less.

I go into the kitchen and open the fridge. For a second, I'm tempted by the carton of orange juice, but instead, I grab the jug of chilled water and fill up a pint glass. I down it in one gulp. I fill it back up and down it again.

"Max?" Robin calls from the hallway.

"Ready!" I shout back.

I'm super-bloated. I know water doesn't make me put on weight, but I still feel disgusting.

You *are* disgusting.

I'm not hungry anymore, though. That's something.

"So, have you found somewhere for your cache yet?"

It's too dark to go back to the Common, so we're walking into town. We've just passed Silk Dragon, the Chinese takeout we always go to. The smell kills me. Chinese is my absolute favorite food.

I shrug.

"It's okay, you don't have to tell me where," he says, grinning. "Anyone visited yet?"

"No," I say. "It sucks."

"They'll come," he says. "I don't know if you've noticed, but Bolford isn't exactly New York City."

The bloated feeling gets better as I walk. In fact, I feel okay, or as okay as I ever feel. Okay-ish.

"Hey, did Mum tell you about the weekend after next?" Robin says.

"I don't think so."

"Uncle Rich and Auntie Jess are going to Brighton, so I'm going to stay at their place and look after James and Louise. You can come with me if you like."

James has this thing about staying over at other people's houses. The thing being, he can't stand it. He says it disrupts his routine. James is kind of . . . particular. For example, he has his own plate and cutlery, which he uses for every single meal. When he goes on holiday, or around to anyone's house, he takes them with him. I used to think this was kind of ridiculous, but these days, I'm not exactly one to judge.

"Maybe," I say.

"Might be nice to give Mum and Dad some time to themselves."

I look up at him. A lump forms in my throat, about the size of a tennis ball. I'm not upset exactly. More embarrassed. He means, it might be nice to give Mum and Dad a break from me.

"It's up to you, little bro," he says quickly. "But I wouldn't mind the company. I might even let you pick the film, as long as you don't pick some documentary on bird migration again."

We carry on walking. Neither of us says anything for a while. We have one of those extending leashes, and Sultan's way out in front of us, looking for stuff he can scarf down before we notice it. Sultan likes walking down the high street best, because there's always discarded food about. He treats it like one of those sushi restaurants with a conveyor belt, where you reach out and grab whatever you want.

I feel weird. Not hungry exactly, but like my body has just realized whatever I drank two pints of wasn't food and is about to launch a rebellion. A deep, sick feeling fills my stomach. My brother's now talking about films we could watch, but I'm finding it hard to concentrate on what he's saying. His voice seems far away, like an announcement on a train you can't quite hear.

"How about *Die Hard*?" he says.

I turn to look at him, maybe respond, but it's cloudy. There's this sharp feeling building in my left shoulder, a pulsing pain that seems to come from nowhere.

And then everything goes black.

February 4

Dear Ana,

I'm an idiot. I'm a complete, total, 100 percent idiot.
The biggest idiot in the entire world.

I didn't eat any food all day, then drank two pints
of water, then went for a walk.

What exactly did I expect would happen?

I had to tell Robin. It was the only way I could
stop him from taking me to the hospital. He was
convinced I was about to keel over and die, right in
front of him.

So I spilled the beans. Sort of. I explained that
I fainted because I hadn't eaten since breakfast. I
didn't tell him about the water thing. Even so, he
was pretty mad.

Robin: "Jesus Christ, Max. This isn't a game."

Me: "I'm sorry."

"You could have split your head open."

"I know."

"You could have died."

I didn't know how to respond to that. He was
right: I could have died. It's not like you have any
control over which way you fall when you faint. You
just drop and smash into whatever's near you. The
curb. The road. A glass window.

We sat there on the pavement for ages, saying

92

nothing. Robin hugged Sultan, to keep him from coming over and licking my face, but after a while, Sultan gave up. He lay down on the pavement, looking glum. Good work, Max, you somehow managed to ruin your dog's day, as well as your brother's.

Once my head cleared, I got up, and we started walking back.

I tried to make a joke to break the mood. I was like, "I think my body's telling me to say no to *Die Hard*." Robin hates any kind of tension or conflict. Even when he was a teenager, if he flew off the handle about something, he came around in about five minutes. I figured that as soon as I tried to make up for stuff he would forgive me.

Nope. Instead he turned around and repeated the last four words he'd said to me, which felt about thirty times as brutal because of the fact he was repeating them like that.

You could have died.

8

My sessions with Lindsay always come around quicker than I'm expecting. Right after each one, I feel this huge sense of relief because I've got two clear weeks. That lasts about three days. Then I'm starting to think that it's only a few days till the halfway point. And suddenly, my next appointment is closer than my last one. It's like I'm standing on the track as the train hurtles closer and closer, and all I know how to do is count how long I have left.

Because I always have to be counting something.

We start with my weigh-in. I step-touch the scales with my foot, wait for the display to flash, then step on. I sort of push down onto the scales, tensing my legs, because I want the number to be as big as possible.

The bigger that number is, the less I have to eat.

It thinks for a moment, then spits out a result. A pound and a half more than I was expecting.

I weighed myself this morning, right before I drank two pints of water. I haven't been to the loo since, and I'm wearing exactly the same clothes. So I had a number in my head: the exact weight I knew I'd be. Two pounds heavier than I was when I got up this morning.

But this number—the number I'm now staring at—is higher. Bigger. Fatter.

For a moment, I'm happy, because if Lindsay thinks I'm putting on weight, she won't put as much pressure on me. But then I think, how come they're different? What's going on? Maybe these scales are wrong. But the ones in a hospital are going to be pretty accurate, right?

Which means my scales at home are wrong. I'm heavier than I think.

Are you eating doughnuts in your sleep or something?

"Everything all right, Max?" Lindsay says.

I don't respond.

Since the Incident, I've felt pretty awful about

myself. Like, even more so than usual. You know when you buy a tub of raspberries, and they look healthy enough, but the next day, every single one is covered in mold? It's kind of like that. When I blacked out, it flipped some kind of switch, and since then I've felt guilty about everything, all the time.

About making Robin cover for me.

About being a dick to Ram.

About lying to Lindsay.

This last one has actually led to some progress: I've started eating chocolate bars. Kind of. On Saturday, we went to this National Trust estate for a walk, and I surprised everyone by having a Twister from the van. Yesterday, I had two fingers of a Kit Kat. I nearly had a Creme Egg this morning, too (yep, it's February 8, and they are already in the shops), but I chickened out at the last minute, because I was worried about what Lindsay might add to my diet plan today.

I was really happy about all of this until fifteen seconds ago.

Do you reckon your mum and dad got special scales to trick you into eating more?

Shut up shut up *SHUT UP*.

I want to throw up. I want to get everything I've eaten over the past two weeks out of my body.

"You've lost a bit of weight since last time," Lindsay is saying.

It takes me a moment to process it. I feel like a blue whale. I feel like, in the past few days, I've eaten more food than I have in my entire life up to that point. Mentally, I'm laying out all my meals on a table, like in those shows where they show a family how disgustingly unhealthy their diet is by piling table after table with all the chips and cookies and frozen meals they've eaten in a month.

And she's telling me I've *lost* weight.

"So we need to talk about that," she carries on. "And adjust our plan a little."

Coming in today, I figured there were two possible outcomes:

1. I've put on weight. In which case I'd be upset, but Lindsay would be happy. Maybe she'd leave me alone for a bit.
2. I've lost weight. In which case I'd be thrilled, but Lindsay would probably be mad at me and make me do things I really, really don't want to do.

Now I'm realizing there's a third way: I can lose weight and still feel terrible. Great.

"Okay," I mumble, even though it feels like the least-okay thing in the world.

"Don't worry about that for now," Lindsay says. I guess she can tell how nervous I am. She gestures for me to sit down. "We'll talk about it later. Tell me how things have been since our last session."

I always thought psychologists made you lie on couches, but Lindsay has these molded plastic chairs. They're pretty uncomfortable—or at least, they are for me. At home, I pretty much always sit on a cushion these days because my bony ass doesn't really provide much cushioning of its own.

I wriggle around to find a good position. Maybe this is part of the treatment: They make you sit on the world's least comfortable chair to show you you're skinny.

Lindsay always starts by asking how things have been and what I've been up to. I never have a good answer. It's not that I'm trying to come up with a lie or anything. It's just that when you're anorexic, you don't do very much. *Well, Lindsay, I mainly read books and slept and studied for exams, because my life is tragic and lonely. How about you?*

The only new things I've done in the past two weeks are a) try (and mostly fail) to eat chocolate bars; b) drink too much water, faint, and nearly kill myself; and c) wander around looking for geocaches or checking my own. I don't want to tell her about any of these things. But I've got to say something, and the last one seems like the safest option.

"I've been . . . orienteering."

"O-kay," says Lindsay cautiously.

I look up at her. Normally, Lindsay is ridiculously enthusiastic about pretty much anything I say to her, and especially anything about my hobbies. Before Christmas, I told her about when Dad took me to Brockholes and we saw a bittern. We ran fifteen minutes over the end of our session because she asked so many questions.

There's a long pause. "Max," she says eventually. "We talked about running."

Of course, she thinks I've just found a workaround. I guess orienteering wasn't the best way to describe it. "It's not *that* kind of orienteering," I explain. "I don't run."

I'm worried she won't believe me. I wouldn't. But she looks relieved and sits back in her chair. "All right," she says. "So, what do you do?"

It's at this point I realize, there's no way of explaining geocaching to someone who's never heard of it that doesn't make it sound crazy. *Um, strangers leave boxes hidden in the woods, and I find them and see what they've put in them.* Or: *I crawl around under park benches and shove my hand into storm drains looking for bits of paper.* See what I mean?

So I keep it vague. "You have a map and a few clues, but it's not a race. It's more like a puzzle. I go with Robin sometimes."

That last part seems to reassure her. She smiles. I guess my parents have told her that my brother is a responsible adult (which is true as long as he's not on a mountain bike).

We talk about geocaching some more. Things are going well. I'm not even too worried about the scales—after all, I've still lost weight. But then Lindsay drops a total bombshell.

"Max, your parents are going to join us in a moment, if that's all right."

"Why?" I hear myself saying—shouting—as soon

as the words hit me, like a tennis player hitting a volley right back over the net.

"I'm really happy the effort you've been putting in. But to be honest, we haven't made enough progress with your weight. Your BMI is currently . . ."

She looks down at her notes. But before she can read the number, I tell her, "—."

Then I realize what I've just said. *My BMI is —.*

Lindsay looks up at me. I look down at my lap. I'm trying to process the two bits of news I've got in the last thirty seconds.

Mum and Dad are coming to my session for some reason.

My BMI has hit —.

Let me ask you a question: What's the most important number in your life? I watched a film once, a romantic comedy, about a mathematician who falls in love with the police officer who pulls him over for speeding. While they're talking at the side of the road, the mathematician says, "Pi is the most important number in the universe." The officer responds, "I don't think that's going to hold up in court." Okay, so it was a super-cheesy movie. But I thought that line was pretty funny.

Anyway, for me, my BMI—which stands for body mass index—is the most important number in the universe. It's actually a pretty simple equation: Your BMI is your weight in kilograms, divided by the square of your height in meters. Doctors use it to figure out whether you're under- or overweight.

I'm four feet eleven. One and a half meters. Square that, and you get about 2.28. How many times does 2.28 go into —? The numbers are hard, but I don't need to work them out, because I've got the whole table memorized.

My magic number is now —, which means, for the first time ever, I'm clinically underweight. Lindsay says BMIs are only a rough measure, and that for my body shape I've actually been underweight for a while. But now it's official.

"That's right," says Lindsay, after a long, horrible pause. "And that's not where we need it to be, Max." She leans toward me, smiling. "That's why I want to talk to you and your parents today. I want us all to come up with a plan together."

I don't say anything.

She asks me about how games have been, now

that I'm not playing rugby. But all I can think about is what's going to happen when Mum and Dad get here.

Eventually, her phone rings. "Hello? Perfect. I'll be out in a minute." She turns to me. "They're here, Max. Will you be okay for a sec if I go and fetch them?"

She says it like I'm a five-year-old or some psycho on a ward. Does she think I'm going to jump out of the window or something?

"Whatever," I say.

When Mum comes in, she beams at me and says, "Hi, love!" in this super-happy, really fake-sounding voice. Dad smiles and nods, but doesn't say anything. He looks kind of sheepish.

Because he's kind of guilty. They both are.

They sit down, and we talk bullshit for a while. *How's everything, any plans for the summer holidays,* et cetera. I'm trying to act cool, like I don't even care they're here. But quietly, I'm freaking out. Is Lindsay going to confront me about the chocolate bars in front of Mum and Dad? *Did Max mention this to you at all, by the way?* Maybe all this time, they've been sending her daily updates, so Lindsay can see if my diary checks out.

They're conspiring to make you fat.

Dad's rabbiting on about how we're going camping again this year. He has this whole speech about the social benefits of camping and why the Howarths *love to camp*. (He's never actually asked me or Robin for confirmation of this.)

"You know, it gives the kids real respect for the planet they live on. And a real appreciation for any food that doesn't come from a tin, ha-ha. But seriously, you know how much Max loves birds. And his brother is training to be a furniture maker. He's very into conservation. Have you ever heard the saying: *Take nothing but photographs, leave nothing but footprints?* That's the mentality camping gives you . . ."

I look across at Mum, who seems like she's not even listening. She usually groans at this speech and says things like, *Joe, why don't you go ahead and give them a pamphlet?* all the way through, even if she laughs at all of Dad's jokes. But today, she's sitting there in silence, with her hands in her lap. She's been doing that a lot lately.

Even Lindsay looks like she doesn't really want to be listening to Dad's speech. She has the face of someone who's waiting for a polite moment to interrupt. Unfortunately for Lindsay, it's at least ten minutes before one arrives.

"Have you ever tried camping, Dr. Hughes?" Dad finally asks.

"I'm afraid not," replies Lindsay. And then, before Dad can move on to his Camping for Beginners spiel, she adds: "And I'd love to talk about that *after* our session, Mr. Howarth. For now, I think we need to move on."

"Yes, of course," says Dad. He looks only a little disappointed.

"As you know, I've been working with Max for nearly four months now. And I think we've really got to know each other, which is great." She smiles at each of us in turn, ending with me. "I'm really happy about how engaged you are with your treatment, Max, and I think now is a good time to reflect on what we've achieved so far and what we still need to crack. Does that make sense?"

I nod. This is, like, the most patronizing Lindsay's ever been. Normally, it's Mum and Dad doing the whole talk-to-Max-really-slowly-and-gently routine.

Like as well as being an anorexic, I've also turned into a simpleton. Sure, Lindsay's always ultra-nice, but she talks to me like a normal human being.

Or at least, she used to.

"It makes total sense," Dad confirms.

I nod. Mum doesn't react.

"Max, you've been keeping a diary of the things you eat for me," she says.

And you've been making half of it up, I add in my head.

You don't have a choice. If they got their way, you'd be obese.

"We started on December first, so that makes four months now. And you were keeping your own records before then too, weren't you?"

"Yes," I say. What am I supposed to say? She knows I was.

"That's been really helpful for me because I've built up a picture of your eating patterns. But I'm worried it's started to control"—there's that word again—"the way you eat. So, I'd like to try pausing your diary for a couple of weeks."

You. Are. Capital. S. Screwed. If you don't keep a record of everything, you'll go psycho in about two minutes.

Helpful, Ana. Thanks.

I go to say something, but I stop myself at the last minute and end up opening and closing my mouth like a goldfish.

"Yes, Max?" Lindsay says. She always catches when you're on the verge of saying something.

What I was about to say was, *That's the point.* Controlling the way I eat is the whole point. If I don't keep track of everything, I panic. That's why I started doing it before I'd even met Lindsay. Because if I panic, it's much worse. For everyone.

How can she not see that?

If she stops me from using my diary, I'll have to keep track of everything in my head. Tomorrow morning I'll eat my slice of toast and think of the number of calories, and then I'll hold that number in my head all morning, reciting it, bouncing it around like a rubber ball. At lunchtime, I'll add more numbers: a ham sandwich, an apple. The sums are easy to start with. But you know when you're doing, say, laps in a swimming pool, and you're trying to remember how many laps you've done? As soon as you start thinking too much about it, you get confused. Am I on lap fourteen or was I just *thinking* about lap fourteen? As soon as you start thinking forward or back, your mind starts swimming, too. When I'm sitting in geography, stomach growling, I'll start thinking about the bag of chips I probably won't eat when I get home. I'll picture myself laying out the chips, pouring away the crumbs so I know I'm under, then calculating the calories in each one. I'll count up, imagining myself biting into each one, feeling the salt and fat burst in my mouth . . . and then Stu will say something to me, or Mr. French will ask us to turn to page 344 in our textbook, and I'll forget what number I'm actually on. I'll panic and start counting again from the beginning of the day. And I know it'll happen over and over: all day, every day, like that game where you're packing a suitcase and you have to recite everything people have said before you and then add another thing of your own. Meanwhile, Ana's bombarding me with questions:

Are you sure you didn't put more than an ounce of ham in your sandwich?

Is that your sixth grape, or was the one you just ate your sixth?

How much did that apple weigh again?

You don't know. You're not sure. You're not in control anymore.

I don't know if I mentioned it, but I already think about food 90 percent of the time. If I don't write stuff down, I'm pretty sure I can wave good-bye to the last 10 percent of my sanity.

"Can I ask a question?" Dad says.

"Of course," says Lindsay, swiveling her smile thirty degrees. "Go ahead, Mr. Howarth."

"Rebecca and I," he says, reaching over and putting his hand on Mum's. I could swear she flinches. "We've been trying our best to make this work for Max." He looks at me. "Because we love you, buddy. We'll do whatever we have to. And that diary . . . well, I think you're right, Dr. Hughes. You're dead right. That diary's now in charge. And to be honest, it puts a big strain on the family."

He turns to look at Mum, like this comment is aimed especially at her. She smiles weakly at him. I reckon she's thinking the same thing I am: *What am I supposed to say to that?*

Dad carries on. "But at the same time, it's given Max a way to organize things. And I worry about taking it away."

"I understand," says Lindsay. "Max, what do you think about that?"

"Um," I mumble.

I should be happy, because Dad's stuck up for the whole diary idea. But I'm not even thinking about that. I'm focusing on what Dad said: I put *a big strain on the family*. Okay, this isn't exactly new information. For instance, Robin told me the exact same thing three days ago. But it's new to hear Dad say it.

"It's . . . I don't know," I stutter eventually.

"That's okay," says Lindsay. "I think your dad makes an excellent point. This could be a little disruptive. At the same time, I do want to try it because I think it might help you be a little more relaxed around food. So how about we give it a go for two weeks, and we'll talk about how it went in our next session. If we need to come up with an alternative plan, that's fine. And, Mr. Howarth, if you have any concerns at all, you can call me anytime. Okay?"

Dad actually gets up and shakes Lindsay's hand at this point, like he's just bought a used car from her. With his genes, no wonder I'm such a weirdo.

February 13
Dear Ana,

Some days are normal. Some days, everything is
okay, and I eat three square meals, pretty much,
even if those squares are ridiculously small squares.

Some days, I can almost pretend there's nothing
wrong.

Today I got up, ate my toast, and took Sultan for
a walk on the Common. When I got home, I read a
book for a bit, then played Zelda. Then I helped
Mum make lunch: quiche and salad. And I ate it all
without making a fuss.

No, it's more than that. I enjoyed it. I enjoyed
eating my lunch! I wasn't adding up the numbers in
my head with every mouthful or worrying about
whether my slice of quiche was bigger or smaller
than Mum's or whether it represented exactly
a quarter of the total. I was just . . . eating it.
Chewing it, swallowing it, tasting it.

I didn't even think about you once.

After lunch, I did some math homework until
Robin came home. He's been at the workshop a
lot lately; it kind of feels like he's been avoiding
me since the Incident. But today, he asked me if I
wanted to go to the Common and look at birds. To

be clear, Robin has zero interest in looking at birds. But that made it even nicer, like he was doing it for me. We didn't see anything particularly special: coots, mallards, herring gulls, Canada geese, and one shelduck. But I didn't care.

Tea was okay, too. We had oven pizza—margherita, which is my favorite because the toppings are basically uniform, so there's no decision you have to make about which slice has the most ham, or the least. I cut my slice with protractor precision, made a little salad, did the numbers, made sure I was happy before digging in. And it was all fine. We had a completely normal conversation about the new tapir enclosure at the zoo. The only wobble was dessert, when I said I'd have some apple pie, then, uh . . . I kind of ended up feeding most of it to Sultan under the table. But it wasn't a big deal.

The whole day was completely uneventful. Completely normal.

It was the best day I've had in weeks.

And now I'm sitting here, trying to figure out why. What's the pattern? Is there some kind of rule I'm missing? What made today different from yesterday or the day before? How did I manage to stay in control? Because if I can find out what happened, I can repeat it. I can stack up normal days until I'm living a normal life.

Maybe it was to do with the cooking: I was always involved. Or maybe it was because I only ate things that divided into easy-to-measure portions. But then I remember the last time I felt normal. It was about two weeks ago, and I'm pretty sure we had spaghetti with meatballs—aka, the most impossible-to-portion food in the world.

That blows that theory.

Is it because I'm not keeping a food diary anymore? Maybe—I have to admit, it's not been as bad as I thought it would be. But that's mostly because I've been reciting the numbers like some kind of monk's chant so there's no way I can lose track. And like I said, this isn't the first time I've felt like this.

Maybe it was the weather or a blip in my brain chemistry, or—who knows—the way the planets were aligned. Was it a full moon? I could be a kind of reverse were-eater: I stop being crazy about food when there's a full moon.

Wait a second—I just realized something. I'm tearing my hair out trying to figure out how to control my anorexia. But needing to control everything is part of the problem. It's

an anorexic's—sorry, a person with anorexia's—
solution. I don't need to give you ground rules, Ana.
I'm sick of rules. What I need to do is kick you out
of my head for good, and never ever let you back in.

9

We're on our way to Auntie Jess's house to babysit for the weekend. I figured it would be a good way to show Robin that I really am sorry about the Incident. Plus, a change of scene is supposed to make you feel better, right?

Robin's really quiet on the drive over. I can't tell if he's decided he's mad at me again or if it's something else.

"How's work?" I ask him, trying to start a conversation.

"Fine."

That's all he says.

When we arrive, Auntie Jess and Uncle Rich are loading stuff into the car. Lots of stuff. They're only going away for two days, but the back seat of the hybrid Uncle Rich keeps telling us about is so full you can barely see through the rear window.

Auntie Jess has made a long list of things we should do while we're staying, and an even longer list of things we shouldn't. For example, we have to make sure James drinks water or Ribena, not Coke. We can't eat the Gouda in the cupboard, which they got from Holland last year and are saving for a special occasion of some kind. We can't use the downstairs toilet. Even though she's written all this down, Auntie Jess still talks us through each item. It takes about an hour. Uncle Rich sits in the car the whole time, beeping the horn every so often and shouting, "Jess, we need to go."

Even Mum, who tries her best not to say anything negative about anyone, admits that her sister is a tad high-maintenance. I guess it runs in the family. On Tuesday, Mum called her to talk through the meal plan for the weekend. We agreed she'd buy stuff in for tonight: steak pies with new potatoes and French beans. Tomorrow morning, Robin and I will go shopping for the rest of the food, so I can keep track of everything.

When Auntie Jess finally leaves, the first thing I do is go to the fridge and check the nutritional information on the steak pies.

It's a lot. I knew it was going to be heavy, but it's way more than I thought. Each one contains more than half the calories I eat in a day. I'm already feeling pretty nervous about this weekend's eating, given a) James and Louise will probably ask awkward questions, because that's what kids do; and b) I'm still getting used to the whole no-diary thing. It wasn't too bad when I was at home because I could work everything out in my head in advance. But I can't do that here. And I'm sharing a room with Robin, so it's not like I can even lie about it.

You'll end up like a sumo wrestler if you eat one of those.

I put the pies down on the side, go over to the fridge, and push against it as hard as I can, because I need to do something with my body other than scream.

A moment later, Robin comes in. "What kid sits down quietly and starts doing watercolors . . ." He's talking about Louise. But he trails off when he sees me. "What's up?"

"I can't eat those pies," I tell him.

"No problem," he says. "But you have to have something else instead."

He doesn't miss a beat. Sometimes, he's exactly like Dad.

We go and peer into the fridge together.

"Cheese?" he says.

A lump of cheese is my usual fallback at home, when Mum and Dad and Robin are having something I don't want to eat. Something I can't eat. It's way easier than meat. Every piece of meat is different: There are seams of fat, dark bits, and light bits. You never know quite what you're going to get. But cheese—at least, hard yellow cheese—is the same all the way through.

I nod.

"But not the Gouda," he says, in this high-pitched voice that doesn't really sound anything like Auntie Jess.

And in spite of everything, I burst out laughing.

~

The next morning, we all walk to the supermarket together. Louise is delighted about this. James isn't. The whole way there, he lists useful things he could be doing if we weren't dragging him to the supermarket—things like putting the washing on, mowing the lawn, and getting ahead with his math homework.

"Sure," says Robin. He gives James a yeah-right look. "Or watching the rest of that season of *Bob's Burgers*."

James scowls.

But Louise is thrilled. She keeps asking me about what we're having. And then suggesting changes. *I LOVE pizza. Can we have ice cream instead of yogurt?* I'm not sure how to tell her, *If we do that, I'll go Hulk-crazy on you.*

As usual, Robin knows what to do. "Signed off by your mum," he explains. "She'll go nuts if we change things now."

Louise nods solemnly.

I spent hours figuring out the meal plan for this weekend. It goes like this:

Friday
Tea
Steak pie, new potatoes, and French beans
Sponge cake

Saturday

Breakfast

Toast and cereal

Lunch

Ham-and-tomato sandwiches

Yogurt

Tea

Pizza, garlic bread, and salad

Sliced peaches with cream and digestive biscuits

Sunday

Breakfast

Muesli

Lunch

Shepherd's pie and peas

Apple crumble

Actually, it's more complicated than that. There are really two columns: one for me, one for everyone else. Mine doesn't include sponge cake or garlic bread, and it has stewed fruit instead of crumble . . . you get the picture.

I've stuck to the rules: I haven't written down the calories anywhere. But if you asked me, right now, I could tell you the exact number for every item on that list. Even the ones I'm not actually eating.

When Mum showed it to Auntie Jess, she was delighted. Apparently, she asked if I could plan all of James's and Louise's meals. Turns out I'm much better at feeding other people than I am at feeding Max Howarth.

When we get to the supermarket, Robin grabs a cart and just says, *Lead the way, little bro.* I get the fresh veg first: lettuce, tomatoes, and cucumber for the salad. Carrots for the shepherd's pie. Easy peasy. When we get to the bakery section, James and Louise both demand iced buns. Robin refuses. While they're distracted, I grab the bread I want: Hovis Soft White Medium. I know from looking in their bread bin last night that it isn't what they normally have, and I've been worrying about whether they'll kick up a fuss. I put the loaf in the cart and cover it with a bag of salad so they don't notice it. Fortunately, they're still arguing about the iced buns.

Hey, crazy thought. Maybe they have, like, actual lives, and don't care what kind of bread you get?

When we get back, we have lunch, which goes okay, then watch four episodes of *Bob's Burgers* back to back. There's only one awkward moment, which is when Robin talks about bingeing—as in, on TV—then realizes what he's said, and stops dead and looks at me.

I decide to wind him up and try to act like I'm shocked. Like I'm about to cry. I last for about two seconds, then burst out laughing.

"What's so funny?" James asks.

"Nothing," I say.

He scowls at me.

"Hey," says Robin, pausing the TV and getting up from the sofa. "Who wants to play a board game?"

"Ummm . . . ," I say.

I like board games: They're one of the few social activities that doesn't involve eating or drinking. But James is nine, and Louise is only seven. At our house, we normally play things like Scrabble and Trivial Pursuit, whereas when the Donalds come over, they usually choose the Game of Life, which is what Robin witheringly calls *a game of chance*.

So, yeah, I'm kind of skeptical whether we're going to agree on anything. I give Robin an eyebrow wiggle that I'm hoping he'll interpret as *It will be rubbish* and/or *How about a jigsaw instead?* But either he's ignoring me, or he doesn't understand. He turns to Louise. "Wanna show us what you've got, Louise?"

Before I can say anything, she's bounding up the stairs. We follow her up.

The games cupboard is in Louise's bedroom. Actually, it's pretty much the same size as her bedroom. It's like a walk-in wardrobe, but for games. There are literally hundreds of boxes in there, stacked right up to the ceiling. Board games, jigsaws, boxes of Lego. We all peer in, like Egyptologists who've discovered a new burial chamber.

"Boggle?" says Robin, after maybe twenty seconds.

Louise looks at him with a screwed-up face, like she's been sucking on a lime.

"Okay then," he says breezily. "Um . . . how about Risk?"

"Don't play Risk with *her*," says James. He looks at his sister and narrows his eyes. "She guilt-trips you into un-invading areas you've won, so she can win them back."

"I think that's called diplomacy," says Robin. "Okay then, cards? Farmer's Bridge?"

"Farmer's Bridge?" Louise sniffs the air suspiciously? "I've never played that."

"Me either," says James. "It sounds weird."

"It's great," Robin says. "And super-easy to pick up. Right, Max?"

He reaches into the cupboard and pulls out a Tupperware box stuffed with decks of cards.

"Right," I say, mainly because I don't think there's much point in saying anything else.

Farmer's Bridge actually *is* pretty simple. Each round, you guess how many tricks you're going to win, and you only score if you win exactly that number. You start with one card, then two, then three, and so on all the way up to eight, and then back down. There's a bit of skill in predicting your tricks and knowing when to win or lose them. But it's at least 50 percent luck.

As soon as we sit down at the table, before Robin's even started shuffling the cards, James asks, "Can I have a snack while we play?"

I'm pretty sure my jaw actually drops, like in a cartoon. We finished lunch at 1:30. Since then, James has eaten an apple, a Snickers, and three custard creams. It's 3:26.

"Sure," Robin says. "I think I saw some Doritos in the cupboard. How about those?"

I doubt Auntie Jess would be too keen on this idea,

especially after all those biscuits—which is probably why James looks like he's won the lottery. But I'm not going to get involved. Robin goes into the kitchen, then shouts back to us: "Tangy Cheese or Cool Original?"

"Cool Original!"

"Tangy Cheese!"

They answer at the exact same time, then turn and scowl at each other. They've had this argument before.

But Robin is a peacemaker: He opens both packs and gives them one each. Fine—as long as no one makes me have any. I've not eaten Doritos since I've been ill, but I still know the numbers on the back of the pack. I can recite calorie counts for things I haven't had in years off by heart. I can tell you that the fruit flavors of Pop-Tarts—Frosted Blueberry, Frosted Raspberry, and Strawberry Sensation—are the most calorific. And I can tell you the calories in any dish on the McDonald's menu, even though I've only eaten there once in the past year, and all I had was an apple pie.

Yeah, I know. This is the worst party trick ever. I am the world's most boring encyclopedia.

James doesn't do well in the first couple of rounds, mainly because he's too busy stuffing his face to concentrate. He's like a machine: He scoops up the next handful of Doritos while he's still chewing the last, and crams it in on top, then dips his hand into the bag again. At one point, he turns to look at me like, *What's up?* and I realize I've been staring at him for five minutes.

So he doesn't play well, and neither do I. I wonder whether he's going to get huffy about losing, but he doesn't seem to care much. He finishes the Doritos by pouring the powder at the bottom of the bag into his mouth. Louise is stuffing her face, too, but apparently she can concentrate on eating and kicking our butts at the same time. She's winning by fifty points, and we're only four rounds in.

My phone beeps. I pull it out of my pocket and wake up the screen.

I do a double take.

"Max, it's your turn."

"Hold on a sec," I say.

"Mum says we're not allowed to check our phones at the kitchen table," Louise appeals to Robin.

Robin shakes his head. "You have a phone? What are you, like, five?"

Louise looks furious. "I'm *seven*," she declares.

"Fair enough then. I take it all back. Everything okay, Max?" Robin asks me.

"Yeah. Um, sorry," I mumble. "I have to go to the bathroom. Sorry."

I'd pretty much given up on the idea of anyone visiting. I figured that, somehow, word had got around that the new cache in Bolford is owned by a sad little anorexic, and no one should visit. But now I'm sitting on the toilet, cover down, staring at the first comment ever on my cache:

TFTC! Nicely hidden. :D

The user is called Stallone05. Which is a pretty stupid name. But I don't care.

A complete stranger found my cache and took the time to write a message.

For me. To me.

It might not sound like a big deal. Okay, it probably sounds super-lame. But remember, this is *me*. Max Howarth, the boring, loser anorexic.

The guy who crosses the street to avoid strangers.

The guy who hasn't spoken to anyone outside of my family over the weekend for, like, six months.

Today, a stranger went out of their way get in touch with *me*.

I hear a knock on the door. "Everything okay in there?" asks Robin. And for once, I can give him an honest answer.

"Everything's fine."

After the game—Louise ends up winning by a country mile—I start cooking tea. Well, *cooking* is a bit of a stretch: All I have to do is put the pizza in the oven and make some salad. While I slice cucumbers and tomatoes, Robin lays the table, and James and Louise go back to *Bob's Burgers*.

Twenty minutes later, I call everyone to the table. I've already put a plate with pizza in front of everyone; the salad's in a bowl, except mine, which I've already portioned out on my plate. I know it's sad, but I'm pretty proud of the salad. I cut the vegetables really neatly and laid them in rings on top of the lettuce to make a nice pattern. I even made a vinaigrette.

Just to be clear, you're definitely 100 percent a sad case.

"I'm not hungry," Louise declares as soon as she sees the food. She crosses her arms to emphasize the point.

We take our seats. Louise flops down and sighs, and leans right back in her chair.

"Probably all those Doritos you ate," Robin says. He glances across at James, who is happily cramming a slice of pizza into his mouth. He either hasn't clocked the salad or isn't interested. "It doesn't seem to have bothered your brother much, mind."

James doesn't look up. I'm not sure he actually hears anything over the sound of his jaws gnashing.

"It's no big deal," I say, sticking to my mantra.

But Robin carries on. "You've got to eat it, Louise," he says gently. "Max made it for us."

"All he did was heat up some pizzas," she mutters, pushing her plate away.

"One, don't be rude," Robin says. "Two, that's not the point."

Of course, Louise is right. But it's kind of a low blow. And Robin knows that that's not the only thing I'll be upset about.

Food waste drives me crazy. I'm not sure exactly why. Maybe it's because in my world, food is *every-thing*, and however else I feel about it, I can't imagine not caring about it. I can't imagine happily throwing it away. I get upset about tiny things, like when people peel too much off potatoes or cut the crusts off bread. You can imagine how I felt watching my cousin refuse to eat a whole meal.

Once again, my brother's looking out for me. But if there's one thing I hate more than food waste, it's attention. "It's no big deal," I say again.

Robin gives me a stern look. "It is, Max."

"Why did you eat those Doritos, idiot?" James says to his sister, with a grin.

"You ate them, too," Louise replies accusingly.

"But I'm still eating my tea, aren't I?"

Robin rubs his eyes. "James, you're not really helping." He sounds tired rather than cross. Like he's spent all day looking after three stupid kids, and he's had enough.

"I'm just saying," mutters James, picking up another slice of pizza.

"Well don't. And have some salad, please." Robin turns to Louise and points at the pizza in front of her. "Look, if you eat some of that you can have pudding, okay?"

Which I guess is a good tactic if the person you're talking to actually wants pudding. But Louise lobbied pretty hard for ice cream, and only agreed to have sliced peaches when I told her she could have a scoop of vanilla with her crumble tomorrow.

She sighs and holds her hand to her head, like a character in a Victorian novel. "No peaches for me."

Then James pushes his plate away. There's one half-eaten slice of pizza in front of him. "If she's allowed to skip stuff, how come I have to eat salad?"

My stomach lurches. So all this food's going to waste. Good job, Max.

And you've eaten more than anyone else. Jesus Christ.

You're getting fat, while they stay nice and thin.

"Everyone has to have a bit of salad," Robin says.

"You didn't say anything about salad," says Louise. "You're changing the rules. I thought we had a deal."

Louise will probably tell Auntie Jess, and she'll wind up mad at me or at Mum. *I trusted him to look after them, Becks. But apparently they ate chips and cookies all day.*

I feel that hot, prickling sensation in my spine, like when you've been concentrating on something for too long, and you know that you're about to flip out. I drop my hands into my lap, clasp them together, and squeeze my nails into my palms. In my head, I can see the little white dents in my skin.

"Fine, neither of you has to have salad. But you've got to finish your pizza."

"*Finish* it?" says Louise. "You just said—"

But she doesn't get to finish. I don't let her.

If you put a lid on something and keep heating it, the pressure grows. That's me: the human pressure cooker. The boy who's been listening to every single little gripe, all day long, and trying to pretend he's cool with it. The boy who's found a way to control everything except himself. I can't even describe what I'm feeling exactly. I don't know how to categorize it. Shame. Anger. Envy. Fear. They all meld into one: one white-hot ball of emotion that's way, way too big to fit inside me.

The pressure grows and grows and grows. And at some point, it's got to find a way out.

I grab the glass in front of me, stand up, and hurl it at the wall. There's a shimmering crash when it hits. I watch everyone flinch. They turn toward me in slo-mo, mouths and eyes wide-open. Pieces of glass skitter into every corner of the room.

And I hear myself screaming.

"SHUT UP! WHY CAN'T YOU ALL JUST SHUT UP?"

~

My left foot is stinging.

It's the first thing I notice, the first thing that drifts into my head. I know it's a cliché, but everything happened in a blur. Another fight-or-flight response. But the pain from my foot bursts the bubble. I stop dead, look around, and realize I'm already halfway home.

I wiggle my toes. My sock feels wet. I know it's not good for me to bleed, because of how low my iron is. I sit down on the pavement and take off my shoe and sock. It looks bad at first: My sock is strawberry-brown, soaked with sweat and blood, but when I bend my foot around, I can see how small the cut is. Dad loves telling people how the Howarths have great circulation. I mean, mine's not as good as it used to be—but I guess it's still all right.

I can't see any glass. I really don't want to think about whether there's glass inside the wound, because then I'll definitely faint. As soon as the thought enters my head, my vision starts to go cloudy. I get on all fours, so my head isn't too much higher than the rest of my body. It's pretty hard for me to faint like that— and even if I do, I'm probably not going to break anything.

I figure that the glass, or some of it, could be loose in my shoe, or stuck on my sock. Sure enough, when I turn my shoe over and shake it, I hear the tinkle of something bouncing off the pavement.

I just hope that was all of it.

Nice work, idiot. If your cousins didn't think you were a fruitcake before, they definitely do now. What next?

"I don't know, Ana," I reply out loud.

It's too dark to go to the Common. The way I see it, I've got two options. I can go back to Auntie Jess's and face James, Louise, and Robin. Or I can go home and face Mum and Dad. Right now, they both seem equally terrible. My cheeks start tingling just thinking about it. All I want to do is hide.

You should do something really crazy, like burn down that factory or rob a bank. That would be cool.

But I've got to face them eventually. And sooner is probably better than later.

I pull my damp sock and shoe back on, stand up, and test my weight on my foot. It's sore, but it's bearable—as long as I don't think about it too much.

I take a deep breath and start walking.

And Ana starts talking again. To keep me company, I guess. Cheers, Ana.

You're stupid. You're pathetic. You've screwed everything up . . .

When you picture someone with anorexia, who do you see? A girl, right? Clever. Pretty. She goes to the kind of school where they wear blazers and put on monthly piano recitals, and where there aren't any boys at all. Her parents put her under tons of pressure—to get As, to pass her piano exams, to get into Oxbridge—and some of the other girls bully her. She starves herself because she's trying to fit in with the cool girls, the bullies, or because she feels like her whole life is out of her hands and she can't escape; and the way she eats, the way she looks, the number she sees on the scales every morning . . . it's the only thing she can control.

I've never spoken to a girl like that. I mean, I've never spoken to anyone else with anorexia, as far as I know. Maybe that's exactly what some anorexics are like. I'll be honest: Some of the girls on the forums sound exactly like that.

But for me, it's different. My parents never put me under any pressure—or at least, not about stuff like that. I don't have a single clue where I'll go for university or if I'll go at all. I get picked on sometimes, but no more than anyone else. And I definitely, definitely don't want to be friends with Darren and Shinji.

Oh, and in case you haven't noticed, I'm about as cool and pretty as a slug.

Look at any website or newspaper article about anorexia, and they'll usually blame the beauty industry for promoting *unrealistic beauty standards for women*, which basically means that they make women feel fat and ugly so they can sell them diets and clothes and makeup. I think that's true. But it's not the whole story. Because *hello, I'm an anorexic, too*. And last time I checked, no one's trying to sell me makeup.

It's worse for girls. It must be. Their friends all tell them how good they look, how jealous they are, ask them to share their slimming secrets. I don't know what that feels like. I mean, I used to get called chubby sometimes, and now I don't. But that isn't the same. No one's actually telling me I look better this way.

On the other hand, when it comes to recovery, all that shit might take the pressure off. *Fine, I went a bit overboard there. But when everyone was telling me how good I looked, who could blame me? When you filled my brain with images of stick-thin girls and diet tips and exercise regimes, what did you expect?*

Me, I don't have anyone else to blame. I made that nagging voice up for myself. I gave her a name, showed her how to keep me in line. It's kind of impressive, actually, how I managed to screw my brain up all by myself.

Men can be muscly, as well as skinny. Even I know that. If I look at a picture of some football player, I can see that they're in shape. I can see they look good.

So why do I want to be stick-thin?

Now that I think of it, it's kind of funny that Ana, my inner anorexic, is pretty much the stereo-typical cool girl, the one who's bullying the shy, high-achieving girl with the demanding parents. Even in my head, anorexia's a disease for posh girls.

Man up, Max, for God's sake.

~

Even before I go inside the house, I know something's not right. There's only one car in the drive, and all the lights are on downstairs. I guess that wouldn't be strange in anyone else's house—it's not exactly late—but Dad is crazy about saving electricity. When we were little, he used to deduct five pence from our pocket money every time we left a light on accidentally.

For a moment, I'm happy: Finally, I've caught Dad breaking the rules. But then I get this weird, churning feeling in my stomach, like something bad is about to happen. Like this is the first scene in a horror movie. I try to tell myself that this feeling is pretty normal for me now, which is true. Another fun symptom of anorexia: You spend hours imagining all the terrible things that could happen to you and your family. All day long—or more commonly, all night long—I imagine terrorist attacks, house fires, kidnappings. Last night, I dreamed that Sultan got hit by a car.

"You're being stupid," I say out loud, trying to convince myself. It doesn't work. I take a gulp of air, then push open the front door.

"Hello?"

The voice comes from the lounge, and it's quickly followed by a volley of barks from Sultan. I feel a surge of happiness. Dad's here. Dad's alive! I start walking down the hall, without replying: I'm so relieved I've forgotten that he wasn't expecting me home.

"Who's there?" Dad shouts.

I reach the door to the lounge, peer around it. "It's me," I say. Sultan comes over, tail ablaze. I stroke his ears.

"Max," Dad says curiously, like he was expecting it to be someone else. He's standing in the middle of the room, looking lost. It doesn't look like he got up when I came in; it looks like he's been there for ages. "You scared me."

"I'm sorry," I reply. I look up at him properly. His eyes are red. He looks *tired*. I thought he only looked like that when I was around.

Sultan, satisfied that I'm a) a member of the pack and b) not about to feed him or take him for a walk, ambles over to the fireplace and slumps down on the rug.

"What are you doing home?" Dad asks. I see his face fall, a moment of panic. "Is everything all right? Where's Robin?"

"He's at Auntie Jess's," I say. "With James and Louise. Everything's fine."

"So why are you here?"

I don't say anything because I don't know what to say. I follow Sultan's lead and slump down on the sofa. Dad looks at me for a minute, then sits down next to me, and puts his arm around my shoulder.

We sit there in silence for a while. For a few minutes, I guess. Then, under my breath, I tell him, "I freaked out, Dad."

"It's okay," he says straight back.

"No, it's not. I left Robin on his own. I scared James and Louise. And Auntie Jess is going to flip."

I'm telling Dad what happened—but really, I'm telling myself, too. I hadn't processed any of it until now.

Dad's response is really weird. He laughs. I look up at him.

"She'll come around," he says. "Don't worry. Does Robin know where you are now?"

"I guess not."

He goes to call him. I stay sitting on the sofa. We have this big family portrait that sits on our mantelpiece from when I was six, and Robin was thirteen. Eight years ago. I barely remember going to get it taken, but Mum and Dad have filled in the blanks over the years. Mum made Robin wear a shirt and tie. He wasn't happy about it. He was a pretty moody teenager. (At least, I thought so at the time. It's all relative I guess.) About ten minutes before we were supposed to leave, he scrunched the shirt Mum had laid out for him into a big ball. Mum was furious. By the time she'd ironed it again, we were late. In the picture, you can see Dad's forehead is glistening slightly, and Mum's cheeks are red. Meanwhile, Robin is scowling like an eagle owl. Apparently, the photographer shot a whole roll of film, and Robin was scowling in every single photo. Mum tells this story every Christmas; she'll never let Robin forget it.

In that photo, I'm the one who looks happy and carefree. The only one. Now, eight years later, I'm the scowling teenager. I'm the one making everyone's life difficult. Will I grow out of it, like Robin did? Or am I too screwed up for that?

"Okay," says Dad, coming back into the room. "All

sorted. Robin says they ate everything in the end. Louise even had the peaches."

Which—guess what—makes me feel about a thousand times worse.

"Did you eat?" Dad says.

I had like five bites. "Yes," I tell him.

"I was about to make some noodles. Are you sure you don't—"

I cut him off. "I'm fine. Hey, where's Mum?" Because when was the last time Mum was out at 8:00 p.m. on a Saturday?

I see something strange in Dad's face—a flicker, like he was thrown off by the question somehow. But it only lasts a moment. He gives me one of his big goofy smiles. "She's having dinner with Clare and Bill."

"How come you didn't go? Are you ill?" I tilt my head. "You do look pretty tired."

"Gee, thanks. I just didn't really feel like it. Plus," he adds, pointing to the book on the table, "that thing doesn't read itself, you know."

The book is *Moby-Dick*. Dad's been reading it since before Christmas. The other day he said to me, *You know, I used to read a book a day before I had kids.*

Reading a book doesn't seem like a good enough reason not to go out. But what do I know?

Dad looks at his watch. "I'm happy to drive you back over to Auntie Jess's if you'd like."

"That's okay," I say. "Unless you want to get rid of me."

I meant it as a joke. Mostly. But Dad grabs my shoulders and gives me this super-serious look.

"I never want to get rid of you, Max. You shouldn't ever think that."

"Thanks?" I say, pulling a stop-being-a-freak-Dad face.

And then we both start laughing.

When you're anorexic, the line between happiness and sadness is thinner than spider silk. It takes the tiniest thought, the smallest push, to move you from one to the other. To ruin the best day ever or make a nightmare seem okay. I live on a knife-edge. I teeter back and forth; a feeling can last a second or an hour or a day. Sometimes, I'm in control just long enough that I think I've found a way to balance. To stay on the line everyone else seems to stay on without really thinking about it.

Then the universe gives me a shove.

I wake up when I hear the front door open. I check my phone: 3:02. I don't think Mum's ever stayed out past midnight before. I listen as she shuffles about downstairs, hanging her coat in the hallway, going to the bathroom, getting a glass of water from the kitchen. She pads gently up the stairs and opens the door to a room she's never slept in before, as far as I know: Robin's room. It clicks behind her. And then everything's quiet again.

March 3

Dear Ana,

Evie is weird. Like, super-weird. I mean, I know I'm
not exactly one to talk. But if there was a competition to find the world's Most Screwed-Up Teenager,
I think we'd both make the playoffs.

Today, in English, she did the weirdest thing
yet. We're studying this book called *Holes*, which is
about these kids who have to dig holes in the desert
as punishment for things they've done wrong. It's
pretty good, I guess, although it kind of makes me
sad that I can't do proper exercise anymore. I don't
think this is the reaction you're supposed to have.

Anyway, Evie was sitting right in front of me, so
I couldn't help watching what she was doing. What
she was doing was plucking the hairs out of her
eyebrow, one by one. That's eyebrow singular: the
left one.

But that wasn't even the weirdest thing.

Halfway through the lesson, Mr. French—yep,
our English teacher is called Mr. French—asked us
what symbols there are in the book. English teachers
believe everything in a book symbolizes something or
other, from the weather to the color of the main
character's T-shirt. I reckon that most of the time

the writer needed to pick a color, and they could just as easily have picked blue instead of orange.

Anyway, Mr. French decided to pick on me.

Mr. French: "Max, can you tell me what the most important symbol in *Holes* is?"

Me: "Ummm . . ."

I was hoping he'd just tell me or pick on someone else. But he didn't. Mr. French has serious stamina. So eventually, I gave him the best answer I had.

"Holes?"

I got a laugh for that, a real one. And right in front of me, there was this huge snort, like an elephant sneezing. Which made everyone laugh again. "Very droll, Mr. Howarth," said Mr. French, before telling us what the actual main symbol in the book is. (Onions, in case you're wondering.)

As soon as he looked away, Evie spun around and stared at me. Her left eyebrow was pretty much bare. She looked kind of crazy.

What? I mouthed at her. And okay, I'm not 100 percent sure what she mouthed back. I might have got it wrong. But I know what it looked like.

I love you.

Then she burst out laughing and turned back to face the front of the class.

At this point, I'm pretty used to people mocking me. But Evie has a grand total of zero friends at

Deanwater High. And one eyebrow. She spends most of her time standing across the playground from me, Stu, and Ram, just staring. In my opinion, she's definitely not in any position to mock.

At the end of class, I went up to her and said hi. I wanted to ask her what she'd said without telling her what I thought she'd said. But I didn't get the chance. She took one look at me, rolled her eyes, and said, "Leave me alone, dickhead."

Somehow, I now have two crazy girls in my life.

10

"There's a new one," Robin announces. "Come on."

I'm stretched out on the sofa, not watching TV. I don't react for a moment because I'm too surprised.

"Heellooo?" Robin says, waving his hand in front of my face like I'm a broken robot. "Is this thing on?"

I pick up the remote, pause. "Where?"

"I'll show you."

After what happened at Auntie Jess's house, I kind of assumed that was it: I'd blown it. Robin would never ever talk to me again. Sure enough, he's barely said a word to me for three weeks. In fact, he's gone out of his way to not even see me. For example, I'm pretty sure lumber companies don't normally deliver at 8:00 p.m., right when we normally have dinner.

So, yeah. It's kind of a shock when he launches into conversation like it's nothing.

I get my shoes and my fleece, and we set out toward town. Robin doesn't say anything else on the way. Ana starts to spin crazy theories, like, he's going to take me to the woods and kill me, or just tie me to a tree and leave me there.

It's like when you have mice: You have to take them at least a mile away to get rid of them, otherwise they come right back.

Even I can see she's gone off the deep end today.

Twenty minutes later, we're by the Starbucks on Station Road, trying to look for a geocache without looking like drug dealers. Our outfits don't exactly help. Robin is wearing his workshop jeans, which are speckled with blobs of paint and varnish and glue, plus a white T-shirt. I'm in some old combat trousers with holes in the knees, and an orange T-shirt that I got when we went to Amsterdam five years ago (it was big on me then, but still, I'm wearing a nine-year-old's T-shirt, and it's not even tight), and a purple fleece. If a police officer strolled by right now, I wouldn't blame him for asking what's going on here.

The clue just says "Itsy bitsy," which we assume means it's something to do with a drainpipe; there are two running down the wall between Starbucks and the charity shop next door. Nothing else seems plausible. Sometimes, the tagged location is off by a few meters. But it's never more than that.

"Itsy bitsy," Robin murmurs to himself for the fifth time, as though if he'd said it enough times, the cache might magically reveal itself. His eyes slowly climb the drainpipe.

"Anyone found it yet?" I ask.

Most caches get muggled eventually. That means someone who doesn't know about geocaching finds it and moves it, or destroys it. If a cache hasn't been found for a while, there's a good chance it's been muggled.

"First one was two days ago," Robin says, running his hand behind the pipe. "And the guy said, 'Very clever,' which I reckon means it's well hidden."

"Okay," I say, sagging slightly.

We search for ages. We don't, like, actually want to get arrested, so we keep doing these slow walks back and forth. Robin jokes that we should have brought stick-on mustaches and changes of clothes, in case anyone is watching us. I laugh, but not because he's actually funny—he isn't. I'm just relieved he's talking to me. I still can't work out if he's just forgotten he's mad at me or he's trying to show me that it's over.

Anyway, we think we're being pretty subtle until this old lady with a shopping cart comes up to us and says, *Are you* still *bothering that squirrel?* So much for being super-sleuths.

Eventually, Robin gives me this pained look and shrugs. "I give up." Me and Robin are similar in lots of ways, and one of them is, we both hate giving up on stuff.

"It could have been muggled in the past two days," I point out.

He nods. "Maybe." But you can tell he doesn't believe it. I don't either, really. I was just trying to make him feel better. He points at Starbucks and says, "Hey, you want to get a drink? My treat."

"Um, sure."

Robin has a super-mega-triple-double caramel latte, or something. I have a tap water.

"Want anything to eat?" he asks me, grinning. He does this sometimes: jokes about it. I'm cool with it. In fact, I kind of like it. It breaks the tension. Unfortunately, Mum and Dad will never, ever get to this point. I tried to make a joke to Mum a couple of weeks ago. We were out walking Sultan, and we had to cross a cattle grid. I said, *I better go around or I'll fall through*. Robin would have laughed his head off at this for sure. But Mum looked like I'd punched her in the gut.

It's different with Robin.

"You know what, I'm good," I tell him. "Thanks, though."

"Suit yourself, stickman," he replies. "I'm having a muffin."

I laugh. *Stickman* is new. It's a lot better than *little bro*.

"What's the occasion?" I ask him as we sit down.

He gives me a strange look. I probably shouldn't say anything. As Dad says, *Don't look a gift horse in the mouth*. But I don't understand why he's being so nice to me, after ignoring me for almost a month.

"Do I need an excuse to treat my little bro to a, um, tap water?"

"In my experience, yes." On top of everything else, Robin earns like zero pounds a week, and he's like Dad: He never spends it. We're not exactly the kind of family that just decides to go to Starbucks.

"Then prepare for a new experience. I want to hear how everything's going. Tell me: What's new at Deanwater?"

I shrug. "School is school."

"Any new faces? How's Miss Jacobs?"

Miss Jacobs taught Robin math. She also taught him how to love. Okay, I'm kidding. But . . . Miss Jacobs doesn't look like other math teachers. She's six feet tall, and she has this amazing raven-black hair. She's pretty fit. Robin was in her first-ever class, when she was straight out of teacher training college, which I guess would make her twenty-two or something. And, um, he was a big fan. Even now, asking me about her, he looks a little misty-eyed.

"I told you, I don't have her this year."

Robin shakes his head. "It's a cruel world."

"There's this new girl in my class," I say, before I think about what I'm saying.

Robin raises an eyebrow. "Oh?"

"It doesn't matter," I say quickly.

"It definitely does. Go on. What's her name?"

And against my better judgment, I tell him. "Evie."

"Even?"

Well, I did kind of mumble. "Ee-vee."

"Oh, cute," Robin says. He takes a sip of his drink and makes this if-you-know-what-I-mean face.

"Robin," I say.

"It *is* cute," he says. "I've never met an Evie before. *Ee-vee*. Nice."

"I don't fancy her," I tell him. "It's not like that."

He spreads his arms, like Jesus at the Last Supper. "Little bro," he says. "Who said anything about fancying? I"—he draws out the *I*—"didn't mention anything of the sort. No, little bro, you brought that up all on your own."

I scowl at him.

"I'm just saying." He shrugs, then takes another sip of his drink, then waits a beat. "I hope you and Evie are very happy together."

Before he even finishes speaking, he braces himself for a punch on the arm. I don't disappoint him.

"Anyway," he says. "I have some news."

"I knew it," I say.

He breaks a big chunk of his muffin and crams it into his mouth. We look at each other while he chews. I tap my wrist where my watch would be—I've stopped wearing it, because it just looks silly now—as if to say *Spit it out then.*

I get bored of waiting and take a sip of my water. Eventually, after like thirty seconds, he swallows the muffin. He waits a beat before speaking.

"I'm moving out."

I sputter and manage to spill water all down my front. "Shit," I say. Then I look at him. I want to say a thousand things—mostly things that, if I said them in school, would get me immediate detention. I want to ask him whether it's because of what happened with James and Louise. I want to ask him how he could do this. I want to plead with him to stay, and I want to tell him to get lost because we'll be just fine without him.

Instead I say, "How come?"

He sniffs. I can't tell if he's upset or bored or embarrassed. "It's time. Mum and Dad have enough to worry about these days without me knocking around."

I look down at my lap. I know exactly what he means. And before I can stop myself, I feel my shoulders shaking.

"Oh, bro . . . I didn't mean that."

I look up at him. There are these bright spotlights on the ceiling, and the tears streak the light across my eyes, like when you're driving through rain and the streetlights become big orange brushstrokes.

"It's not like that," he says. "It's just . . . I mean . . . with Mum's work and everything . . ."

He stumbles, trying to deflect the blame onto

anything but me. He thinks I'm crying because I've just found out that I'm a burden to Mum and Dad. But that's not the reason. I already know I'm a burden to Mum and Dad; it doesn't take a genius to figure that one out.

I'm crying because I just lost the only person I can really talk to.

I'm crying because now I'm totally alone.

March 11
Dear Ana,

Today I saw Lindsay for the first time in over a month, because she's been on holiday. It wasn't too bad. I've lost half a pound, which is somehow enough to make me feel okay, but not enough to freak Lindsay out. The perfect amount.

Even so, she decided to make up two new rules. As if I don't have enough rules in my life already.

Rule One: the not-keeping-a-food-diary thing is now permanent. Actually, I'm not as bothered about this as I thought I'd be. At this point, I pretty much know how many calories there are in everything anyway. And I hate to admit it, but since I stopped writing everything down, I do seem to spend less time worrying about it.

Rule Two: I have to start taking vitamins. Technically, this isn't Lindsay's rule. It's from my nutritionist, Dr. Roberts. I'm okay with this because he's given me regular ones—not flavored or chewable or whatever. As long as it doesn't seem like food and contains absolutely zero calories, it's okay.

We spent most of my session talking about Lindsay's holiday, which got me thinking about last summer—aka, the time when you first decided to climb inside my head. Okay, so I still don't have a clue why I ended up like this. But I do know when it happened. The two-week period when my life started to fall apart.

Robin called it the Last Great Hurrah. He'd decided it wasn't cool to keep going on holiday with your family in your twenties, but that he'd come one more time. He said it like he was doing us a massive favor. I'm sure it was nothing to do with the fact that he was totally broke.

We went to Venice and Verona for two weeks. We arrived in the middle of a heat wave: It was 35°C the day we landed, and that was the coolest it got. Luckily, we weren't camping—Dad decided that because it was Robin's last holiday, we'd stay in hotels instead. On the downside, he also decided to save two euros a day on the rental car by not getting AC.

Naturally, because we're Howarths, we didn't let the heat slow us down. During the daytime, we traipsed around museums and churches and gardens. We went to Saint Mark's Square and Juliet's balcony, and we saw an opera, which is four hours of my life I'll never get back. (The opera was in Verona's Roman amphitheater. Thankfully, it started at sunset, or else I'm pretty sure we would have baked to death.) At one point Robin said to me, I can't believe I chose to come on this holiday.

Because it was so hot, none of us really felt like eating much in the daytime, except for the odd ice cream. So, our evening meal was pretty much the only thing we ate. And going out to restaurants on holiday was kind of new for us because we usually cooked our own meals at the campsite.

The only problem was, it was expensive, especially in Venice. Robin didn't seem to notice. He kept ordering these steaks that were, like, thirty euros, as well as a starter and a pizza. And because it was the Last Great Hurrah, Dad didn't say anything. But I saw him and Mum looking at each other, like, Ouch, and then Mum would say, I think I'm going to have a salad, and Dad would have some plain tomato pasta or whatever.

And I didn't want to make things worse. So I had salad, too. It wasn't so bad, actually—it turns out, if you don't eat all day, you kind of go past hunger. I mean, I'd been drinking Cokes and eating ice cream, so I wasn't exactly starving. But still.

It's not like I immediately became an anorexic. When we got home, I went back to having seconds every time we ate and, you know, actually eating lunch. But I reckon Italy planted a seed. Now I knew that I could not eat and still get on with my life.

When school started again and Ram was off sick and Stu was at football training most lunchtimes

and I had to eat on my own, I knew I could just . . .
not do it. I've always been kind of self-conscious
about eating anyway (I mean, no one likes eating on
their own in public, right?). So I thought, why put
myself through it?

The answer's pretty obvious now. Not putting
myself through it meant giving you the chance to
climb into my head. It's a whole lot easier to stop
eating than to stop not eating. But I didn't know
that at the time.

11

Robin's moving out today. Me and Mum are helping.

He's renting a flat in Chorley: five minutes' walk from the workshop, twenty minutes' drive from home. It's *tiny*. If he stretches out, Robin can touch all four bedroom walls at once. (He shows me as soon as he arrives; he seems weirdly happy about it.) There's no kitchen, just a row of cabinets and a hotplate along one wall of the living room. There isn't even room for a microwave, which is Robin's go-to method of cooking. He says he doesn't need one.

It makes zero sense. His room at home is almost as big as this entire flat. We've got a shed to store his mountain bike in—whereas here, he has to put it in the hallway, right next to the sign that says NO BIKES OR PRAMS.

"So, what do you think?" he asks me, as we traipse

up the stairs for about the fiftieth time. Robin's carrying two massive boxes; I can only manage a tote bag full of clothes.

"I don't get it," I tell him honestly.

He laughs. "One day you'll understand."

That pisses me off because it's super-patronizing. Like when Robin tells Mum he never wants kids, and she says *You'll change your mind someday.* He gets mad at that. But apparently, it's okay for him to do it.

There is an upside to all this, though. I'm getting Robin's room, which means I'll finally have room to put all my posters up. There are two I've wanted up for ages. One is a guide to all the raptors—that means birds of prey—you can see in Europe. I got it for my birthday last year. The other is a Peters projection world map. Regular world maps are Mercator projections. They have straight longitude lines, but all the countries and islands are stretched to fit on a flat surface, so nothing's the right size, especially if it's near the poles. For example, Greenland is about ten times its actual size on a Mercator. Peters projections show all the countries to scale. In my opinion, they are much better maps, as long as you aren't using them to navigate with.

On the whole, though, I'd probably still rather have Robin. Even if he is a pain in the ass sometimes.

"Is that it?" Mum says, as we put the final boxes down in the living room.

"That's it," Robin says.

"Phew," says Mum. "Oh, I almost forgot! Wait here." She zooms back out of the door.

Dad isn't here. For some reason, he picked today as the day to finally finish building his rock garden, which basically means wheelbarrowing the three tons of rock that have been sitting in our driveway for six months along the side of the house and dumping them next to the pond. I'm not sure why he's picked today to do this. Maybe he's upset Robin's leaving, too, and wanted an excuse not to come. But that's not really like Dad. I thought Mum would be furious about it, but if she is, she's hiding it well.

Me and Robin stand in the living room, waiting for Mum. It feels awkward, even though Robin's basically the only person I never feel awkward around. He's opened a box of kitchen stuff—cutlery, pans—and now we're both staring at it.

He fishes out a honey dipper and waggles it at me. "Oh, good, I'm glad Mum packed this. I've been worrying about how I'll dispense honey in my new home."

I laugh.

"Hey," he says, pointing at me with the dipper. "How's your you-know-what?"

I shrug. What do I even say to that? He's moving out, and he's asking me about my stupid cache. "It's fine," I mutter.

"Any good visitors lately?"

"Nah."

That isn't exactly true. The other day, there was a really weird note in my logbook. It just said:

Sorry I was a doofus to you.

Ever since I found it, I've been racking my brains about who it's from and what it means. Until twenty seconds ago, I thought it might have been from Robin. But either he's a much better actor than I realized, or it wasn't him.

It could be someone from school, but there are only three people at school who owe me an apology: Darren, Shinji, and Evie. I can rule out the first two right off the bat: The chances of Darren or Shinji ever apologizing for anything are zilch. It's more likely that the Sahara will freeze over tomorrow.

That leaves Evie. I mean, I guess it could be her. She was acting pretty strange in English the other day. But she doesn't exactly seem like the type to apologize. Or the type to use the word *doofus*.

It could be from a stranger. Maybe someone mistook my cache for someone else's. Or maybe they were just messing about, trying to freak me out.

Robin shakes his head. "That one on Station Road is still bugging me. 'Itsy bitsy.' It's got to be the drainpipe, right?"

I shrug. "I think so."

Mum comes back carrying a present, wrapped in some of Dad's carefully recycled Christmas wrapping paper.

"What's this?"

"A little housewarming gift." She hands it to Robin.

Robin carefully unwraps a cardboard box, then removes the lid. Inside is a loaf of bread, a candle, and a bottle of wine. Robin looks confused. I'm thinking Mum's gone loopy and really should have asked me what Robin's into if this is the best she could come up with.

Mum catches Robin's face and laughs. "They're traditional," she explains. "Bread so you're never hungry, wine so you're never thirsty, and a candle so your home is always filled with light."

"Er, thanks, Mum," Robin says. He looks at me and rolls his eyes.

I laugh.

"That's the last time I get you a present, Robin," Mum says. Then she puts on her Serious Mum face. "Don't leave the candle unattended, please. And, for God's sake, share that bottle of wine with someone. Ffion, for instance. Now, who wants a cup of tea?"

"Please," Robin says.

"I'm fine," I say. Like she was expecting any other answer. I turn to Robin. "Who's Ffion?"

Robin waves a hand. "She's nobody."

"I hope you don't tell her that," says Mum.

"All right, fine," Robin says. He turns to me. "She's my Evie."

April 4

Dear Ana,

I'm sitting in the room that was Robin's room seven
days ago. Dad said I should move in straightaway—
apparently, it will "help us adjust." But so far, we've
only moved my bed and my desk and my chest of
drawers. There are no books or posters or anything.
It's kind of bare and kind of sad.

Today, I read this thing online about Zeno's Paradox, which is an example of what Dad calls a thought
experiment. Say you have a race between a tortoise
and a hare, and the hare is ten times as fast, but you
give the tortoise a hundred-meter head start. By
the time the hare has run those hundred meters, the
tortoise has shuffled ten meters forward. And once
the hare has covered those ten meters, the tortoise
has moved another meter ahead. If you keep breaking
it down, the hare never actually overtakes the tortoise. Even though it's ten times as fast.

Zeno has been screwing with my head all day. Of
course, it doesn't actually work like that. Trust me,
when my dad drives down the motorway at sixty
miles per hour, people overtake him all the time. But
the point is, when you look at a snapshot, nothing
really makes sense.

At least, I think that's what the point is.

It reminds me of this story that Mr. Sumner, my primary school principal, used to tell at the end of assembly. (Mr. Sumner told a story every day, but he only knew about ten, so we got to know each one pretty well.) It goes like this: Once, a group of travelers stop near a village. They're hungry, but they don't have any food with them, so they fill a huge cauldron with river water and put a big stone in the bottom. A passing villager asks them what they're doing. "We're making stone soup," they say. "It's almost ready—but we could do with a little bit of carrot to make it extra-tasty." So he goes and brings them some carrots and heads on his way. Then another villager comes. This time they say, "A few herbs would really help bring out the flavor." And so on. Each villager who comes past brings them a little something—a handful of salt, some beans, a chicken carcass—until, eventually, the travelers really do have a nourishing, delicious soup, which they share with all the villagers.

Anorexia is the same thing in reverse. It's Zeno's Paradox in super-slow motion. You keep taking stuff away: food. Friends. Family. Until one day you realize there's nothing left. The hare's overtaken the tortoise. The soup is just water.

Okay, I'm not sure that made any sense at all. It's, like, 00:36 now. I should probably go to bed. I wish Robin were here.

12

"We're going to the zoo," Ram announces trium-
phantly. He shrugs his backpack off and pulls out his
lunchbox.

"What, right now?"

"That's dead funny, Stu. You're a regular come-
dian," says Ram.

Stu puffs out his cheeks and nods. "I try."

"It's a good idea, isn't it?" Ram carries on. "I want
to see the lion feeding. I've heard they catapult a goat
over the fence."

"Sounds idyllic. Anyway, I'm pretty sure going to
the zoo was Max's—"

"May ninth. You better both be free."

Stu leans back in his chair and shrugs. "I'll have to
check my diary."

"Move over, loser."

The voice comes from behind me. I watch Ram's and Stu's eyes bulge in unison. I don't move because I don't need to: There's loads of room.

"C'mon, I ain't got all day."

I shuffle my chair about a quarter of an inch to the right, and Evie sits down, satisfied. I'm thinking it was less about the room and more about making me move for her.

We all bring a packed lunch, and normally, we eat in the playground. Sort of to avoid situations like this. But today, it's raining like crazy—*like Thor's piss* is how Dad put it this morning. So we're all crammed into the Big Hall.

I say *crammed*, but whenever we sit inside, there's almost always an empty seat next to me. More than 850 students in one assembly hall, and somehow, there's still plenty of room for avoiding Max. Today, I watched three separate people spot the empty seat, look at me, then find some way of sardining themselves onto another table.

Evie digs into her satchel and pulls out her lunchbox. As soon she takes the lid off, Ram leans in. "What you got there?" he asks. He tries to say it casually, like he's asking about the weather or if we have math today. But it's pretty obvious why he's asking.

If it wasn't for Ram's appetite, I'm not sure our friendship would've made it through the past six months. He's a bottomless pit; he can put away anything you give him and more. I still eat my lunch every day, but the extra snacks I bring to school—the snacks Mum and Dad and Lindsay think (or at least hope) I'm eating? They all go to Ram. At this point, I'm basically bribing him to be my friend with chips and chocolate bars.

But apparently, one supplier isn't enough.

"My lunch," Evie says. She looks him dead in the eye, then adds, "For me."

I snort. Evie may be a fruitcake, but she can be pretty funny.

"That a jam sandwich?" Ram says, as Evie unwraps a foil parcel, like an archaeologist unwrapping a mummy.

Evie looks at him like she might slap him. Eventually, she sighs and nods.

"And Mini Cheddars," Ram adds. "Nice."

"Nothing gets past you," Evie says.

Me and Stu look at each other, trying not to laugh.

Evie pulls her phone and a book out of her bag, and places them both next to her lunchbox.

"And I thought you were here for the scintillating conversation," says Stu.

Stu hates it when people use their phones in front of him. When I first met him, I couldn't work it out. This is a guy who carries a phone, headphones, a smart watch, and at least one Nintendo console with him at all times. But then I went to his house. Stu's family is Quaker, which means they're the nicest people on earth and put a lot of emphasis on face-to-face interaction. He's allowed to use all the technology he wants, as long as it never gets in the way of a conversation. I've never seen him even glance at his phone without asking the permission of everyone he's with first.

Evie doesn't clock Stu's comment. Her phone's in her lap, and she's busy sending a long series of emoji to someone or other.

Ram looks nervous. "You know they'll take it off you if they see it, right?"

"I know," replies Evie, cool as cucumber dip.

She opens the book and slots her phone into a deep hole cut into the pages. She turns down the brightness—so it doesn't catch your eye, I guess—and then she resumes what seems to be her favorite activity: scrolling.

"Niiice," says Ram.

Stu scowls. If he was unhappy about the phone thing, I can't even imagine how he feels about the book. I remember him laying into me once for turning down the corner of a page to mark my place. (I've said it before and I'll say it again: Stu's a total nerd, and it's a bloody good thing he can play football.)

Ram, Stu, and I drift back to the conversation we were having before Evie arrived.

"How many people are coming?" I ask.

Ram twitches his nose for a moment. "Just you guys," he says quietly.

"Hold on a second," Stu says. "I thought you were having some huge party. The biggest social event of the year, you said."

"Yeah, well, I changed my mind, didn't I?" Ram barks.

"All right, I was only asking," Stu says.

I get the feeling there's something Ram isn't telling us. But I'm also getting the feeling he doesn't particularly want to tell us.

"What's all this then?" Evie asks, without looking

up from her book, aka her phone.

"Er . . . my birthday party," Ram says. When she doesn't reply, he adds, "We're going to the zoo."

"Sounds shit," Evie says.

"She's such a charmer," Stu says. He plucks a cherry tomato from his lunchbox and pops it into his mouth.

"Aren't you going to invite me?" Evie asks. To be clear, she still hasn't looked up from her phone. Stu's now staring at her, like, with his mouth hanging open slightly. I can see some tomato seeds. It's pretty gross.

"Am I?" asks Ram.

"I wouldn't," Stu mutters.

"There's no need to be rude," Evie says. "Dick-head."

Stu doesn't even know how to respond to that. He looks at both of us, as if to say, *Am I hearing this correctly?*

"If it sounds shit, why do you want to come?" Ram asks.

"Because Max will be there, of course. I *luuuurve* him, don't I, Max?" She flutters her eyelids at me, then bursts out laughing.

"Um," I say. What the hell am I supposed to say to that?

"Fair enough," Ram says. "I tell you what: You can come to my party if you give me those Mini Cheddars."

"Deal," Evie says. She picks the bag up by the corner and tosses it at Ram. "I don't even like them."

"Well, now I'm *really* looking forward to this party," Stu says, slumping his chin on his hands.

"Anyway," Evie says, closing the book with her phone inside, putting it on top of her lunchbox. "I'd love to stay and chat, but I've got places to be. By the way, Ram, you should share those with Max." She's pointing at the Mini Cheddars. "He's looking pretty skinny."

She laughs again, then picks up her rucksack, and runs off.

"What was that about?" says Ram, opening the Mini Cheddars and offering them to me and Stu.

I shake my head. I feel as though my cheeks could melt a block of steel right now. "Beats me."

April 9
Dear Ana,

I nearly lost it with Mum tonight. She's on this
diet where she basically only eats at dinnertime.
For breakfast and lunch, she has juice or soup. Okay,
so I'm not exactly qualified to lecture people on
healthy eating, but it doesn't sound healthy. At
least it's better than last year, when she did that
one where she only ate raw foods.

Anyway, this evening she came home complaining
about how hungry she was. Dad was like, "Have a
snack then," and Mum replied, "It's not that easy."
Then she turned to me and added. "Max knows what
it's like. Don't you, love?"

Um, no I don't.

It's not Mum's fault, but what she said kind
of made me want to scream. It happens all the
time. Whenever someone talks about anorexia in
a magazine or on TV, they basically treat it like a
really strict diet. That's like treating the Pacific
Ocean as if it were a really big paddling pool. And
then telling someone who's spent the last six
months in a submarine that you know exactly how
they feel.

I get that diets suck, and that loads of people—
especially women—are under pressure to lose

weight. But it's totally, totally different. You know why? Because when you're on a diet, there's an end point. Because when you're on a diet, you <u>want</u> people to notice. Because when you're on a diet, you don't have some psycho called Ana whispering in your ear 24/7.

Sorry, Ana. But it's true.

13

I just heard it. The first one this year. I look at my phone to double-check the date.

April 11.

Too early. I must have made a mistake.

But then I hear it again.

Wow.

April 11.

Usually, the first time anyone in the whole of England hears a cuckoo is about April 10, in either Devon or Cornwall. They don't get up here until at least the twentieth. But they're getting earlier and earlier.

Cuckoos are the coolest and weirdest—and evilest—birds in the world. Instead of raising their own chicks, they lay eggs in other birds' nest, so those birds do all the hard work for them. And then, when a cuckoo chick hatches, it pushes all the other eggs out of the nest so it gets all the food. Evil, right?

You'd think the bird raising the chick would notice. All I can say is, the phrase *bird-brained* exists for a reason. But it definitely, definitely doesn't apply to cuckoos.

A cuckoo call is slap-in-the-face obvious, once you know what you're looking for. I mean listening for. You can't miss it. It sounds—well, it sounds like someone saying *cuckoo*. It's only the males you hear. The females, who do all the sneaky egg-laying, tend to keep quiet. (As Dad puts it: *I wonder why.*)

I head to the lake. That weird message I got in my cache—*Sorry I was a doofus to you*—is still bugging me. I want to check if any other caches nearby have had anything similar.

But at the cache under the bench, it's all the usual stuff: *Nice work! TFTC*, et cetera. I can't help noticing that this cache gets way more visitors than mine, though. For example, seven people have visited since April 1. I'm lucky to get two a week.

It's like your geocache is radiating the same loser aura as you. Impressive.

Just as I'm putting the cache back, someone very close behind me shouts, "What are *you* up to, Max?"

Super-loud, right in my ear.

A girl's voice.

Naturally, I smack my head on the bench in surprise. And then, as I crawl out from underneath it, I nearly lose my trousers.

I got this pair only a month ago, and they're already getting loose.

Once I'm free, I look up. And guess who I see standing over me?

"Looking for a bag of chips, Max? Maybe a Snickers?"

"No," I shoot back, a hot, angry word that spills from my mouth like a flame, even though I know she's not really asking.

She shakes her head at me. "I'm *joking*, dickhead. You need to chill out." She sniffs thoughtfully. "Although, you really could use a meal or two. So, what *are* you doing under a park bench?"

"Nothing," I reply. When I first went to high school, Robin taught me his one golden rule: *Deny everything they can't prove.* According to Robin, this rule was what got him through secondary school—

and I have to say, it's worked pretty well for me so far. "What are you doing here, anyway?" I ask, knocking the ball back into her court.

Evie crosses her arms and gives me a no-bullshit look. The kind of look cops give in movies, right before the perp breaks down and tells them everything. "Pretty sure I asked first."

I stick to the script. "I'm not doing anything."

"Yeah, right," Evie says with an eye roll.

Evie's wearing cutoff jeans, purple Converse, and a white T-shirt that says BLAME IT ON THE DISCO in big black letters across the chest. Her rabbit-brown hair is tied up, but her bangs hang down over her eyes. It must be super-annoying.

I have no idea what to do next. All the advice I've read about muggles says not to get spotted; it doesn't tell you what happens when you do. Maybe I'm supposed to convert her, to bring her into the geocaching community. Maybe I'm supposed to move the cache to a new location and fess up online.

Or maybe it's never happened before. Maybe there's no advice because no one has ever been stupid enough to get into this situation.

I realize I'm still crouched on all fours like Gollum or something. I jump up and dust the dirt off my knees.

Evie digs into her back pocket and pulls out a box of Nerds. Who eats Nerds anymore? She opens the box and lifts it to her mouth, ready to pour, then stops. "I'm still waiting for an answer."

Maybe the Robin Howarth technique isn't foolproof after all.

I point at the bench. "There's a geocache under there."

"A what?"

"A geocache. It's a little box you have to try and find."

She scrunches up her face. "Why?"

"For fun. Look." I pull out my phone. "You have this app, which gives you the location. And when you find one, you write in the logbook."

"That sounds stupid," Evie says.

I shrug. "Suit yourself." Evie seems to think everything's stupid.

She slumps down on the bench and pulls out her phone. For a moment, I think she's going to give it a go—geocaching, I mean. But instead, she starts scrolling through photos, like I'm not even there. I stand there for a bit, hoping maybe the ground will open up and swallow me. Or her.

She thinks you're a loser. And she's right.

I can't decide whether to leg it, or to play it cool and stroll off casually. On the one hand, I don't want her telling people that I'm the kind of total weirdo who runs off in the middle of a conversation. On the other, I'm pretty sure they already know. Plus, it's not like she actually has anyone to tell. She's as much of a loner as I am. No, wait, she's *more* of a loner—at least I've got Ram and Stu.

I turn to go.

"So, what's the deal with Deanwater?"

I turn back to her. Naturally, she hasn't looked up from her phone or anything. I frown, not that she can see me frowning. "What do you mean?"

"Everyone's so uptight. At my old school, we did whatever we wanted."

Like telling people you love them and calling them dickheads and playing with your phone the whole time? That's what I want to say because, right now, Evie's really pissing me off. "So why did you move?" I ask her.

That makes her look up. She looks at me like I've

punched her on the nose.

"I didn't want to, idiot. They *made* me move."

"How come? And who's *they*?"

"God, you ask stupid questions," she says, shaking her head at me. "I was kicked out."

"Oh," I say. I want to ask why, but I'm not sure if I should. I never am with Evie.

She gives me another psycho grin. It's the sort of grin the bad guy in a film pulls when he's captured the good guy and he's explaining his evil genius plan before he shoots him. Evie's grin gives me major creeps.

"Why?" I can't help it. It just comes out, somewhere between a croak and a whisper. A crisper?

Evie doesn't flinch. "Because Amelia Jones is a bloody rat, that's why."

Of course, this just opens up ten more questions. Who is Amelia Jones? What was she squealing on Evie about? Had Evie actually done anything wrong? I feel like I've regressed to that toddler stage when you ask questions constantly. *Where are we going? The supermarket. Why are we going to the supermarket? Because we need milk. Why do we need milk? Because we put it in our tea. Why do we put it in our tea?*

Et cetera.

"I wish that bird would shut up," she mutters.

She means the cuckoo. She has a point, I guess. It's pretty loud. It can't be more than a couple of trees away. I consider telling her that she should be happy: Hearing a cuckoo on April 11 is kind of amazing. But I have a hunch she won't take that very well.

She jumps up off the bench. "Do you like Nerds?" she says, thrusting the box in my direction. Somehow, Evie even manages to handle a box of Nerds like it's a lethal weapon. I guess for me, it kind of is.

"No thanks," I murmur.

"Of course you don't," she says. "Anyway, I've downloaded the app." She turns her phone so I can see. It's the home screen of the geocaching app. That means she must have already set up an account. "What happens next?"

I show her the one under the bench first. I take out the logbook and the pencil, show her all the messages people have left. She tells me it's *the lamest thing I've ever seen.*

"I can't believe you waste your time doing this," she says.

I shift from foot to foot, like Sonic the Hedgehog. What do I say to that?

It's not like you have anything better to do, is it?

Harsh, but fair.

Then I have an idea.

"Yeah, this one's pretty lame. But *this one*"—I hand my phone to her—"this one's super-cool. Amazing, actually. I'm not sure you're ready to see it."

She takes my phone and stares at it for, like, fifteen seconds. Like she's paused due to a bad connection. Meanwhile, my mind is racing with ideas of how she's going to react. Is she going to smash my phone into the ground? Is she going to cry? Is she going to punch me?

Nope.

She looks up at me for a second. I swear her eyes change color, like traffic lights. A flash of green. A flicker of amber. A blaze of red.

But for Evie, red doesn't mean stop. Evie doesn't live by the rules of normal human beings.

"I'm ready," she says, all cocky. "But there's one thing you should know."

"What?" I ask.

Then she does it again. Mouths three words that make zero sense, but even so, make my spine feel like it's being tickled from the inside.

I love you.

And before I can react, she's gone. She's legged it. *With my phone.* I run after her, but there are thick gorse bushes all around the lake: If you want to disappear, it's pretty easy. And apparently, I'm not the only person around here who's into that.

Evie's like quantum mechanics, or relatively. Occasionally, you think you've got your head around her. But you're always wrong.

I do know one thing, though.

I know where she's going.

~

She's so fast she must actually be a witch. She must be able to fly or teleport or . . . *something.* I know the Common like it's my bedroom, and I know exactly where I'm going. Plus, I'm the second-fastest runner in our year.

Or at least, the second-fastest boy.

She beats me there. And you know what? She doesn't even seem tired.

I, on the other hand, am gasping. Like, I literally can't speak for a good thirty seconds. I double over, with my hands braced on my knees, breathing like Darth Vader on sports day.

She looks at me, amused.

"What . . . was that . . . all . . . about?" I eventually manage.

She shrugs. "It's a race, isn't it?"

I give up trying to stand and sit down on the pavement. In the gutter. I can feel sweat running down my back and pooling in my ass crack. Nice.

"Not really," I tell her.

"Oh," she says.

"Can I have my phone back?" I ask.

"Oh yeah," she says. "Sorry."

Did she just apologize to me? I didn't think she even knew the word *sorry.*

"What about the bit . . ." I trail off.

"What bit?" she says, tilting her head like a dog.

The bit where you told me you loved me. But I can't ask that: It sounds properly mental.

"Never mind," I tell her.

"O-kay," she says slowly. "Anyway, you were right."

"I was? About what?"

"About this cache. It's pretty cool."

"You mean . . ."

No way. There's no way she's found it already. The other week, Robin and I were here for forty-five minutes. I shake my head.

She holds up a little disc of metal about the size of a bottle cap. No wait, bigger. The wheel on a wheelie suitcase. "Tell me, Max. What does it feel like to be beaten by a girl?"

I guess she's figured out that I've never found this cache before.

"It's not . . . I've just . . ."

"Forgotten how to speak?" Evie suggests.

She twists the disc, so it springs into two pieces, and offers them to me like communion wafers. I take them, turn them over in my hands. One is a flat disc of metal with a threaded edge. Nothing special. But inside the other, there's a thin ticker tape of paper, coiled like a snail's shell, and underneath that, a single pencil lead slotted into a groove in the metal. It's amazing. It's as intricate and precise as a pocket watch.

"Woah," I say.

"Clever, huh?" Evie says.

"Where was it?"

She shows me. It was set into the middle of a drain cover—specifically, a drain cover with eight spokes radiating from its center, like spiders' legs. Drains. Spiders. Itsy Bitsy. I look up. We're standing literally opposite the front door of Starbucks, exactly where it's tagged. Geocaching has a habit of making you feel really, really stupid sometimes.

"Can I ask you a question?" I blurt. I want to ask it before my brain—or Ana, or both—tells me not to.

"Mmm," Evie says, nodding her head.

"How come you, er . . . Why did you . . ."

Evie smirks. "Spit it out, Max."

"What did you mouth to me before? And the other day?"

"Elephant juice," she replies cheerily.

"Huh?"

"Look at my lips." She says it again: "Ell-ee-fant-joos."

Then I understand; it looks like *I love you.*

"That's what you were saying?"

She nods.

"Um, why?"

"It's funny."

"Okay," I say quietly.

Long pause.

Wait a minute. Did you actually, seriously think she loved you?

Shut up, Ana.

HA! This is priceless! Even your parents don't love you, Max. Come on.

But how come she . . .

"You know what?" Evie says, snapping me out of my argument with Ana. I guess I'm grateful for that at least.

"What?" I say. I'm thinking, what's she going to say now? Maybe she's about to tell me I'm looking awfully chubby today, or that she snuck into my house this morning and murdered my parents. My stomach feels like it weighs about three tons.

"You're pretty cool, Max Howarth."

April 26

Dear Ana,

I try not to think about how things were before because it makes me feel way too guilty. Not long ago, we were a totally normal family. We went for walks. We had people over for BBQs. I'm not saying it was perfect or anything, I mean, what family is perfect? We argued all the time. Especially with Robin. Until recently, Robin was kind of a pain in the ass. He used to lock himself in his room for hours, playing heavy metal at, like, 120 decibels, and ignoring Mum when she hammered on the door. And/or he used to go mountain biking in the middle of the night and not tell Mum and Dad, so they pretty much freaked out when they realized he wasn't there.

I was a pain, too—but in different ways. Like when I bought some sketchy PC games from eBay and managed to wipe the hard drive of every computer in the house. Or when Stu was trying to teach me and Ram how to not suck at football, and we were practicing keepy-uppies in the back garden, and Ram booted the ball into Dad's greenhouse and smashed three windows.

But it was all normal stuff. My parents didn't have to keep making excuses for why they couldn't have people over for dinner. When we argued, they didn't spend the next two days worrying about whether I would binge or cut my arms or worse. And I didn't wake up every morning wondering whether today would be the day I finally end up in the hospital.

When you're anorexic, there is no normal. Ever. It's like you've dropped some dye into a swimming pool: it slowly spreads through the water, turning everything the same color. Now Mum can't go to the post office without seeing a flyer for karate classes at the leisure center and thinking about how I couldn't do them even if I wanted to because my bones might break. Dad can't do the washing without noticing that I haven't bought any new clothes in a year, and knowing why: 1) because all my old ones still fit; and 2) because the thought of going into a shop and trying on clothes makes me want to dig a tunnel a thousand feet under the ground and never ever come out.

Okay, so you're only in my head. But everyone I know has to deal with you, too. Day in, day out. And they didn't sign up for any of this. If I were them, I would have shoved me and you in a clinic somewhere a long, long time ago.

14

I've never seen this many people in one place before. It's like a royal wedding or something. But with penguins. We're right by the front: me, Stu, Ram, and Evie. Ram's dad drove us here, although he didn't actually come into the zoo; he's shopping at the outlet village instead. Just the thought of spending all day shopping—looking at yourself in the mirror, taking clothes on and off—makes me shudder.

"How much longer?" Stu asks.

I pull my watch out of my pocket—that's where I keep it now—and take a look. "Five minutes."

The penguin enclosure is a big peanut-shaped pool surrounded by flat rocks. There's a little jetty that sticks out over the water in the middle, for the penguins to dive off. Ten minutes ago, it was covered in snoozing Humboldt penguins—but now they're all up and chattering, looking around for the keeper. I guess they know what's up.

"I hope this is better than the lion," Ram grumbles.

The lion feeding didn't quite live up to Ram's expectations. There was no catapult and no goat. Instead, the keeper climbed a tower and threw a leg of mutton over the fence. The lion grabbed it and took it right to the back of the enclosure, behind the trees, out of sight. That was it. (Ram's review: *This is bullshit.*)

"Different kettle of fish," Stu says, nodding wisely. Then he adds, "If you'll excuse the pun."

"You're as bad as my dad," I tell him.

Eventually, a woman steps over the barrier a couple of yards along from us. Penguins shuffle toward her like happy zombies. She's wearing a green sweater and carrying a bucket of fish and a megaphone.

"Welcome to Chester Zoo, everyone. Are you ready to feed some penguins?" She has one of those singsong, ultra-happy voices. Like her vocal cords have been dipped in sherbet.

"Yaaaaaay!" everyone cheers. Well, everyone except us—because we're all busy. Evie is texting someone, while Stu stares at her with his judgiest judgy face. Meanwhile, Ram is trying to impress the zookeeper.

He has his arms crossed over his chest, and he's standing at a forty-five-degree angle to her. He once told me that this was his *signature move*. In Ram's head, he looks like Rambo. In everyone else's, he's more like the boss from *The Office*.

Also, the zookeeper is now standing ten yards away, in front of several hundred people, and, um, definitely isn't looking at Ram.

And me? Call me crazy, but I'm actually looking at the penguins. There's this one who's doing laps: hopping down the jetty, diving in, zooming to the edge of the pool, then doing a very ungainly climb out. I don't know whether he (or she*) normally does this or if it's an excited feeding-time thing. Like a dog chasing its tail.

"Humboldt penguins can swim at twenty miles per hour," I say, to no one in particular.

---

*Zoology-fact klaxon: I have no idea which, because penguins don't show sexual dimorphism, which is a fancy way of saying males and females look the same. Actually, male Humboldts are slightly bigger, but that doesn't really help you tell them apart: It could just be a big female or a small male or whatever.

Bonus zoology-fact klaxon: The reason penguins don't show sexual dimorphism is that they mate for life, so there's not much competition for mates. No one needs to show off. *It's like when I married your mum and started wearing socks and sandals again*—that's how Dad explained it to me.

"Packham strikes again!" says Stu, and we all laugh. Even Evie laughs.

They came up with this nickname two hours ago, in the tropical house, when I was telling him how there's no real difference between frogs and toads. *You're like that nature guy off the telly,* Stu told me. I wasn't sure what he was talking about for a second, but Evie immediately replied, *Chris Packham! Yeah, he really is. Max, you should be a zookeeper or something.*

That made me feel good because being a zookeeper would be amazing. I've noticed it today: I feel confident talking about stuff like this. Today, I've actually spoken up in conversations for the first time in weeks. I've *started* conversations. I guess it's because it's not subjective. No one's asking for my opinion on whether spiders are insects or not. No one's asking me to express my feelings. Have you ever noticed that 99 percent of the conversations you have are about your feelings? *How are you? What do you want to do today?* I'm terrible at answering questions like that.

But facts? I can do facts. Especially facts about frogs and toads and spiders and penguins. I even think I could do what the penguin woman is doing right now: stand up in front of a bunch of people and talk facts. As long as it's *just* facts.

"Big deal," Ram says, breaking my train of thought. "My dad does ninety on the motorway sometimes."

"Then he should slow down," Stu says seriously. Sometimes, it feels like Stu was born forty.

"Can anyone tell me where Humboldt penguins come from?" says the woman. About fifty hands go up. Another fifty people shout out answers. *South Africa! Japan! Barnsley!*

She walks over to a little girl who's shorter than the fence. Her dad is holding her up so she can see.

The woman angles the megaphone so the girl can talk through it. But she gets shy and starts crying.

She moves the megaphone away, leans toward the girl, and whispers in her ear. And you can see the girl's face light up. The transformation's kind of amazing. One minute, this girl is bawling; the next, it's like someone told her she can move into Disneyland, permanently.

And that's the bit I couldn't do. The touchy-feely bit. The bit where you have to tell someone it's okay and make a joke, or whatever she just did.

I guess I should stick to my get-a-PhD-and-become-a-zoologist plan.

"Dimple here knows the right answer," the zookeeper says, walking back out across the rocks. "Humboldt penguins are from South America. They live on the beach in Chile and Peru. I'm pretty jealous of them, to be honest!"

"Bet you knew that," Evie whispers to me.

I did—well, the South America bit, anyway. But how do you say yes without sounding like a total know-it-all? I lower my head. I can feel my cheeks glowing neon.

See what I mean? As soon as it's anything other than facts, I'm lost.

"Now, can anyone tell me what a Humboldt penguin's favorite food is?"

Evie jabs me in the ribs. Which hurts a lot, when your ribs are the tiniest fraction of an inch below your skin.

"Put your hand up."

I shake my head.

"C'mon, Max. I know you know the answer."

"It doesn't matter," I say out of the corner of my mouth.

She puts her hand up and shouts, "We know!"

I turn on her and hiss, *"What are you doing?"* I grab her arm, pull it down. She instinctively pulls away from me and whacks it on the fence.

"Ow!" she shouts.

And her face drops.

Like she's thinking, *Wow.*

Like she can see the psycho in my eyes.

Like she's terrified of me.

"All right," says the keeper. "A lot of enthusiasm from over there." She points at us, takes a few steps in our direction. "What's the answer, guys?"

I freeze. My limbs turn liquid. My stomach is churning like a washing machine. Everything slows down, and the *baBOOM-baBOOM* of my heartbeat drowns out the babble of the crowd.

It's Ram who steps in. "Um, fish fingers?" Right after he says it, he glances at me and winks. I'm pretty sure no one else sees it.

And just like that, the tension breaks. Everyone's laughing. The world returns to normal speed.

"Not quite," says the zookeeper, with a patient smile. An I've-heard-that-one-approximately-376-times smile.

Evie turns to Ram. "Good one, dickhead. Packham totally knew the answer."

"Herring," I say under my breath. "Probably other stuff, too."

"In the wild, these guys eat mostly anchovies, herring, and smelt," the keeper says into her megaphone, like she's my backup singer.

Evie jabs Ram in the ribs this time. "See?"

"Whatever," Ram says.

"I think our friend simply wanted to be noticed," Stu says, draping an arm around Ram's shoulders. Ram, annoyed, shrugs it off. Evie and Stu burst out laughing.

We listen to the keeper for a while. She's now explaining how penguins feed their young.

"Little penguins can't chew their own food, so their mum and dad do it for them, then regurgitate the liquid." About two hundred kids make an *ewww* noise at once. "It's the penguin equivalent of baby food!"

Revelation: Talking about animal biology can make me feel faint, too, if it's all about how animals throw up. I brace myself against the fence and try to tune her out.

My mind keeps whirring, though. I think about how much easier my life would be if throwing up was an ordinary part of life. Something you just did. Then I realize, *Wait a minute. I'm actually, literally feeling jealous of a penguin. BECAUSE THEY GET TO THROW UP!*

The feeding itself is great. The penguins huddle around the keeper, squawking impatiently at her. She throws fish into the water and they do big, looping dives, to catch the fish from below. It's like Cirque du Soleil or something.

When it's over, Ram sniffs the air. "That was cool. Better than the lion."

"What next, birthday boy?" asks Evie.

Ram shrugs.

"We could go to the bat house," I say quietly. Then I do an immediate or-whatever shrug. I can't believe I actually expressed an opinion, just like that, without anyone asking me. "I mean, if you guys want."

Ram raises an eyebrow. "Is it cool?" Ram treats cool like this absolute quality: Everything in the world is either cool or not cool. There's no middle ground.

"I think so," I answer.

He clicks his fingers, and points at me. "Packham, lead the way."

I want to go to the bat house for two reasons:

1. Bats are awesome.
2. It's basically pitch-black.

You go through an airlock, with sheets of plastic hanging down to stop the bats from getting out, and walk into a giant cave as high and wide as a football stadium, as dark as the woods on a new moon. There are bats everywhere: hanging from wires, circling the roof. You can see them when you look up, because there are little pinpricks of light, like stars I guess. But at eye level, you can't really see anything.

Here's the thing: I'm never not thinking about people looking at my body. Even when I'm just with my parents. Even when I'm totally alone. It starts with Ana asking a question, like,

Hey, remember that bottle of water you drank at lunchtime?

And it's like a snowball at the top of a hill: Once it's started, I can't stop it. I can't shut her up.

It makes your belly stick out. You look totally bloated—like Santa Claus. Someone's probably looking at you, right now, and thinking, What a lard-ass.

That's why hanging out in pitch-black caves seems like a pretty good idea. Maybe I should become a troglodyte.

"Coooooool!" Evie says as we shuffle inside.

There's a single walkway that loops through the cave. There are tons of people, but you can only see them when they are right in front of you. A slightly darker patch in the inky blackness.

"Yeah," agrees Ram. "Turns out this was a pretty good idea, Packham. Though it does smell a bit."

"You get used to it," I tell him. Then play it back to myself. Oh God. Cringe cringe cringe. I managed to make it sound like I spend every weekend in a bat cave. Covered in bat poo.

"Um, if you say so."

"Tell us about the bats, Packham," says Evie.

I shrug, like, *What do you want to know?* Then I remember that no one can see me. "Um, there are two types of bats in here. The big ones up there are fruit bats, from Madagascar."

"So they don't drink your blood?" Ram asks. He sounds really disappointed.

"That's vampire bats. And they don't actually drink people's blood, you know."

"Lame," Ram says. Then he shrieks. "Oh my God! I swear that one almost hit me."

"They won't hit you," I tell him. "The little ones that are flying around are, um . . ." I can't think of the name. I experience some internal turbulence, like inside me there's a pot of water with a lid on it, and as the water comes to the boil, it rattles away.

Two seconds later, Evie's phone screen lights up her face. She looks like she's about to tell a ghost story.

"Evie," I hiss. "You can't—"

"Seba's bat?" she suggests. Before I can answer, her thumb twitches, and the screen flicks off, plunging us back into darkness.

"Right. Seba's bat. Anyway, they echolocate. Even if it's pitch-black, they know exactly where you are."

"So it flew right past my ear for the kicks? Little bastard," Ram grumbles.

"You mean they can see us?" Evie asks.

"Kind of," I tell her. I'd never thought of it like that. I guess I've only made myself invisible to humans. But on reflection, I don't really mind too much if bats think I'm fat.

"Hey," Ram says. "Where's Stu? *Stu!*"

No answer. I thought Stu was right behind us

when we came in. Maybe he is, and he's just screwing with us.

"Have you seen Stu?" Ram asks. I don't know who he's asking. It sounds like he's a few yards behind us.

"Ain't seen much since I came in here to be honest with you," someone replies.

"*Stu!*" Ram shouts again, getting more distant. "Max, Evie, we'll catch up with you guys."

Which means it's just me and Evie. The moment I think it, I can feel my cheeks turning beet red. Good job she can't see me.

I was pretty surprised she even came. I figured she'd tell us she was busy at the last minute. Or she was washing her hair. But when Ram's dad came and picked me up this morning, she was already in the car. (I asked her if she lived near Ram's dad, in an attempt to be a normal human being who *makes conversation.* But she was super-weird about it. *Kind of,* she replied. *Not really. I mean, closer than you, I guess? I'm not really sure. Ha-ha! Where are we again?*)

As usual, she's spent most of today glued to her phone. She's taken a minimum of five pictures of every animal we've seen, and like a hundred of the penguins. She must have a wicked-big hard drive somewhere.

"This is pretty cool, you know, Max," Evie tells me. She's been calling me Packham all day. It feels important that she's now calling me Max, but I'm not quite sure how.

I want to tell her I'm sorry, about before. I want to laugh it off, make some stupid joke about needing to be more chilled out like a penguin—anything. But I'm scared of drawing attention to it. If I bring it up, I'm just ruining another moment, aren't I? And it's not like Evie's never been weird around me.

I wish I could describe how it feels. How the panic builds, like a wave crashing over me. How in my head I'm telling myself: *This isn't a big deal. No one cares. Even if you make a total fool of yourself, no one will remember.* But at the same time, Ana's screaming:

Everyone will look at you and laugh at you. Even if you can't see them laughing, they're being polite. The moment you turn your head . . .

And suddenly I'm freaking out. I'll do whatever it takes to get out of the situation, to end the moment. My nerves prickle all over, and I can't think.

I feel like a psycho. Maybe I am a psycho.

You can control most things that happen in your

life, but you can't control what goes on inside your head.

"There's only one problem," Evie continues.

"What?" I say. My heart goes from the *Jaws* theme all the way up to drum and bass. Right at that moment, a bat brushes past my head, moving the hairs on my temple without hitting me. Because I'm on edge, I jump out of my skin. For the second time in thirty seconds, being in a pitch-black room saves me from looking like a total idiot.

"It's too dark to take a picture," Evie says.

"Then don't," I reply, more bluntly than I mean to.

Nicely played, Max. Are you trying to make her hate you?

But I can't help it: The whole let's-take-loads-of-pictures-instead-of-looking-at-stuff thing bugs me. If you go to a reserve to look at birds, there are always these guys—it's always guys—with massive zoom lenses, trying to get the perfect shot, fiddling with meters and cable releases and God knows what else, getting in your way, when all you want to do is look at birds.

"Wow. Chill out, Packham," she says. I'm back to Packham again.

"Sorry. But how come you take so many pictures?"

I don't see her cross her arms. But I can feel it. A little wall of tension shoots up between us. "To remember stuff."

"That's what your memory is for," I say.

"Yeah, well, my memory's pretty rubbish."

"But, like, do you really need to remember *everything*? Is every single moment of your life important?"

"No," she says slowly. It sounds like she's really considering her response. "But that's the thing with memories, isn't it? You don't know what's important until later. Hey, I wonder where they've got to," she says, and even I can read the subtext: *Please change the subject.*

"Yeah," I mumble.

"Do you think Stu chickened out?"

"Dunno," I say. "Maybe, I guess?" I'm still thinking about the memory thing. How many memories from the past nine months would I actually want to save? Right now, I can't think of any. At all.

"Wow, what's got into you? You sound like someone stole your last Rolo all of a sudden. *Ow!*" she shrieks.

"What?"

"A bat just flew into me."

"Really? I mean, they know exactly where you are . . ."

"Max, listen to me," Evie says. "One of the little shits hit me. Maybe he's got a broken radar or maybe he's stupid or nasty or something. I don't know."

"Okay," I say, laughing.

"You don't believe me!"

"I do," I say. But my voice is kind of high-pitched. Even I can tell it's probably not very convincing. "Maybe I'd believe you if you had a photo."

"It's not funny!" she says. And then something hits me, too, square on the shoulder: Evie's fist. Considering she can't see a thing, it's a pretty good hit.

"Hey, one just flew into me, too," I say.

"Oh, you smartass. You think you're *sooo* funny! *Ow!* That was another one! Right, that's it. Get me out of here immediately, Packham."

I flinch when she grabs my hand, but it's cool, because she just thinks it's bat-related. Not oh-my-God-Evie-is-holding-my-hand-related.

It's warm. And soft. And, um, kind of clammy.

But I don't mind one bit.

May 9
Dear Ana,

SHE HELD MY HAND. Voluntarily. Because she wanted to. She reached out and grabbed it, just like that.

Naturally, you started freaking me out immediately.

—Can she feel how bony it is?

—She's doing it out of pity.

—Or maybe she's scared, because you took her to a freaking BAT CAVE, like some psycho murderer.

Cheers, Ana.

But she didn't let go. Even when we came out of the cave and into the light, and she could see exactly where she was going and there were no bats flying into her or nearly into her. She did drop it when we saw Ram and Stu, though. Dropped it like it was hot coal. That didn't make me feel great.

Now there are about a million questions bouncing around my head:

—What happens next? Are we, like, together? Does she want to be together? Was the whole "elephant juice" thing a cover, and she was actually into me from the start?

—Can she tell I'm ill? Like, she calls me skinny all the time, jokes about it—but does she realize

I'm vital-organs-may-go-on-strike-at-any-moment skinny?

—If she doesn't, how will she react? What if, like, she wants to go swimming or something, and she sees me with my top off—sees my skeleton ribs, and the big dark triangles above my collar bones? Will she want to stick around then—or will she drop me like she dropped my hand?

Here's the thing, Ana: I kind of need you to get lost for a bit now. I need to show Evie I can be normal, just for a little bit. So how about a deal? How about I stick to my regular diet, and you don't make me freak out about every little thing? How about I stay in control, and you stay in control, and we see how that goes? Is that too much to ask?

15

I'm playing *Zelda* when Mum comes in. Stu's way ahead of me, despite the fact he's always at football practice, so I'm trying to catch up. It's almost dinnertime, and tonight, it's one of my favorites: quiche. People think anorexics don't like food, but they're wrong. I can 100 percent guarantee you that I like food more than you do. I *love* food. That's why I think about it for sixteen hours a day.

"What's this?" Mum says, holding up my notebook.

My stomach lurches, like I've gone over a speed bump at a hundred miles an hour. "It's nothing," I murmur. I can feel my cheeks burning. There may be no iron left in my blood, but I can still blush.

"Sweetheart," Mum says, in that I'm-going-to-give-you-the-chance-to-be-straight-with-me voice that parents use all the time.

"Honestly, it's nothing. It's not what you think," I say.

She thinks it's my food diary. She thinks I'm still secretly recording everything I eat, so I can make sure the numbers keep going down, down, down, a little lower every day. I guess I am still doing that—but only in my head.

I never told Mum about the *other* diary. The thoughts-and-feelings diary. The one where I tell Ana exactly how much I hate her and my family and myself. The one that doesn't contain any sums, because there's no sum you can do to make yourself happy (believe me, I've tried).

It was in the bottom of my sock drawer. It's not like I wasn't allowed to keep it or anything. I just didn't want anyone else to see it. The stuff I wrote there was between me and Ana, you know?

Come to think of it, why was she looking in my sock drawer?

"Max," Mum says, in the same voice as before. *This is your chance to fess up.*

"Where did you find it?"

"It doesn't matter where I found it—"

"Were you going through my stuff?"

"No, love, I wasn't—"

"You don't have any right to go through my stuff," I tell her.

The more I think about it, the angrier I get. It's like my blood is suddenly on fire.

She's spying on you.

She's going to try and get you hospitalized.

She wants to get rid of you.

"Max, listen to me."

"Did you read it?"

"Max, listen—"

"*DID YOU READ IT?*" I scream, flinging myself toward Mum. I grab for the diary and rip it out of Mum's hand, somehow, with all my puny strength. Or maybe she let go, I'm not sure. My hand pings back and hits . . . something. There's a beat of nothing, where all I can hear is the roar inside my head.

That's when I leave my body. Now I'm in a first-person film, and everything that's happening is happening to someone else. I don't feel myself turn. I don't feel myself run toward the door. Even the pain in my finger—*What did I hit it on?*—feels distant. It doesn't hurt, exactly. It's just a sensation I'm aware of, like white noise. There's a moment of clarity, when I look at myself, or this person who used to be me, and think, *Who is he? Why is he running away, again, when there's nothing really wrong? Why is he so mad at his mum?*

And then it's me again. I can tell because it suddenly feels like someone is trying to shove wires down the blood vessels in my finger. The pain makes me want to scream.

I turn to look at Mum. She's kneeling on the floor, head bent over, shoulders shaking. And she's clutching at her face.

"It's not what you think," I tell her again.

Then I'm gone.

~

These days, I seem to spend most of my life running away from things. These days, the people I fight with are the ones I love most. Lindsay says it's normal. Lindsay says that we all hurt people we love, sometimes. We shouldn't blame ourselves for it. We should just do our best to show them how sorry we are.

But when I felt that sting in my finger, my first

thought was *Have I broken it? Am I now so weak that my bones snap like little twigs?* And it must have taken me ten seconds, maybe more, to even think about Mum. To turn and look and try to figure out if she was okay.

Did I just hit my mum in the face?

Writing down everything I eat doesn't work. And apparently, writing down my feelings doesn't work, either. I'm still selfish. I'm still scared. This is still happening to me. And the people around me have to bend, like branches in a storm, if they want to avoid being broken. They have to accept me being stupid and scary and angry all the time.

Even then, they might not be safe.

Maybe that's why Robin left.

Ana picks this moment to chip in.

One by one, you're driving your whole family away.

When I ran out on that meal with Robin, Louise, and James, I didn't know where I was going. But this time I do. Across the heath, around the lake. I've been here so many times, I can count the distances between every little landmark. It used to take me thirteen seconds and thirty-four steps to run from the bench with the cache, to the next one along (IN MEMORY OF RACHEL DOBIN, WHO LOVED THIS PLACE). Today, it's thirty-eight steps, and probably more like fifteen seconds. Ugh. When you've lost all the fat you can lose, you start digesting your muscles. You get out of breath more easily, and you don't move as quickly.

I'm slowing down. That's what old people say, isn't it? It's what they say on TV anyway. I remember this line from something or other: *We only get one body, and eventually it gives up on us.* It can happen slowly, or it can happen fast. It's all down to how you treat it. And how lucky you are.

Turn left at the fourth bench along going clockwise and into the birch trees. I watch my feet carefully: I've tripped over these roots more times than I can remember and fallen flat on my face. If I fall like that now, my bones would shatter. I read this post on a forum once, where a girl was explaining how she trained herself to stop putting her hands out when she fell over. Wrists break easily and take ages to heal. If your bones are weak, you're better off twisting and landing on your side. You may crack a rib, but probably not—and even then, you'll be better off.

I reach the oak tree, spring up onto the low branch, and grab the cache. One by one, I tear the pages out of my diary and stuff them inside.

Dear Ana, I can't talk to you anymore.

Maybe no one will read them. Maybe everyone will. I don't care. I just don't want to choose. I don't want to be in control anymore.

~

I tiptoe into the house with a lump the size of Jupiter in my throat.

~~Maybe they've already called the police.~~

Maybe they're finally going to send me to a mental ward.

But it's like any other evening. Dad looks up from his crossword and says, *Hi, buddy.* I wave at him, without saying anything, and run up the stairs. I can't face seeing Mum, not yet. My only objective is to get to my room as quickly as possible.

But she comes out of the office as I'm going past the door.

"Oh, hi, love. I didn't hear you come in," she says in this really cheery voice and beams at me.

What the hell is going on?

I can't even process what she's saying. I kind of nod at her and stumble past like a zombie. I get to my room, close the door, and slump down on my bed.

Did I imagine the last half hour of my life? Am I in a nightmare? Did I hit her so hard she lost her memory?

My finger doesn't hurt at all anymore.

Luckily, Ana's there to fill in the blanks.

Don't be an idiot. Didn't you see the way she flinched before she put that smile on? She's terrified of you. She thinks you're about to lose it completely. By the way, take a look at your desk.

What?

Your pen's out.

So what?

So your mum wasn't going through your stuff, you idiot. You left your stupid little diary on your stupid little desk.

16

Ram looks like he's going to faint.

"That was the worst ninety minutes of my life."

"The worst ninety minutes of your life *so far*," Stu says cheerily, squeezing between us and throwing an arm around both our shoulders. I flinch, but I don't think he clocks it.

Practice exams: tests that have no purpose except to make teenagers anxious and miserable. Even more anxious and miserable. The good news is, I'm nearly through. I have two left—German and physics— both tomorrow. After that, there are three completely pointless days back in normal lessons, then it's summer. And I won't have to pretend to be normal anymore.

"Don't worry," I reassure Ram. "They don't count for anything." This is approximately the 257th time I've told him this.

He ignores me. "What did you put for the last question?"

"Don't answer him," Stu warns. This week, we've learned that his no-spoilers philosophy extends to exams.

"Why not?" Ram asks, shrugging Stu's arm off and turning to face us. "I want to know."

Stu massages his temples. "How many times do we have to go through this? Because it's done now. Knowing what we put won't change anything. It'll just make you worry more." Stu Swindells: the philosopher of Deanwater High. Maybe he'll end up becoming a psychologist like Lindsay. I reckon he'd be good at it.

Evie bursts into the hall, looking mad, and comes and joins us. "What did you idiots put for question seven? The one with the picture?"

Stu holds up his palm, ready to drop some knowledge. He's probably going to tell us to drink green tea and meditate or something. But before he can, Ram blurts out, "Xylem."

"Oh God, I put phloem."

They turn to Stu and me.

"Who's right?" Evie says.

"Me, when I said you shouldn't talk about it," Stu says with a shake of his head.

And I just shrug. Before they said anything, I was pretty sure the labeled bit of the diagram was actually the cortex. Now I feel like maybe I made a mistake. Ana is machine-gunning anxious thoughts through my brain.

You sure screwed that one up.

Why do you even care? It's a one-mark question on a test that doesn't even matter.

Pretty embarrassing, though.

"Anyway, do you want to go get lunch in town?" Ram says, rubbing his stomach. "I could eat an elephant."

He seems to be over the practice exam. I'm kind of annoyed at how he immediately forgets about it—whereas I'm still fizzing with anxiety and will be for days. Not to mention the usual lurching feeling when someone starts talking about food.

I glance at Evie, who still looks twitchy. For a moment, I'm glad. Then I realize this makes me the worst friend in the entire world.

She's probably not even twitchy about the exam.

She's probably twitchy about being around you.

This triggers the thought loop I've been running through for the past couple of weeks, since the zoo.

Is she into me?

Yeah, right. She grabbed your hand because she was scared, Max. Because you took her to a bat cave.

But then she held on to it.

For like thirty seconds, until she saw someone else and remembered what the hell she was doing. It's not exactly Romeo and Juliet, Max.

Maybe I should ask her out.

Oh, good idea! Maybe you could take her to a restaurant and watch her eat for two hours?

"Sure," she says vaguely.

And Stu nods.

Ram looks at me. "Max?"

I want to say yes. A lot. But I know it will be horrible. I know they'll pick some sandwich shop where you don't know what you get until it arrives, so I'll have no idea how many calories are inside. Maybe they'll have bags of chips or something—but then, Ram will ask me for a chip, maybe offer to swap one, and they won't be the same size. Or even worse, Evie will ask for one.

They already think you're a freak. Don't make it worse.

All of this runs through my head before I answer.

"I've got stuff to do at home," I mumble.

I watch their faces drop into expressions that say, *You're a rubbish friend.*

Wow, they must really hate you. They'll probably cut you loose soon. Over the summer, maybe. Next year, you'll come back, and they'll just blank you.

I quickly add, "I'll walk into town with you, though."

We head toward town. Evie and Ram keep asking each other questions about the exam. Mainly to shut them up, Stu starts telling us about his summer holiday: The Swindells are going walking in the Scottish Highlands.

"Snore," says Evie. She pulls her phone out of her pocket and starts scrolling.

"For how long?" Ram asks.

"All summer. We're renting a campervan."

"You're kidding."

"Mum and Dad want to *get away from the hustle and bustle,* so we can *reconnect with each other.*"

"Stu, your house is like Zen garden," Ram says. "And I'm pretty sure your parents are surgically joined."

"You're preaching to the choir," Stu says. "Anyway, what are you doing?"

"Mum's taking me to France. Again. Last time, we stayed in this little cottage in the middle of nowhere. There was nothing to do except read a book."

Stu and I both make that-sounds-all-right faces. Ram catches us.

"Oh, shut up. It's boring. But the day after I get back, I'm going to Portugal with my dad. Mad, right?"

"Divorce has its advantages," Stu says with a shrug.

Ram nods enthusiastically, like one of those dogs you put on the dashboard of your car. "We went to the same place a couple of years ago. It's all-inclusive, and they have this amazing unlimited breakfast buffet. Plus, all the girls walk around in bikinis the entire time."

"Sounds idyllic."

"What about you, Max?" Ram asks.

Long story. Mum and Dad finally announced the plan on Sunday. I've been asking for weeks because I want to start sorting out my food plan. Well, it turns out that this year—I can't believe I'm actually saying this—we're going *back to Italy*. Aka, the place that turned me into an anorexic.

The conversation went like this:

Mum: We're going to Italy again this year, love.
Dad: We're going to stay near Lake Garda for ten days. Does that sound all right to you?
Me: Is Robin coming?
Mum: Not this year, I'm afraid, love.
Me: Okay.
Dad: We're going to have a great time.
Mum: A really great time.

That was it. Notice how I never responded to the last bit. Because I didn't have a clue what to say.

We're going back to Italy. I'm going back to Italy.

I'm terrified.

You're going to lose it completely.

Italy's a big country. Lake Garda isn't the same as Venice. And maybe what happened last time would have happened wherever I was. There are plenty of anorexics in France and Germany and America, after all.

But it doesn't have to be rational. I'm living proof of that. You can know something makes zero sense and still let it control your whole world. Like when people get mugged and end up moving cities, because they're scared to walk down their own street.

"Max?"

It's Ram. From five yards in front. Because I stopped walking in the street. It's like I'm going out of my way to look like as big a weirdo as possible.

"Uh, sorry," I mumble, scooting to catch up. "We're going to Italy."

"Pizza," says Ram, with moony eyes. "Pasta. Ice cream. *Niiice.*"

"Yeah," I say, though I feel sick thinking about it.

Evie, as usual, joins the conversation without looking up from her phone. "Aren't you going to ask where *I'm* going?"

"You seemed busy," Stu replies icily. He still gets mad about the phone thing.

"Where are you going?" Ram asks.

She actually looks up at us when she answers. "I'm going to France with Ben and Jacob, and *the other girls aren't coming!*"

She smiles like the Cheshire Cat. Evie *never* smiles. I swear her eyes change color—from green to luminous turquoise. You can't help but stare.

"Who are Ben and Jacob?" I ask.

"Who are the other girls?" Ram asks.

Stu's still trying not to look interested, but you can tell he's dying to know, too.

"Ben and Jacob are my parents," Evie says. *"Obviously."*

Ram, Stu, and I all give one another the same what-the-hell? look. There's a really long pause.

"What?" Evie says eventually.

"You call your parents by their first names?" says Stu.

Evie's eyes flick to the side. If you weren't looking for it, you definitely wouldn't have noticed. But I *was* looking for it. It's the first time I've ever seen her look the tiniest bit unsure of herself.

"Yep," she chirps. She starts stuffing her things into her rucksack. "Anyway, I'd love to stay and chat, but I've got places to be."

"But I thought we we're going to—" Ram begins.

"Can't," Evie says abruptly. "Sorry. I'll see you losers tomorrow."

Then she marches off in the direction of Redlands, which I'm pretty sure is the opposite direction to her house.

"Weird," says Ram, as he watches her walk away. He shrugs, then turns to Stu. "Nando's?"

17

We **haven't heard** from Robin for two weeks. When he first moved out, he came over for dinner pretty much every other night. Then suddenly, he stopped. Mum reckons he's got a girlfriend—probably that Ffion he mentioned. Either that, or he's learned how to cook.

Last week, I really wanted to text him and complain about the practice exams, but I didn't. I didn't want to bug him. I'm pretty sure my neediness was what made him move out in the first place. I didn't want to make things worse.

But the night before we go to Italy, he texts me.

All set for camping? :D

I reply within a minute. So much for not being needy.

Me: We're leaving in 12 hours. Take a guess.

Robin: I'm guessing Dad's already put the stuff in the car, and set . . . 5 alarms?

Me: 6. And we're leaving at 11 a.m. for a 5 p.m. flight.

Robin: A new record!

Me: He's also turned the central heating off already, in case we forget. It's FREEZING.

Robin: Textbook Dad. Has Mum had a go at him yet?

Me: She went to bed an hour ago. She said she had a headache.

Robin: I don't blame her.

Me: I can't believe you're not coming.

I know I shouldn't say it, because it makes me sound pathetic, and probably makes Robin feel bad. But I can't help it.

Pfft. You'll have much more fun without me. Now get some sleep! You know Dad's going to make you do an inventory of all the stuff you're taking at 8 a.m.

I lie awake for ages. Hours, probably, but I don't look at my phone because I don't want to know how long because that will just stress me out more. Worries whir around my head like the blades of a ceiling fan. I worry about forgetting the food I need for tomorrow—the food I'm taking to eat at the airport, so I know exactly what I've got. I worry about whether the stuff in the camp shop will all have calorie numbers on it, and what I'll do if it doesn't. Most of all, I worry about eating out. About staring at a menu that's just pizza and pasta, carbs on carbs on carbs, and not knowing what to do.

I worry until I exhaust myself, until my brain literally can't wrap itself around anything else for me to worry about it. And then I pass out.

~

Anyone could find it, you know. Your tragic little diary: all those pathetic thoughts and feelings you were stupid enough to write down. Someone's probably reading it right now and laughing their head off, and texting the funniest lines to their friends. It wouldn't be hard for them to figure out who you are. You weren't exactly subtle. Once they've pieced it together, your humiliation will be complete. But you won't know a thing about it until September, when you go into school and realize everyone's laughing at you. Even Stu and Ram and Evie, because—well, they've done their best, but it'll be way too embarrassing to stay friends with you after this.

I swear I jump six feet out of my bed. I'm sweating, and my breath is ragged, like I've just sprinted a hundred meters. I can't remember what I was dreaming about. All that's left is one thought looping through my head:

You've got to get rid of the diary.

I look at my phone: 5:23 a.m. I'd go now, but Dad sleeps like a field mouse; he'd hear. Better to wait until after we've done the stupid inventory. Then I'll have an hour or so to myself.

What was I thinking? Why did I leave all my sad, lame boy-with-a-girl's-disease thoughts in my cache, where anyone can find them and read them? Including, y'know,

- My brother, who's already left home because he finds me too difficult to live with.
- My best friends, who I've spent six months hiding it from.
- Evie, aka the only girl who's ever shown any interest in me whatsoever.
- *Literally every other human being on earth.*

～

We're leaving in an hour.

I walk across the Common on autopilot. I only clock where I am once I reach the oak tree; I must be *really* tired today. I'm holding the slice of toast Mum thrust into my hand when I said I needed to skip breakfast. She made me promise I'd eat it, and I don't want to let her down. Not this time.

I take a look around for muggles—I've started being a bit more careful since Evie—then boost myself up, grab the cache, and slide it open.

"You're kidding," I say to no one. Or to my cache or to the tree, I'm not sure. I take out the logbook and leaf through it, to double-check.

Meanwhile, Ana starts up.

Told you, you daft prick. Someone's taken it. Soon, everyone will be reading all that stupid shit you wrote.

Maybe I didn't even leave anything in my cache. Maybe I dreamed the whole thing. I was in kind of a crazy mood, after all.

Sure, keep telling yourself that.

I open the logbook again, and turn to the most recent page, just to see if anyone's written, *What's with the dumb diary?* There are five new entries.

Most of them are the same old thing: *TFTC—Sarah, Handforth*. But one leaps out at me.

It says, *I'll check back on Tuesday*. And I recognize the username: Stallone05. The first person who visited my cache.

Check back for what?

I look into the cache again to check I haven't missed anything. Then I see them. The diary pages were there all along; they were wedged into the join of the wood.

But when I pull them out, I realize the paper is different—blue instead of white. And the handwriting is a lot, lot neater than mine.

Because it's not my diary.

It's a reply.

18

Surprise, surprise, we're at the airport four hours early. We always are. Usually, Dad leaves enough time that even if all the trains are cancelled, and our car breaks down, and all the taxis in England suddenly vaporize, we'll still have enough time to walk to the airport and make our flight.

Dad also thinks airport cafés are totally over-priced and refuses to go to them. So today, as usual, we end up sitting on the hard plastic seats next to our gate for two hours. I have to keep getting up and walk around because it hurts my bony ass so much.

The flight is fine, except my ears go crazy with the pressure changes. I used to have a piece of candy to help sort it out, but that's definitely off the cards now. And I'm too shy to ask the flight attendant for water. So I just swallow air, over and over. It hurts like hell.

We land at the Milan airport, collect our bags, pick up the rental car, then drive east. We're staying at a campsite right next to Lake Garda, two hours away. Dad, naturally, refuses to pay for a GPS. Instead, we have a Northern Italy road map that folds out to roughly the size of a swimming pool, which Mum spends most of the journey wrestling with.

Mum and Dad have the same conversation about twenty times in four hours (yes, it ends up taking four hours):

Dad: We're coming up to a junction. Can you check whether we want to stay on E64?

Mum: Hold on, let me find it.

Dad: Okay.

[*Rustling noises*]

Dad: We're nearly at the junction.

Mum: Did we pass Stezzano already?

Dad: I'm not sure.

[*Long silence*]

Dad: Any idea?

Mum: I think we should stay on the highway.

[*More rustling noises*]

Mum, two minutes later, sheepishly: I think we should have turned off back there.

I've been dreading this holiday for months, but now that it's here, I'm kind of excited. Maybe it's partly because I have two whole weeks where I don't have to worry about making excuses not to see people or do stuff. But I'm also wondering whether maybe, just maybe, this is my chance to change things. Maybe I'll figure out *why* I got ill last summer—and maybe, if I do that, I can make myself better.

It kind of makes sense, right?

I have the note with me. Right after I found it, I got a text from Mum. Taxi leaving in 15 minutes! I sprinted home, and by the time I got there, Mum, Dad, and all of our bags were already in the taxi. I didn't get a chance to go inside the house. I just slipped the note into my pocket.

I didn't want to read it until I was on my own. I knew Mum and Dad would've worried about it, and I already give them plenty to worry about. We checked in and went through security; I could feel it in my pocket, weighing me down, like the ring in *The Lord of the Rings*. Then, as soon as we were on the other side of security, I went and found a bathroom to read it.

Wow. I mean, like, wow. I don't know what to say.

I'm sorry for all the crap you've gone through.

I don't really know what to say, except YOU'RE NOT ALONE. I guess it can be hard to feel that way sometimes. But even from the stuff you wrote . . . Just because people don't always get exactly how you're feeling, doesn't mean they don't care.

I know it's not the same, but my family's pretty screwed up, too. And for a long time, I felt like it was all my fault. I didn't even have any brothers or sisters to blame it on.

But I was wrong. And guess what? You're wrong, too. Because NONE OF THIS IS YOUR FAULT!!!

You've just got to deal with your crap and keep putting one foot in front of the other.

When things are crap, my dad always says the same thing to me: Tomorrow will be different. He doesn't literally mean tomorrow. It's more like, things always change eventually. Even if they feel like they never will.

I've got to go now. But if you leave another note, I'll write back. I'll keep checking.

Remember: TOMORROW WILL BE DIFFERENT!

E

It's got to be Evie. It can't be Robin, because of all the family stuff, and Evie's the only other person I know who's ever even heard of a geocache. Plus, it's signed with an E. But there's one bit that doesn't make sense. The other day at lunch, she was definitely talking about her siblings—but now, apparently, she's an only child?

Maybe she *was* an only child, but she isn't anymore.

Or maybe she's just being weird again.

And then another thought hits me: *I wrote about her in my diary.* Oh God oh God oh God. All that stuff about her holding my hand . . . *OH GOD.* Even worse, I don't have any kind of record, so I can't find out exactly what I did write. I just get to stew about it.

And for the next two weeks, I can't even reply.

~

The first surprise of the holiday comes when we finally arrive at the campsite.

The man at the gate hands Dad a key. "Numero trentadue, signore."

"Grazie," Dad replies.

"What's that for?" I ask Dad as we drive on into the site.

Dad shrugs. "Maybe the showers are locked," he says.

Which makes zero sense. "Then don't we need one each?" I ask. I'm not exactly keen on the idea of checking in with Mum and Dad every time I want to go to the loo.

Dad smiles into the rearview mirror. "We'll be there in a minute. Why don't we wait and see?" As if the showers were the Magic Kingdom or something.

To be fair, the campsite's actually pretty cool. There's a pool with waterslides, about a hundred Ping-Pong tables, and a beach. It's set in this huge forest, and there are loads of nature trails leading up into the hills. There aren't any geocaches, though: I've already checked.

Dad pulls up in front of this big log cabin, like the ones they have in ski resorts.

"We're here," he says.

I say, "Where's the field?" There are trees all around us. I laugh. "Did you park on it again, Dad?"

Mum and Dad look at each other, grinning.

"What?" I ask. "What's going on?"

"We decided to do something different this year, love," Mum says. "Since Liberace decided to sit this one out."

"What do you mean?"

Suddenly, my heart is doing death-metal beating. Anxiety is one part of anorexia no one really talks about, probably because it's not the part that kills you. But it feels like a wind blowing inside you twenty-four hours a day. Sometimes, it's so strong it can knock you over; sometimes, it's a rippling breeze you barely notice. But it's always there.

Dad turns around, sees my expression, and laughs right in my face. "We got a cabin."

"So you can have a room all to yourself," says Mum.

"And a proper kitchen!" Dad adds.

Oh.

Wow.

This might not sound like much, but the Howarths

always—*always*—go for the cheapest possible option in every situation. Always 100 percent guaranteed. It's like a family policy. When we got the Eurostar to France two years ago, business-class seats were a whole two pounds more expensive, and we *still* went economy. Now Mum and Dad are telling me they've spent probably two or three times what they normally do for accommodation, so I can have my own room and cook the things I want to cook.

WOW.

It's probably the nicest thing anyone's ever done for me.

I look from Mum to Dad, and back again. They both have the same expression on their faces: excited, but also kind of scared about how I'm going to react. I can tell they weighed everything up, discussed all the options, probably even asked Lindsay, who probably told them I needed my space, and that having a kitchen would allow me to stick as closely as possible to my home routine.

It's all for me.

I'm so happy I can barely speak. "Thank you," is about all I can manage.

"You're welcome," Dad says. "Now, why don't you two have a look around, and I'll bring the bags in?" He hands me the key.

Mum and me go inside. And it's . . . amazing. There's a massive kitchen, with an oven, a microwave, four burners, a giant fridge-freezer. There's every kind of pan you could think of. Chef's knives. Wooden spoons. There's even a set of scales, though I brought mine anyway.

The cabin is decorated like a chalet. The walls are made of wood, and there's a wood-burning stove, wooden shutters, a wooden dining table with wooden chairs. The whole downstairs area—kitchen, dining room, and lounge—is one big open space. And upstairs, there are two big bedrooms—*I have a double bed!*—and a bathroom.

Oh, and for some reason, there's a cuckoo clock in every single room. Seriously.

I guess it's a little cheesy. But I don't care. For a good ten minutes, I'm over the moon. I forget about everything I've been worrying about during the three-hour flight, the four-hour drive. And, you know, the last nine months.

And then, there it comes again. Maybe the wind

isn't the best analogy. The anxiety's more like a river: It has to flow somewhere. If you try to block it off, it finds another route to the sea. As soon as one thing seems okay, Ana finds something else for me to worry about.

This place must've been expensive. A lot more expensive than a field. Is that why Robin isn't here? Because Mum and Dad couldn't afford for him to come?

Or was it because he hates you? Or was it a bit of both?

Dad totters through the door, loaded up with bags. He drops them with a satisfied sigh, like someone who's just drunk a Coca-Cola in an ad. "So, what do you think?" he says.

I think a lot of things. But each good thought has a nasty sidekick, courtesy of Ana.

I can cook whatever I like.

. . . but your mum and dad will worry if you don't eat it all.

Wow, my room's big.

. . . and you're mostly going to lie awake in it, crying like a baby.

It's like having a debate with the smartest person in

the world. Every time I think I've made a good point—
wham—she demolishes my argument, and makes me
feel like a total idiot.

"It's great," I reply. "Thanks, Dad."

Dad nods enthusiastically. I turn to look at Mum.
She's beaming so hard I want to cry.

I pick up my bag and take it up to my room. I shut
the door and lean against it. I close my eyes. My Zen
period lasted all of five minutes. Now, I'm a bag of
nerves—and on top of that, I feel super-guilty. Why
can't I be happy when my parents have done all this
for me?

"Want a drink, Max?" Mum shouts from the
kitchen. "We're having hot chocolate!"

I slump down on my huge, soft double bed. "I'm
fine," I shout back.

19

Here are my top five tips for going on holiday with an anorexic:

1. **Get ready to spend a lot of time in museums.** People with eating disorders are kind of obsessive. We want to see and do everything—and I mean *everything*. If you take me to the Louvre, I'll look at every single picture and read every single sign (which apparently takes three months) because I hate the idea of missing out on stuff. This is true even when every sign is in a language I don't actually speak.
2. **Don't ask us about it afterward.** The only problem is, I won't actually take much of the

stuff on those signs in. I'm too tired. Don't ask me if I read the bit about Da Vinci's childhood, because if I missed it or can't remember it, I'll be upset.

3. **Eating out is tricky.** When you order at a restaurant, you never know quite what you're going to get, unless you're at McDonald's or something. (Anorexics like McDonald's a *lot* more than you'd think.) Counter service is great, because we get to see the food before we order it. Even better if it's already in portions. Buffets are harder, because it's way too easy to lose control and overeat. The worst possible option is sharing food with other people on the table. Never, ever, ever take an anorexic for tapas.

4. **Don't go to the beach.** Trust me. You don't want to see an anorexic with their top off— and they want you to see them about a million times less. If you *have* to go to a beach, make sure there's somewhere they can sit in the shade with a book, or find them a private cove, or whatever.

5. **Watch how much water we drink.** Some anorexics don't drink enough water, because when you're stick-thin, even a glass of water makes you feel bloated. Others drink loads, to fill their stomachs with something that isn't food. Both of these can be pretty dangerous, especially on holiday.

Oh, and here's a bonus one: Please don't play Billy Joel's greatest hits on every single car journey. That's not an anorexia thing. It's a my-parents thing.

~

The fourth night of the trip, July 23, is Mum and Dad's wedding anniversary. Most couples would go out for a romantic meal or whatever, and leave their kids in peace. But we aren't most families. Mum has this cringey line: *Our children are the most important part of our marriage.* Which means me and Robin get to go to their romantic dinners, too.

Tonight, we go to this posh restaurant right by the lake. We sit outside. There are little tea lights all around the garden, and a big white canopy overhead.

"It's very romantic," says Dad as our waiter leads us to our table.

I make my I-want-to-spew face. Mum doesn't exactly look convinced, either.

When they come to take our drinks order, Mum chooses some wine—a carafe, because Dad's driving, so it's basically just for her. But then she asks for three glasses.

I look at her.

"You can have a glass if you want, Max."

Dad nods in agreement.

Wow. *Wow.* My parents are nuts about alcohol, drugs, and anything else that's even a little bit bad for you. When Robin was thirteen, they banned him from eating Pop-Tarts. They may as well have just offered me my first hit of heroin.

How do I say no?

"Are you sure?" I ask, hoping they'll change their mind.

"It's a special occasion," Mum says.

"Our anniversary," Dad adds. It's weird: He looks at Mum when he says it, as if she maybe needs reminding of this fact. I want to say: *I reckon she knows, Dad.*

Then the waiter comes back, carrying the carafe of wine, and says, "Who will taste-a the wine?" He's got this really strong accent, like he's playing an Italian waiter in a cheesy movie, except it's for real.

Dad looks at me. I'm about to shake my head when he says, "Max, want to do the honors?" The waiter switches direction.

Oh God. I'm not sure why my parents think the rules don't apply here. I guess they're assuming I'll be so excited about having a drink, I'll forget that, y'know, *I'm bloody anorexic.* Or maybe it's a holiday thing—Mum always says her diet doesn't count when she's on holiday.

Unfortunately, mine does. However much I want to, I can't shut Ana up.

Alcohol's really calorific. There are like a million calories in one sip of wine.

The waiter pours a little into my glass and looks at me expectantly. I look at Dad, then Mum. There's this horrible silence that lasts about three ice ages. It's like a total standoff.

Mum grins at me, and it makes me want to snap: *This isn't funny, Mum.* "You know, Max, most of the flavor comes from the smell," she says. She reaches over, grabs the glass, and does an exaggerated sniff. "Many oenophiles just smell it to see if it's good."

"Eno—what?"

"Oenophiles," Dad chips in. "Wine experts."

Mum's eyes flick to Dad. She looks mad at him for some reason.

"Um, okay," I say. I'm pretty certain Mum and Dad have never ever not tasted the wine they're supposed to be tasting. But I'm happy to run with it.

Mum hands the glass back to me, grinning again. I hold the cup of the glass with both hands—I'm shaking so much I'm worried I'll drop it—and sniff. I have no idea what I'm even supposed to be smelling.

"It's good?" the waiter says. He looks kind of mad, too, like, *Why is this stupid teenager wasting my time?*

I nod at him. He smiles a big fake smile, then pours glasses for Mum and Dad, then tops mine off. Mum gives me this big, cheesy thumbs-up.

"I'm still going to drink it," I say when the waiter's gone. Then I add: "Hopefully."

I mean it, too. Sometimes, it's not the food exactly, but the pressure of the moment. Once the moment is over, you stop freaking out and feel a bit stronger.

"I know," Mum says. She reaches over and lays her hand on mine. "But you don't have to, love. It's okay."

Mum and Dad didn't get this idea at all to start with. If I couldn't eat something there and then, they'd assume the sky was falling in. But I guess they've got used to it. To me. To Ana.

For a moment, I'm really happy. Then I remember I still have to order food.

Go wild, fatty. Gotta work on that belly.

The menu's all in Italian, but I can work most of it out. It's a posh restaurant, so there's no pizza, which is my go-to order, because at least you know exactly what you're getting then. At this kind of place, you're supposed to order a starter, pasta, and then a main course. I guess that's what Mum and Dad will be doing. When you're anorexic, you spend a lot of time sitting around watching other people eat. It's crazy-boring.

Eventually, I decide on a caprese salad.

Good choice. As long as it's not drowning in oil.

I know the waiter's going to say something like, *Is that all?* at which point I will totally die inside. But I know I'll feel worse if I order something else. Plus, we've come up with an okay way of dealing with this situation. Dad will say something like, "He's going to share with me," and they'll bring out an extra plate, and we'll smear a bit of sauce on it or whatever. It works fine as long as the restaurant is big enough that there aren't waiters around all the time. I think it will work here.

And you know what? It's okay. Everything is okay. I pick at my caprese salad for two hours while Mum and Dad eat their way through a plate of meat and olives, then pasta, then steak (Mum) and duck (Dad), but I don't even mind, because it's their anniversary, and they deserve to have a nice night. Sure enough, my salad is swimming in olive oil, but I don't freak out. I just pick out each bit and let it drain off before eating it. I mean, I've got plenty of time to kill.

I even drink the wine—some of it. Mum asks me how it tastes, and I say it's delicious, because I don't want to say, *It's like sour fruit juice and I can't believe I wasted calories on this.* The worst thing? I only had a sip, but I have no clue how many calories that is, so I have to count it as a whole glass.

It doesn't matter. Everything's okay.

But then, Mum and Dad fall out.

Big time.

Have you ever noticed how the biggest arguments start with the most stupid things? I remember one Easter, when I was about ten, Mum and Auntie Jess had a massive argument—like screaming-and-shouting-and-storming-out-of-the-house-and-not-talking-for-a-couple-of-months-afterward massive—about whether you should hang clothes on radiators. Seriously.

Well, tonight, it starts with dessert.

Dad, to Mum: Do you want dessert?

Mum: I don't mind.

Dad: It's up to you.

Mum: Why is it up to me?

Dad: I just mean I'm not fussed.

Mum: Why do I have to make all the decisions? Why can you never be bothered?

Dad: Come off it, Becks.

Mum: Every time we do anything, it's, like, "Becks, you choose."

Dad: It's called being polite.

"It's polite to *ask*," Mum says. Her voice goes weak and wobbly and high-pitched; I can tell she's about to cry. "But it's not always my responsibility to make a decision. I should be allowed to bounce the odd ball back into your court, you know?"

"You are."

"It doesn't feel like it."

"We'll have dessert."

"I don't *want* dessert. That's not the point. For God's sake, Joe. Are you listening to me?"

"Of course," says Dad.

And so am I. I'm listening as my mum rips the guts out of my dad in the middle of a restaurant. On their anniversary. Over nothing.

I mean, yeah. She has a point. Dad is terrible at making decisions, and it can be annoying sometimes, especially when the decision doesn't matter at all. Like, for instance, there are two Indian takeaways near us, both the same distance away, but in opposite directions. And whenever we get takeaway Dad spends twenty minutes going around the house asking our opinions—*Robin, you like bhuna, don't you? Do they do that at the Mahal?*—when what he should really do is just pick one.

But it always comes from a good place, you know?

That's how it feels to me, anyway. Like he wants us to have what we want.

And it's not really that big a deal. Is it?

Mum seems to think it is.

We don't get dessert. Dad makes a point of asking to see the menu—even I can tell this is a bad call—but neither of them reads it. Mum finishes her wine and reaches over and grabs my glass without even looking at me, and finishes that, too. When the waiter comes back around, Dad asks for the bill.

"Il conto, per favore."

Then we sit in silence for about ten minutes.

Then the waiter comes back, and Dad pays, and we all say thank you.

Then we get into the car and drive back to our campsite.

I guess there's a bright side to all this. For once, the argument isn't my fault.

20

Tomorrow will be *different.* The phrase from the letter echoes around inside my head. What I want to know is, different *how*?

Tomorrow, the number on my calendar will be one higher.

Tomorrow, I'll probably have finished the book I'm reading.

Tomorrow, if I'm lucky, I might see a honey buzzard.

What else?

So, I know Evie—or whoever wrote that note— said that it doesn't actually mean tomorrow. It's more like: at some point in the future, your life will be totally different to how it is today. But I can't help thinking about it that way. Anorexia kills 20 percent of the people who get it. There's a pretty good chance

I don't have that many tomorrows left. I've got to think short-term.

~

We're supposed to be going to Sirmione this morning, which is a little town built on a peninsula that juts out into the lake. There's a big medieval castle right on the water; our guidebook describes it as *breathtaking*.

When I wake up, I dig around in my suitcase, and pull out one of the three books I've brought with me: a guide to the birds of Northern Italy. I turn to the page with the folded-down corner: buzzards. I want to check which habitat is best for seeing honey buzzards again.

Honey Buzzard. *Pernis apivorus*. Family: Accipitridae. L 52–59 cm, WS 113–115 cm. Summer visitor (late Apr–Sep). Common. Breeds mainly in forest clearings in mountainous areas.

Identification

Slightly larger than Common Buzzard. The key differences are slimmer neck . . .

It's not like honey buzzards are particularly rare or anything. But we barely get them in England, and

I like the name, I guess. I'd love to see a lammergeier, too. But you don't get them outside of the Alps—and even there, they're pretty hard to see.

Then I start flicking through all the other birds I might come across: warblers, pygmy owls, alpine swifts. I think I saw a crag martin, *Ptyonoprogne rupestris*, yesterday, but I didn't have my binoculars with me so I couldn't tell for sure. Italy isn't really known for its birds, but I'm making the best of it. I've got to do something to fill my time, right?

~

I'm not exactly looking forward to breakfast, and not just for the normal reasons. Here's the thing: Italy is great at most kinds of food, but they can't do breakfast. You get a cappuccino or a hot chocolate (or if you're me, a black tea or a glass of water), and a stale roll. That's it. We've been eating at the campsite most days, so it doesn't really matter—I've been having cornflakes. But today, we're planning to leave early and eat breakfast in Sirmione.

I check my phone: 8:37 a.m. We were supposed to leave before eight, and Dad's pretty uptight about sticking to schedules. I can count the number of times he's been late for anything on one hand. I get up and go to find him.

Instead, I find Mum. She's sitting in the kitchen eating a slice of toast on her own. There wasn't any bread in the house last night, so she must've been out already without me hearing.

She doesn't say anything when I walk into the room, which is weird. Mum greets me with a cheery *Morning, love!* every day, even if we've argued or whatever. But she just looks at me.

"Where's Dad?" I ask.

She flinches slightly—the kind of flinch that would make Dad say, *Someone walking on your grave?*

"Your dad's gone out."

"Where? Aren't we going to Sirmione?"

"Not today, love."

I feel a little twinge of relief when she says love. I thought she might be cross with me.

"How come?"

"We're just not," Mum says abruptly. She gives me a please-can-you-drop-it look.

"Okay."

Then she does a 180°, and gives me this huge, mushy smile. Mum sucks at losing her temper. She normally apologizes after about seven seconds, and still feels guilty about it days afterward. "How about you go bird-watching today? There was that one you wanted to find . . ."

"A honey buzzard. But I'm not sure I'll see one this close to the lake." There's this bird-watching motto: *If you're happy to see a sparrow, you're never disappointed.* Which means, basically: Don't get your hopes up. Birders love lame mottos. Another one is *Once bittern, twice shy.* When you're starting out, you think you've seen all these rare birds, like bitterns and lammergeiers. But 99 percent of the time, you haven't.

"But there's a chance?"

It's funny. Mum's never taken much interest in my bird-watching before—it's much more Dad's thing. But right now, she's giving me this pleading look, as if me seeing a honey buzzard would pretty much make her year.

"Yes," I say. I don't want to let her down. "Especially if I walk up into the hills."

Another mushy smile. "That's good. Make sure you take your phone."

I'm confused. Is she asking me to go out, or telling

me? "What are you going to do? When's Dad coming back?"

"I'm going to read for a bit, love. Be back for lunch, okay?"

I know I should leave it there, but I have this heavy feeling in my stomach, like I'm going over a speed bump. Like the universe's tilted on its side, and we're about to fall off. "Mum," I say.

"What is it, Max?"

"Is everything all right?"

She kneads her eyeballs. Which is never good. "Can you just do what I asked?"

I don't say anything else. I go to my room, get my stuff, and leave. As soon as I close the door, I realize I haven't had any breakfast.

I carry on walking.

~

There are a dozen paths that run from the campsite into the woods, along the lake, up into foothills. No one uses any of them, except for the one that goes straight to the beach. Twenty yards from the door of our cabin, I'm totally alone.

It's sunny, but it's cold in the forest: You can feel the temperature drop the moment you step under the trees. The sun jabs its way through the beech canopy, casting leopard spots on the ground, which dance in the breeze coming off the lake.

I go along the main path leading away from the campsite until I hit a junction. Four paths. One loops around to the far end of the beach, where the rock pools are, where I spent most of yesterday looking for crabs. One is marked ALL'AUTOSTRADA: "to the motorway." The other two are nature trails. I take a look at my campsite map. The right-hand one hugs the lake and leads to a little village called Entera. The other curves up into the foothills, then back down on the other side of the campsite.

I take that one. It'll be quieter—not that there are exactly a ton of people around—and I'll have a better chance of seeing a buzzard if I'm higher up.

I walk for a bit, scanning the canopy for birds. I see Italian sparrows browsing on the ground, and a couple of redstarts. *If you're happy to see a sparrow, you're never disappointed,* I tell myself.

The path climbs pretty quickly out of the lake valley. After a few minutes, I'm puffing. I think my anemia's getting worse. I sit down on a rock to catch my breath. I check my phone, to see if there are any geocaches near here, even though I've already checked a bunch of times, and I know there aren't.

And I tell myself I'm having fun.

You can't even get your own parents to hang out with you.

Sometimes it feels like the worst part of anorexia isn't anything to do with food. It's not about how scared I am of getting fat or my next meal, or any of that stuff. Sometimes, it feels like the worst part is the way Ana sucks the fun out of everything I do. Even when I'm doing stuff I enjoy—looking for birds, or watching a film, or whatever—I feel rubbish after about ten seconds.

I'm anemic: There's not enough iron in my blood, and the color's slowly draining out of me. And at the same time, my world is turning gray. I'm sitting in a forest. The leaves above me are lime and emerald, depending on how the sun's hitting them. Below me, the lake is a deep, shimmering blue. I'm wearing red sneakers, a yellow T-shirt. But it all *feels* gray.

When I get back, Dad's unloading the car. I'm a little nervous about what he's chosen for lunch, without my input: This definitely isn't the deal. But I can't complain too much, because it's bound to be less stressful than eating out in Sirmione would've been.

"Hi, Dad," I say. I'm surprised at how happy I am to see him. I guess I didn't realize how worried I was until now. "No honey buzzards, *again,* but I did see . . ." I peter out when he looks up, and I catch his face. "What's wrong?"

Then I notice a lot of things all at once.

The suitcase in the trunk.

The file of documents Dad's holding.

The jacket he's got slung over his arm, even though it's 32 degrees Celsius here.

Dad isn't unloading the car.

He's leaving.

August 2

Sorry I haven't written back until now. I went on
holiday right after I got your last note. Hopefully
you haven't got bored and given up or whatever.

Anyway, the holiday was a total disaster. My mum
and dad had this massive argument, and Dad ended
up leaving the holiday early. Then me and Mum sat
around for a week with nothing to do. She tried to
tell me it wasn't a big deal. Dad just went home early
because there are elections soon. (My dad works for
the county council.) But I'm not stupid. He's never
even worked late before, let alone skipped a holiday.
I wanted to call her a liar, and make her tell me
what was really going on. But I made the mistake
of looking her in the eye.

Fun fact: You stop looking people in the eye when
you're like me. Aka, when you're anorexic. (Now that
I know someone's reading this, it feels weird writing
that word. I've been keeping it secret for so long.)
I'm not sure why it happens exactly. I guess you're
sort of scared of what you might see.

Anyway, when I looked properly at my mum for
the first time in weeks, I saw how upset she was.
With me. With my dad. With everything. So I went
along with it. I pretended Dad was busy, and everything was okay.

For the rest of the holiday, we basically stayed around the campsite. We didn't have much choice: Dad took the rental car with him when he left. Mum didn't feel like doing much. She mainly just read her book in the cabin, or sometimes by the pool. I spent the whole week walking around Lake Garda, looking for birds. But I didn't see the one I really wanted to see.

July 27th was actually my birthday, and it was the worst day of all. It's the first birthday I've had since being ill, and, well, it wasn't exactly a cake-walk. No pun intended. We agreed the day before that I wouldn't open any presents until I got home, so I could do it with Dad, too. I went for a walk by myself, and while I was out, Mum went to the camp shop and got loads of ingredients to make a cake, which was really nice of her, because she definitely wasn't in the mood. The problem was neither of us actually wanted to eat any cake. At home, we'd feed it to my dad and my brother, but they weren't there. I ended up breaking it into crumbs and feeding it to the birds.

When we finally got home, Mum and Dad acted all happy and smiley. Dad said he'd missed us, as if he'd never been there and we'd just decided to go on holiday without him. He gave me a big hug, even though he hates hugging me now, because I'm so thin.

I started to wonder if maybe everything will work out. But he didn't give Mum a hug.

Since then, everything's been really tense. It's like . . . my parents have been walking on eggshells around me for a year. And now, they're walking on eggshells around each other, too. I have no idea what's going to happen, but it doesn't feel good.

Sorry, this is super-boring. I'll shut up now. Thanks for writing to me. And if you don't want to write back, I won't blame you.

M

August 12

OMG, THE SAME THING HAPPENED TO ME! I
must've gone away like the exact day you sent
that. That sounds like a big fat lie, doesn't it? But
I promise, I'm not bullshitting you. By the time that
letter arrived, I was already on a plane.

So, um, yeah. Hopefully you're still hanging in
there?

I'm not going to lie, your life sounds like a mess.
Total car crash, to be honest. So how about I tell
you what's going on in my life? It might make you
feel a bit better.

It was supposed to be just me and my dad
going on holiday. But at the last minute, Dad
told me Katya was coming, too. "Who the hell is
Katya?" you ask? GOOD QUESTION, my friend. I'd
never even heard of Katya before I found out
I was going on holiday with her. You know why?
Because Dad only met her TWO WEEKS AGO.

Well, I can inform you that Katya is a complete
bitch. She tried to be nice to me for like five
minutes, but got upset that I didn't immediately
start pretending that she was my new mum. And
Dad took her side, because he starts acting like
a total idiot whenever some woman he fancies
shows up. Apparently, I "wasn't trying hard enough,"
and I needed to "understand that he had feelings,

too." Which I do. The only problem was, Dad felt the need to express those feelings by taking Katya back to his hotel room roughly every five minutes. If you know what I mean.

I spent the whole holiday kicking around the pool on my own, while my dad screwed some woman called Katya. Katya what? Come to think of it, I don't have a honking clue what her last name is. I bet Dad doesn't either.

But hey, maybe tomorrow really will be different, and my dad will dump Katya, and your mum and dad will sort things out, and everything will be sweet. You never know, right?

The good news is, I'm back for the rest of the summer now. I'll check you-know-where again tomorrow.

E

P.S. Happy birthday! You never said what presents you got. Spill the beans!

August 14

Okay, you'll probably think I'm a total weirdo when I tell you what I got. But you asked, so here goes:

—A new phone. That's not too weird I guess.

—A coat. By which I mean a massive furry parka. Who gets a coat in the middle of August, right? But I'm freezing all the time.

—A soft toy fox. It's for my dog, Sultan. Sultan's birthday is two days after mine, so he always gets a present on my birthday, too (except this year I had to give it to him when we got back from Italy). I'm not gonna lie, he looks pretty cute carrying a toy fox around in his mouth.

—A bee hotel. You're probably wondering what the hell that is. The name pretty much covers it: It's a hotel for bees. There are porters and a swimming pool and . . . okay, I'm lying. It's basically a set of little tubes for rare bees to make nests in. My brother made it for me.

—A TON of books. Including two copies of this one I really wanted, called The Life of a Cuckoo. Somehow my mum and my dad both bought it for me. Given everything that's going on, it was a bit awkward.

You're probably thinking, "Um, why did you ask

for a book about cuckoos?" Allow me to nerd out for a minute. I don't know if you're into birds or whatever, but cuckoos are kind of amazing. Instead of raising their own chicks, they lay them in other birds' nests, so the chicks grow up surrounded by complete strangers. And as soon as they hatch, they kill the other chicks, and gobble all of the food. The new parents don't even realize what's going on. Crazy, right?

I guess being on your own makes you tough. Come to think of it: If Katya starts giving you shit again, you should definitely go all cuckoo on her. Wait—brain wave! I have a spare copy of this book anyway. I'll leave it in my cache for you. Maybe it will inspire you, ha-ha.

Anyway, things have got better here since I last wrote. It doesn't seem quite as tense. Tonight, we're all having dinner as a family—my brother's coming over, too. I'm thinking maybe my mum and dad have worked things out. I guess I'll find out.

I'll write back soon.

M

21

My first-ever memory is from the Cheshire County Show, age four, when a goat head-butted my ice cream out of my hand. My second-ever memory is from a holiday to the Black Forest. It must've been the following summer, when I was five. We were at a campsite deep in the forest, where one night they spit-roasted a whole wild boar. I remember walking through the trees, under stars so bright they cast shadows in the forest, toward a big, orange fire in the distance.

What's your first memory? What about the first birthday party you can remember, and the first Christmas? I bet at least one of them involves food. I asked Mum and Dad about their first date once. Mum said, "We went to an Italian place. I can't remember much except that your dad had spaghetti with clams, which seemed very grown-up to me."

The big moments in your life, the ones that really matter? They all involve food. We use food to celebrate, to commemorate, to keep kids happy when they're driving us nuts. Food is what keeps us alive. But it's way more than that. For most people—for normal people—it's a pretty big part of what makes their life worth living.

If you're anorexic, you carry these happy food memories around with you, every day. I think about this a lot. Probably too much. If you're addicted to drugs or alcohol, you can always think back to a happier time, before those things were part of your life. But if you're addicted to not eating, every memory you have turns sour on you.

~

This probably won't work.

Lindsay's not stupid. She's bound to see right through it. On the other hand, she's nice enough—trusting enough—that she might believe me.

And it's not like I've got anything to lose.

I weighed myself this morning: —. I'm now five feet tall: half an inch taller than I was the last time I saw Lindsay. The jury's still out on how much anorexia stunts your growth; it probably depends on how long you have it for and how bad it is. But for the first time ever, I'm taller than Aunt Jess.

That means my BMI is now under —. Lindsay's going to hate me.

Since I weighed myself, I've drunk four pints of water, eaten one slice of toast and spread, and half a cucumber, which was the best way I could think of upping my weight without adding too many calories.

Still a few calories, though. You could have done without the toast.

I've also taken the wrappers off two Kit Kat Chunkys and one Snickers. I didn't want to just throw the bars away, so I wrapped them in a tissue and left them in my bedside drawer. I guess I'll give them to Ram when I see him.

There's one wrapper in my pocket and two in my rucksack. I don't know which is where: I thought it would be more natural if I didn't. At some point, if everything goes to plan, I'm going to get my phone out of my pocket and drop a wrapper on the ground. And then, when Lindsay gives me my worksheet—I get one after every session—I'm going to open my rucksack right in front of her.

If you pull this off, she won't bother you. She'll leave you alone.

I'm trying. But she doesn't understand. She needs to think I'm eating, so she can see how hard I'm trying.

It probably won't work. But I've got to do something.

"How was your holiday?"

We've been having this conversation for ten months now. It's always exactly the same. Five minutes of smiley small talk about my life, and then she starts asking the questions I don't want to answer. *How do you feel? Any dizziness, numbness, or pain?*

Bad. Awful. Yes, yes, and yes.

Say whatever you need to say to shut her up.

"It was good," I tell her. "I saw a honey buzzard."

This is my practice lie. The lie before the yeah-I'm-totally-eating-loads-of-chocolate-bars-what-are-you-talking-about lie. I want to see if I crumble under pressure, or if I have some kind of tell Lindsay can spot a mile off.

But she's delighted. She swallows it whole. "That's brilliant, Max!" she says, as if I've just cured cancer.

Then she pauses. Normally, she'd ask about a million follow-up questions. *Where did you see it? Was it flying? Was it a male or a female?* She gets pretty excited when I volunteer any information whatsoever about my life. But right now, she looks a little lost, like she doesn't know what to say next.

Which never happens.

"Max," she says eventually, in that I'm-about-to-say-something-important voice that you can spot a mile off, even if you've never heard it from that person before. "Is there anything else you want to tell me about your holiday? It can help to talk through these things, even if it feels painful."

And then I twig: She knows what happened.

I shake my head.

"These sessions are your chance to get things off your chest," she says. "Anything you say will stay in this room."

She wants me to open up to her. She wants me to say, *My brother left home because he's sick of me, and then my dad left our holiday early because he couldn't stand the idea of spending any more time with my mum, or with me, or with both of us. I haven't seen any of my friends in a month, and I'm not sure I want to, except for the girl who I'm in love with or something, who calls me a dickhead when I see her or ignores me completely, and who still hasn't replied to the note I left her three days ago. Oh, and I'm now officially "dangerously underweight," but I still feel like a whale.*

"I know," I say.

"Max, I know this all must be very upsetting for you. But your mum and dad both want what's best for you. They're both on your side, okay?"

"Okay," I say. It's not okay, but I figure going along with what Lindsay's saying is the best way of ending this conversation ASAP.

"And if you are worried about anything, you can contact me anytime."

I don't say anything.

"So," Lindsay says, trying to sound cheery again. "What have you got planned for the rest of the summer?"

Well, gosh, Lindsay, I'm not sure. I thought I might join a lacrosse team or start learning to play the flute. What does she want from me? I'm going to sit in my room and read and play video games. Like always.

I shrug.

She doesn't miss a beat. "I'm going on holiday next week. To Devon."

"Cool," I say. It's kind of impressive how Lindsay can sustain a conversation all by herself. "Have fun."

"I'm taking my dog with me," she says.

I look up. "I didn't know you had a dog," I say. I know I'm being tricked: This is a way to get me to talk. But I want to know about the dog. Then I think: Could she have made up the dog? Is she allowed to lie to me, like I lie to her? Are there rules about what psychologists can and can't say to get gullible idiots like me to talk?

"I've got an Australian shepherd," Lindsay says.

"Oh, cool," I say. Except I mean it this time. "What's he called?"

"*She's* called Sheila," Lindsay says.

I laugh. It's literally the first time I've laughed in a week. No, wait—the second time. I laughed at Evie's letter, too. "Cool name. She should meet Sultan some time."

Lindsay beams at me. "That would be wonderful, Max. What breed is Sultan again?"

"A red setter."

"I *love* red setters," she says, leaning forward in her chair. If she's lying about wanting our dogs to meet, she's really bloody good at it.

I'm wondering if she's going to do an I-told-you-so. *You see, Max? There's still plenty to be happy about. Go play with your dog and smell the roses.* But she doesn't. She probably wants me to join the dots myself.

"Okay, Max, I think we should probably call it a day."

Wait. What?

We haven't talked about my weight once. She weighed me at the start, as usual, but she hasn't mentioned it at all. I've lost another pound since I was last here. I figured I was at least going to get a lecture. I thought today might be the day Lindsay decided I need inpatient treatment.

But . . . nothing. Has she made a mistake?

Hooray! Mission accomplished. Now get the hell out of there.

"Thanks for coming in today," she says, getting up out of her chair. "Say hello to Sultan for me, won't you?"

22

I've started making a list of all the reasons why—everything I can think of that could have nudged me in Ana's direction. It's not like I think it's going to fix me. I'm starting to doubt that anything can fix me. But ever since Italy, I've had this feeling, like, maybe if I understand better, I can learn how to live with this. We can all learn how to live with Ana.

I haven't written any of it down. From now on, stuff like this stays in my head. But that's okay. It turns out, Ana's made me pretty good at remembering stuff. Finally, I get to use one of her weapons against her.

Reason #1

We're kind of health conscious, as a family. For example, I have never knowingly eaten a meal at home that didn't contain at least one vegetable. Most people would consider this a good thing. But I reckon you can take it too far.

Reason #2

Food is never just food in my house. There's always a conversation. For instance, did you know that almost all bananas are clones, and that in the 1920s, we used to have a tastier kind of banana, but it got wiped out by a fungus? Probably not, right? But I did, because Dad talks about stuff like this 24/7. I guess how I'd put it is, we always put a lot of focus on food. I've been trained to think about where it comes from, who made it, what they got paid. Again, this should be a good thing.

Reason #3

As well as being health conscious, we're also pretty particular. Especially Dad. Sure, he never gets mad, but that's partly because everything in our house is *exactly* the way he wants it to be. All of our books are alphabetized. Our herbs and spices are alphabetized, for crying out loud. Mum's a bit like this, too, and I think it's rubbed off on me, however much I didn't want it to. When I see something slightly out of place, I get this prickly feeling in my neck. I can't stop thinking about it until I've put it right. (Robin is definitely *not* like this, by the way. When he was at home, his bedroom looked like it had been raided by the FBI. I can't even imagine what it's like now that he doesn't have Mum nagging at him all the time.)

Lindsay told me once that anorexia can be related to OCD: People who have one often have the other. I don't have OCD, but I maybe have some of the same traits. Like, when I was little, I always used to wash my hands in this particular way: I'd rub the soap exactly four times across each hand—first the back, then the palm. If I got it wrong, I had to start over. I kind of grew out of it. Or maybe I didn't. Maybe it just grew into something else.

Reason #4

This isn't a new one, but . . . the money/waste thing. For a family who has never been poor, we're totally neurotic about money. And the absolute worst thing that can happen in our house is if we let some food go bad and have to throw it away.

For me, the money part only really kicked in on that first trip to Italy. But I'd probably sucked it up by osmosis before then. Now it's the main thing I think about—when I'm not thinking about food, of course.

Reason #5

My parents want me to be an overachiever. Or to put it another way, they want me to turn out different from Robin. Don't get me wrong: They've never told me this. They never would. But it's true. There was this one evening last year, right before I got ill. I overheard them. Dad was telling Mum about how much I love zoology—which I guess is true—but made me feel like a total dweeb. Anyway, Mum was like, *Do you think we have a science genius on our hands?* Dad replied, *It would be a nice change from a creative genius,* and they both started laughing. This was before Robin got his apprenticeship, when he was just a guy who made the odd birdhouse but didn't really know what to do with his life.

They wanted me to be the stable, sensible, high-flying one. The one who alphabetizes his herbs and spices. The one who's always in control. In which case, this year must have been the biggest letdown in history.

So there you have it. Five reasons why I turned out the way I did, maybe. Do they add up to anorexia? Do they explain why Ana decided to climb into my head? You wouldn't think so, right? Maybe there's some extra element I'm forgetting. Some broken wiring in my brain I don't know about.

What I do know is, I don't see any of these things changing. I'm not sure I even *want* them to change. If finding a way to live with Ana means changing who I am, what am I supposed to do?

~

So far, nothing. I've been to my cache twice since Tuesday. The book is still there. My note's still there.

Third time lucky, right?

I've got Sultan with me today. Walking him is one of the few chores Mum and Dad still ask me to do, but I usually take him to the quiet patch of farmland behind our house, rather than the Common. Because when you're out and about with Sultan, people come up and talk to you all the time. He's too cute. In fact, even when I *don't* have him, they sometimes come up and say, *Where's Sultan?*

Once we get to the heather on the far side of the lake, I reach down and unclip his leash. He trots over to a clump of brambles twenty yards in front of us, roots around. I assume he's looking for somewhere to pee, but when I get closer, I realize he's eating the blackberries.

"You're a smart dog," I tell him. He doesn't look up. When I was little, we used to go blackberry picking every summer. I had always scarfed down at least half of the blackberries by the time we got back. I consider following Sultan's lead and eating some now. Maybe just one, for old time's sake. I go through the numbers in my head, trying to figure out how many calories are in one blackberry.

Too many.

I head toward the oak tree, calling to Sultan every so often so he doesn't get too far behind.

Mum and Dad are planning something for tonight. I'm not sure what exactly. Robin's coming over, and they asked me to make sure I was home and showered by six. Like I have anywhere else to be. *Okay,* I said to Mum. *I'll see if I can squeeze you in.*

It's still going to be there. I know it is. She's already

got bored and moved on. Or, alternative theory: She came, read the note, saw the book, decided I was a psycho, and ran a mile.

Who could blame her?

I hear a scuffle and look up. Sultan's chasing a squirrel, hell for leather. The squirrel zips up a tree, and Sultan stands at the bottom, barking, showing it who's boss. He never managed to catch anything even when he was young, and now, he moves much too slowly. But he'll keep trying. He doesn't give up.

"Sultan!" I call. He ignores me the first time, and the second. "Sultan! *Sultan!*" He looks up at me, like, *Can't you see I'm busy?*

"Suit yourself," I say. I'm at the oak tree now. I boost myself up, reach up to the hole, and pull out the box.

A stream of water pours onto my head and down my neck.

"Bollocks!" I shout.

For a moment, I'm confused. Then it comes back to me: the storm. Last night, I woke up to the sound of rain punching at my window.

Someone didn't put the lid back on properly. They slid it into the groove on one side, but not the other.

Was it me?

I slide the lid off with a jerk, pour out the water, then peer in.

The book is gone. And everything else is soaked.

Including a blue note.

23

"What's up, Grumpy Guts?" Robin says, as soon as I walk through the door. "You look like you've just kissed a trout."

"I saw your car in the drive," I reply. The thing with Robin is, you've got to meet him head-on. Even if you don't feel like it. It's a universal law of big brothers: If you give them an inch, they'll take a mile.

He crosses the kitchen to give me a hug. "Good to see you, little bro."

I shrug. "You too. I guess. Is Dad home?"

"Not yet, love," Mum shouts from the kitchen. Robin rolls his eyes at me, to indicate that he disapproves of her listening to our conversation. "He's stopping at Silk Dragon on his way home."

I'd forgotten we were having takeaway, mainly

because I'm not. Takeaways are an anorexic's worst nightmare. They're greasy, the portions are huge, and (even worse) inconsistent. I have a strict no-takeaways policy, although I did agree to sushi once. Mum usually tries to persuade me to have something, and we end up arguing about it for twenty minutes or so. But today, she says right off the bat, *Are you okay to have something from the cupboard?* So I'm having my go-to cupboard meal: half a can of Heinz Cream of Tomato Soup, and two Ryvita Dark Rye Crispbreads.

Robin asks me if I want to play *Mario Kart,* so we do that for half an hour until Dad gets back.

"You should come stay with me for a weekend," Robin tells me, as we hurtle through Bowser's Castle. He's playing as Koopa Troopa, as always. I'm Yoshi. He'll win by about three seconds. It's pretty nice doing something the same way we've always done it, where I know exactly what to expect. It feels comfortable, like a pair of old jogger bottoms. I can almost pretend things are how they used to be.

"Okay," I say.

"Seriously. I've got a sleeping bag. There's this big wood near my flat, it's probably full of caches."

"Okay."

Robin pauses the game, which is awful *Mario Kart* form. He looks at me. "What's up?"

I don't look back. "Nothing."

"Suit yourself."

He unpauses, and we carry on playing in silence. I'm not trying to be rude. I know Robin's being nice, as usual. But it's exhausting just trying to think of things to say at the moment.

I'm still worrying about the letter. My first thought was that maybe I'd be able to decipher it, but when I unfolded it I realized that was never going to happen. I couldn't even make out a single word. It's a long letter: four sheets of A4. It must've taken ages.

So, what do I do now? Write a reply, like, *Sorry, but could you say that again?*

As if she'd bother. She's probably already regretting replying in the first place. This is the perfect excuse for her to bail.

On the final lap, I'm actually ahead. Just. The course ends with this massive staircase, then a big jump over a fire pit, then a sprint toward the line. I'm on the home straight, when a red shell whacks me from behind, and guess what? Robin beats me by three seconds.

"Thanks for coming," Dad says when he sees Robin. It's weirdly formal, like we're at a funeral or something.

Robin grins at him and nods, like, *No problem, you weirdo.*

Dad's carrying two massive paper takeaway bags. He heaves them onto the kitchen table, then sits down. We sit down, too.

"Listen," Dad says. We listen, but he doesn't actually say anything. He folds and then unfolds his arms. Then crosses his legs.

"Shall we eat first?" Mum says eventually.

First. What's that supposed to mean? What else is happening?

They're finally going to shove you in a mental asylum.

Dad turns to Mum, looking relieved. "Okay."

I microwave my soup while Mum and Dad sort out the takeaway. Saying Dad over-ordered would be a bit like saying Antarctica is chilly. I know I'm not the best judge, but we have a stupid amount of food, including a whole crispy duck, three main dishes, prawn crackers, loads of wontons, and spare ribs. All for three people. Mum empties all the takeaway cartons onto plates. Most families would eat from the cartons, but Mum hates the clutter, so everything goes onto plates and bowls. Mum then spends an hour after we've eaten washing up. Naturally, because Dad is Dad, this includes washing up the cartons so we can use them as storage boxes. I know every family is weird, but I guarantee you mine is the weirdest.

Before Ana arrived, Chinese was my favorite takeaway. And the thing I loved most was prawn crackers. The takeaway we go to, Silk Dragon, always gives you a massive bag, about the size of a parachute. I would've happily eaten them all. I don't miss a lot of food, really. You kind of just tune the idea of food out after a while.

But I miss prawn crackers.

We sit down to eat. The prawn crackers are right in front of me. I want to have one. But . . . they're basically deep-fried flour. If you leave them in the paper bag for half an hour, you can pretty see right through it from all the grease. Plus, they're Robin's favorite, too. I try to think of it as a good deed: I'm letting him polish off the whole bag. *You're welcome, big bro.*

I eat my soup and try not to think about it.

Robin's telling us about his latest project, which is a table made from Japanese larch. He's got a *lot* to say about Japanese larch. Apparently, it has so much resin in it that you don't need to treat it: The wood is self-oiling. Robin seems to think this is an interesting fact.

"You don't even need to treat it," he says, for maybe the fourth time.

I'm still nervous about what Mum said. Do they have something to tell us? If they do, they don't seem to be in a hurry about it. Mum's picking at her food, which always makes me really anxious, because anorexia is part genetic. They found this out by studying twins. Identical twins are more likely to share their anorexia than non-identical ones, which means it's not just about your home environment.

If I'm vulnerable, Mum might be, too.

When they start treating you for anorexia, they always ask about your family history. *Has anyone in your family had an eating disorder?* I said no, but then I realized I had no idea. It's not the kind of thing you tell your kids about, right? Maybe Mum was ill, too. Apparently, anorexics can be split into three roughly equal-size groups: the third who die, the third who recover completely, and the third who relapse. What if Mum used to be sick, and she's come out the other end—and then I make her sick again?

She could do with losing a few pounds.

The thought hits me like a train. I hate myself for thinking it, even if it isn't really me. I don't know anymore. Before I can do anything, I feel the vomit coming. My eyes bulge.

"Max? What's wrong?"

I close my mouth as tight as I can, press my hands over it, and sprint to the bathroom.

~

I'd barely touched my soup. You know when you're sick, and you want to throw up, but there's nothing there? Retching on an empty stomach is even worse than throwing up food. I spit. It feels like my whole digestive tract is on fire.

"Everything okay in there?" Dad calls through

the door.

Not really, I want to tell him. There are two thoughts running through my head:

1. They're going to think I took something.
2. If Mum is sick, watching her son throw up probably isn't going to help.

"I'm fine," I say. It comes out so quiet, I'm not sure Dad will even hear me through the door. But I don't have the energy to be any louder.

"Can I bring you some water?"

"Dad, I'm in a bathroom."

"Okay," Dad says again. He sounds a little sheepish, and I feel bad.

Loads of anorexics take stuff that makes them throw up or go to the loo. I never have. But right now, Dad is standing outside, wondering if I've started trying to destroy my body in a whole new way. And Mum might be wondering about doing the same.

There's only one way to fix this: I have to let them know I'm all right. I have to go out there, eat my soup, smile. Show them I'm in control.

"Hi, Dad," I say as I come out of the bathroom.

"Everything okay?"

"You tell me," he says. He tilts his head and looks hard at me.

"I'm just a bit under the weather today," I say. "But it's nothing to worry about. Honest."

He looks at me with that nervous smile I've gotten used to: that smile that says, *I love you, but I'm scared of you.* I see the same smile on Mum's face when I go back through to the dining room, and on Robin's. It's the look you give a big dog off its leash: friendly but nervous, because you're not quite sure what it'll do.

So I do what Robin would do: I make a joke. "Sorry about that." I do this big, obvious shrug. "I guess I didn't like your Japanese larch story very much."

Robin looks surprised for a second. I'm worried that I've misjudged things, and he's going to be upset. There's a little pause. Then Mum grins and turns to Robin. "He's only saying what everyone's thinking, love."

And we all start laughing our heads off.

When we've finished eating, Dad packs all the spare food into cartons and Tupperwares. And there's a *lot* of spare food. Pretty much half a duck, for instance, and half of Mum's Kung Po chicken. I notice

Robin's polished off all of the prawn crackers, though. I offer to help clean up, because I like knowing exactly what's in the fridge, but Dad tells me to stay and chat to Robin.

"You say it like it's some kind of punishment, Dad," Robin says.

"That depends on whether you're going to carry on telling him about Japanese larch."

Robin crosses his arms like, *I've had enough of this.*

"Leave him be, Joe," Mum says. "Now, who wants a cup of tea?"

I feel good. It's weird: Twenty minutes ago, it was like the world was going to end, and now, I'm having a great time. My mood's kind of like a swift: It can zoom off in any direction, then change course in an instant.

Okay, it probably helped that Mum *did* eat some food in the end.

Robin looks at me like he's going to say something important. Apparently, everyone's in this kind of mood today.

"What?" I ask him. He doesn't respond. "Robin, what?"

He thumbs in the direction of the living room, where my Nintendo is. "Rematch?"

Guess what? Robin wins again, using the exact same cheap and cynical technique: a shell in my back right before the finish line.

"I hate *Mario Kart*," I say. "And you're a terrible person."

"I know, little bro," he says. He pats me on the back, then scoots away before I can punch him.

We drift back into the dining room and sit down with our cups of tea. At which point, Dad gets all serious again. "So, I wanted us . . . *we* wanted us all to have a nice meal together, because we've got some news. Nothing bad." He glances at Mum. "I mean, uh . . ."

Mum cuts in to save him. "I think what your father means is, it's nothing you need to worry about."

"Exactly," Dad says.

"I'm on tenterhooks here," Robin says, and rolls his eyes at me.

But I'm not finding it funny. Something in the way Mum and Dad are acting has put me on edge.

"As you know," Dad carries on, ignoring Robin. He's speaking in little bursts, with long pauses. He sounds like a hermit who's trying to talk for the first time in years. "Your mum and I . . . we've been going through . . . well, a bit of a rough patch lately."

I glance over at Robin. A second ago, he was slumped back in his chair, grinning. Now, he's sat up straight, with this ultra-serious look on his face.

"We love each other very much," Dad says. "But we've decided we need to spend some time apart."

"What do you mean?" Robin says.

Isn't it obvious? I want to scream at him.

Maybe Robin knows exactly what Dad means, he just doesn't want to believe it. On the other hand, I really don't want to have it spelled out. I'm holding on to some tiny, stupid hope that they don't mean what I think they mean. It's like when you know you've given a wrong answer in a test: You don't want to look at the scores, because then there's a chance. If they don't explain, there's a chance this isn't happening.

Too late. Mum gives Robin this stern look and says, "From now on, your dad and I are going to live our own lives. Separately."

"Oh," Robin says. "Shit."

"Language," Dad says. But you can tell from the way he says it he doesn't exactly mind, given the circumstances.

For the second time this evening, I want to throw up. But this time, somehow—God knows how—I hold it in. I hold in the questions, too. More than anything, I want to ask: *What about me? What happens to me?* But if I wasn't ready to hear the other thing, I'm certainly not ready for that.

They are going to get rid of you so bloody fast.

I try not to listen. I picture myself taping her mouth shut and throwing her down a well.

There's one more question, too: an even scarier one. It bounces around inside me, squeezing my organs, kicking me in the stomach, making me feel even more horrible than I already did. Which is kind of impressive. The thing is, with this one, I *definitely* know the answer. There's no fooling myself when it comes to the scariest thought of all. I look at Robin, and he catches my eye, and I know he's thinking the exact same thing I am.

It's my fault.

They're breaking up because of me.

~

I open the fridge.

The orange glow pours out onto me. The kitchen's dark, except for the light from the fridge. It feels a bit like I'm standing in front of an alien spaceship.

Right now, I'm totally cool with being abducted and flown off to Mars.

Robin left in a hurry after dinner, mumbling something about an early start—even though, when he was telling us about Project Larch, he said they couldn't do anything tomorrow because they were waiting for more wood to be delivered. But I don't really blame him for not wanting to stick around.

It must be really late. The main road runs twenty yards behind our back garden, and you can normally hear the odd car going past, even late at night. But now there's nothing.

I start taking boxes out of the fridge, all of the leftovers from last night. There's three bits of sesame toast, some sweet-and-sour pork, some beef and black bean noodles. Plus the duck and a whole thing of rice.

I pour it all out onto a plate.

I look at it.

I gulp.

There's so much food: one huge mound that domes out of the plate like Mount Fuji. Enough for at least two normal people and at least five of me.

But I have to eat it.

Because if I eat it, things are okay.

I'm okay.

Our house won't feel like a prison anymore.

And who knows, maybe our family will stay together.

I'm not stupid. I know it's not going to change things overnight. But if the problem goes away—if I pack Ana's bags and kick her out of the door and never let her back in, Mum and Dad could change their minds.

I *want* to eat it. I want this to all be over. I want to be able to sit down and eat a takeaway with my family, like a normal functioning human being. I want to shove chocolate bars into my mouth and swap sandwiches with my friends. I want to go over to people's houses sometimes, or go to the cinema and eat popcorn. I want to play rugby, even if I'm shit at it. And this Christmas, I want to eat loads and then sleep all afternoon, like everyone else does, like you're *supposed* to, and not worry about it.

And the only way that's going to happen is if I *make* it happen.

I start eating.

And I don't stop.

24

I guess bulimics know how this feels. But I don't. I've never felt like this, not really. The closest I've got is stuffing a Mini Roll in my mouth and swallowing it whole. I felt a rush then: a moment of pure bliss as it slipped down my throat, Ana struck dumb, for once, by the shock of it. After three seconds, the panic hit me. Grabbed me. I took the packet and shoved it into the back of the kitchen cupboard, then ran out of the house to stop myself from giving in. To put myself in control again.

This is that Mini Roll, times a million.

My first-ever binge.

My jaw moves without me thinking about it, like those mechanical ones they use to cut people out of cars. Robotic. Relentless. I feel the lumps of food in my throat—big, ragged lumps, because I'm not chewing. I picture a snake with a series of mouse-shaped lumps along its body.

I bite my cheek, and for a second, I want to scream, but I don't. I control myself. *See? I'm still in control.* It doesn't stop me. Nothing can stop me. Chew, chew, chew, swallow. All of the duck has gone. I start on the rice.

Now there are two voices inside my head: Ana has developed a split personality. My mental health problem has her own mental health problem.

Stop. Stop. STOP. What are you doing? You're disgusting. You're ruining everything.

Keep going. It feels good, admit it. It feels so good to finally EAT. And if you keep it up, your family will love you again.

No—they'll be ashamed of you. Fat, hopeless you. What happened? You used to have willpower.

They can't love you while you're anorexic. They won't. You've got to show them you're okay.

This isn't okay. This is disgusting. And you have no idea how much you're going to regret it.

Five minutes later—probably less—I'm done. The

duck, the wontons, the prawn toast—it's all gone. And for a moment, I feel this rush, like, *I did it. I won!*

Then the pain starts.

When you stop eating, your stomach becomes less elastic. It can't expand like it used to. So if you barely put anything in it for an entire year, and then sit down and eat two days' worth of food in one sitting, you're in trouble.

Snakes can do it. Polar bears can do it. We can't.

The cramps make me double over. I feel like my guts are about to explode all over the floor. I hate myself. And I don't know what to do.

What did I tell you?

I crawl over to the sink, grab the edge, drag myself up. I stick my fingers down my throat. I retch, but nothing comes.

You're rubbish at that, remember? You can't do anything right.

I grab my phone, and google *how to make yourself sick*. The first hit is this herbal remedy website that tells you to drink a mixture of mustard and water.

So I do.

It's one of the worst things I've ever tasted. But it

works. I'm pretty sure no one's ever been this happy about throwing up before. It feels amazing. It hurts, but I don't care: I've not been this happy for ages. Because now I know the secret. I know how to pretend to be normal. How to stay in control, forever. Now I can show Mum and Dad I'm okay. They don't need to know that I'm spewing my guts up every night. I feel like an archaeologist who's just discovered a lost city he's been searching for his whole life.

Then I turn around and see Dad.

Before I even clock what's happening, he's hugging me, and I'm crying into his shoulder. "We're going to fix this," he whispers in my ear. And I try to pretend he's talking about him and Mum, as well as me. But I know he isn't.

~

A conversation I had with Robin, before things got really bad (I thought they were already really bad at the time. But they weren't):

Robin: Do you remember Mum's stopwatch?
I shake my head.

Robin: It was the only way she could get you to do anything when you were little.

It comes back to me gradually, like a ship through mist. When I was little, I put stuff off for hours. Getting up, finishing my tea—anything. But if Mum bet me I couldn't get dressed for school in thirty seconds, I'd be ready in twenty-nine.

Me: Don't put this all on me, Robin. She used it on you too.

Robin: True. She had that lanyard so she could take it everywhere. You know, I wish she'd used it when I was doing my A-levels. Maybe I would've got that A in math then.

I guess Mum's lesson didn't change Robin. But it changed me. Now I count time like I count calories: day in, day out. I can't stop. I count my steps as I walk, and I count the number of days left in the year. When I can't face doing anything else or I can't be bothered, I sit in my room, close my eyes, and start the stopwatch on my phone, and see how close I can get to a minute counting in my head. Usually, I'm a second or two too slow. Even though I know I'm usually a second or two too slow, I can't seem to adjust for it: No matter what I do, it always comes out that way. Like the world is moving too fast for me. Like I'm always chasing things, and I never have time to catch my breath.

It's one week until I go back to school. At the start of the holidays, there were forty-three days on the clock. I thought it was enough time to fix myself—or at least, to start fixing myself. I thought, if I tried really hard, somehow, I'd be able to catch up.

But when it came down to it, the opposite happened. The universe said, *Thanks for trying, Max. But, um, no. Sorry.* Robin left. Mum and Dad broke up. The world is running away from me faster than ever.

I keep speeding up. I keep trying. But I can feel myself fading. Like when you sprint toward the line at the end of a race and your legs start to burn, your body starts to scream no at you. You know you can only keep going for so long. You know you're on borrowed time.

Or maybe it's Zeno's Paradox. Maybe no matter how far I go, how fast I go, I'll never catch up.

My body is breaking in slow motion. I cut myself three weeks ago, chopping a carrot, when we were in

Italy, and it still hasn't healed. If you starve yourself for months, eventually, your body starts giving up.

You can't keep running forever.

～

One week later. To be exact, 159 hours. In that time, an average adult male would have burnt 13,250 calories. Not me, though. Because I haven't left this room in a week. Because I weigh a grand total of —.

You don't need to eat anything. Pinch your skin. See? That's fat. That's pure blubber. There's enough there to last for weeks. Months, probably.

"Hey, buddy," Dad says from the doorway. "Can I come in?"

He doesn't wait for a reply, probably because he knows he isn't getting one. He closes the door behind him and walks over to my bed.

"I brought you some breakfast," he says.

I don't need to look. It's a pot of Shape Up Smooth Strawberry Yoghurt. Four ounces. That's pretty much all I can stomach at this point. Sometimes, I can't even bring myself to eat that.

"You okay?"

I shrug.

I don't get out of bed. I can't sleep. Mostly, I stare at the walls. I never did get around to putting those posters up.

Yeah, you're totally okay! This is exactly how a normal teenager spends their summer. Nothing about this situation screams "freak" at all.

Dad sits down on the edge of the bed. "Listen, I wanted to talk to you about something."

I turn to face him. It takes a while. I have to use my arms to lever myself over. I feel like a whale trying to unbeach itself.

"What's going on?" I mumble.

"I've found a flat," he says.

And it's like that moment on a roller coaster when you think you've reached the bottom, but there's another secret drop. It turns out it's possible to feel even worse than I already did.

"It's right around the corner," he carries on. "You can come over whenever you like."

"That's what Robin said," I say.

"Max," Dad says, in a pained voice. He pinches the bridge of his nose. Until now, I hadn't really clocked how tired he looks. "Your brother is just trying to settle into his new home. Anyway, my place is only a five-minute walk away."

I don't reply. I feel bad, because I know Dad's trying his best, but it's taking all my effort not to scream. I don't have any left over for saying the things I'm supposed to say. I lie back down in the bed.

Dad stares at me for the longest time. I'm waiting for him to say something about how it's all going to be okay or ask me if I want to watch *Springwatch* with him later or something. But he just walks out and softly closes the door behind him. I guess he's used up all his effort, too.

Afterward, I realize it's the longest conversation I've had in two days.

August 30
Dear Ana,

At the start of the year, I told you there were six
people in my life. But then Robin left, and then Dad.
And when Dad left, Mum turned into a zombie.

I was supposed to go see Lindsay yesterday, but I
guess Mum forgot. I didn't say anything. I know how
these things work: NHS referrals are like gold dust
now. Once you've missed your appointment, you're
stuffed.

And there's no way Stu, Ram, or Evie are going to
talk to me when I go back to school. If I even make
it back to school.

I'm supposed to be the one who's disappearing.
But as I do, everyone around me melts away too.

I guess this was your plan all along, right?

I don't care though. It's easier this way. It's
easier to stay in control when there's no one
bothering me. It's easier to be me when no one's
trying to fix me.

After I write this, I'm going outside for the first
time in two weeks, to get rid of the last thing
connecting me to the world: my cache. I've already
taken the listing down. But apparently, it can take a
month to update in some people's apps. And anyway,

that doesn't stop people who already know where it is from finding it. Like Evie, for instance.

I'll be back soon. Then it'll just be me and you. No one else gets it. We're better off on our own.

25

The wind on the Common howls through my clothes and into my joints. I ache all over, like I'm eighty years old.

I walk like an eighty-year-old, too. Slowly, warily, because I'm afraid of tripping over a tree root and shattering my bones. I'm still out of breath, though.

My body's started to properly give up. When I try to stand, my legs judder underneath me, and I imagine them snapping like twigs. I can't even do a single bloody push-up anymore. And when I comb my hair, more and more seems to come out, each strand as brittle as a piece of Shredded Wheat. Noticing this put me off Shredded Wheat forever.

But wait. That's not even the gross stuff.

Gross Thing Number One: My pee has gone sort of . . . foamy. Seriously, it happens. When your kidneys are so screwed they can't filter out protein anymore, *your pee goes foamy.* It looks like the old-man cider Dad drinks sometimes.

Gross Thing Number Two: If I put my hand to my mouth and smell my breath, it's like sweet and sour. Tangy. Fruity. That's the smell of dissolving fat. We did this in biology once. It's called ketosis: When your body runs out of sugar, it starts burning fat. As Dr. Roberts put it, *Ketosis is what your body does when it has no other choice. It's like burning your table and chairs to keep warm, because you've already chopped down all the trees.*

Gross Thing Number Three: This is the worst one by far. I'm turning into a monkey. There are little hairs growing all over my body, the kind newborn babies sometimes have. I can't believe this is my life. I'm fifteen, and half the boys in my class already have beards or at least mustaches, and I'm growing peach fuzz on my face.

Oh, and for some reason, my ankles and knees are swollen. Probably some other fun side effect I don't even know about yet.

Anorexia happens when you're not looking. It's like that game you play when you're little, where you have to sneak up on someone and freeze whenever they turn around. As soon as you let your guard down, it pounces. Because you can always eat less. You can always take away one piece, one mouthful, one calorie. That slice of toast can be slightly thinner. That can of soup can be two portions instead of three. You do that over and over again until you can't survive on what's left.

I've made this journey hundreds of times. Across a shimmering carpet of meadow grass and rye, dotted with purple patches of heather. Past the lake, where the ducks look as unhappy to be outside as I am, and into the birch woods. The leaves are starting to turn already; I guess it's been a long summer. The trees are preparing for a winter without food, where the only way to survive is to manage with less.

If only it were that easy. If only I could just drop my leaves and wait for things to get better.

The oak tree looms over me. I cower away from it, like it's about to attack me or something. I feel dizzy. All right, I always feel dizzy. But this is way worse than my usual haven't-eaten-a-proper-meal-in-months dizzy. It's more the-world-is-a-giant-washing-machine dizzy. I'm pretty sure I'm going to chuck my guts up, even though I haven't eaten anything at all for twenty-four hours.

I stop.

I bend over, rest my hands on my knees. Then I decide even that's too much effort. I slump down on the carpet of leaves that's already forming on the forest floor. The ground is harder than I thought it would be; as I hit the dirt, I hear something snap.

And then I realize I can't get up.

September 1

Dear Ana,

When I first saw Lindsay, she told me that the way to deal with anorexia is to focus on "rational beliefs" about food. It's like, if I can distance myself from it, it won't hurt me anymore.

That's why I tried to think of you as someone else. I gave you a name, and wrote all these letters, to convince myself that you weren't me.

But that was never how it felt. Not really. When the voice inside my head said, "Don't eat that. You'll thank me later," it never really felt like it was coming from someone else. From Ana. Because it wasn't. They were my thoughts. My opinions. My head.

I reckon that's why people with mental health problems get annoyed when other people talk about "voices in your head." Because those voices are your voice—and that makes them way, way scarier.

"There's still fat on your stomach. You could drop another pound, easy."

"Don't give in. Don't eat that. You're better than that."

"The less you eat, the stronger you are."

You don't exist, Ana. And I have zero clue where that leaves me.

On my own, I guess.

26

"**Come on, love,** time to wake up."

"Ugh."

For a moment, I have no idea where I am. Or who's talking to me. Or what's going on. My head feels like it's full of treacle and cotton wool, and I'm pretty sure there are razor blades jabbing into my lower back.

"Come on, otherwise the day will get ahead of us, won't it?"

It's Mum. She always says this: *The day will get ahead of us.* Robin always used to respond, *The day can do what it likes, I'm staying in bed.*

I wince at the metallic screech of the curtains being pulled back. Light pours into the room. I scrunch my eyes tight.

"Max," Mum says.

"Okay, okay," I mumble.

Slowly, I come to my senses. I unscrunch my eyes, just a little, and see a blurry Mum hovering at the end of my bed. She comes over to my bedside table and tidies the books into a neat pile.

"Oh God," I say. "It's today."

"It's going to be okay," Mum replies immediately. She was obviously waiting for me to realize.

Today is September 2: the first day of school. The day that's been approaching forever, like a train hurtling across a huge plain, getting closer so slowly you barely notice, until it's *right there*. Today's the day I'm supposed to face everyone: Ram, Stu, Darren, Shinji, my teachers. And Evie.

I've gone through the conversation a hundred times in my head. They'll ask me what I've been doing all summer, and I'll tell them not too much, normal stuff, and act like everything's fine. Or fine-ish. And then I'll have to pretend I'm interested when they start telling me about their summers. How Ram went on holiday with his mum, then came home for one night, then went away with his dad, which was much better. How the camper Stu's family rented broke down somewhere near Inverness, meaning they had to spend a night in the woods, in the pitch-black, and he was pretty sure he heard a wolf, even though there haven't been wolves in Scotland since the seventeenth century.

Except they won't. I won't. It's not going to happen.

Because I'm not going to school today.

Mum's now making small talk with the old man in the bed opposite me, Bill, who has some kind of bladder infection.

"You know the community garden plots down on Sherbourn Road?" Bill is saying. "I've had one of them for thirty-two years."

"Gosh!" Mum says, like she is stunned by this fact. "What do you grow?"

"All sorts. Tomatoes, cucumbers, carrots, potatoes. Loads of beans. The only problem is, it all needs harvesting now, and I'm stuck in here."

"Oh no!" Mum says. "Isn't there anyone who can pick them for you?"

Mum can be invested in someone else's life within ten seconds of meeting them. The other night, when we were eating (or not eating, in my case) takeaway, Mum said to us, *Remember Sandra the florist? Her daughter's having another baby.* It turned out she'd met Sandra for less than ten minutes, two years before, in the supermarket, and never seen her since. But Mum still wanted to send a card to congratulate her. Robin said, *She'll think you're mental.*

Bill shrugs. "I've tried to get my wife to go, but she says I've got bigger fish to fry right now."

Mum looks horrified. "I'll talk to my other son, Robin. Maybe he can help. Which plot was it again?"

I shake my head, smile a little. I haven't seen Mum like this for ages. *Soft as chalk,* as Dad puts it. When Dad's here, he mostly sits by my bed and reads, or plays cards with me when I'm awake. But Mum spends the whole time talking to other patients. If you walked in, you probably wouldn't guess who she was here for. I kind of prefer it this way. I don't know what to say to Dad half the time.

The downside is, when she leaves, they talk to me about her. *She's nice your mum, isn't she?* And so on. The worst was Paul, who was definitely flirting with Mum. They were laughing their heads off about nothing for a good hour. I stared at Mum, trying to get across a Dad-hasn't-even-moved-all-his-stuff-out-yet vibe. She kept giving me these guilty glances. When she left, Paul said to me, *Your mum's great, you know.*

What a firecracker. I didn't even respond to him: I just turned to face the wall. Luckily, Paul only had kidney stones, which meant he was in and out in a day.

Bye-bye, knobhead.

~

When they brought me in, the doctors diagnosed me with acute renal failure. Basically, my kidneys gave up completely. (That snap I heard? I asked Dr. Singh, the kidney specialist, about it. She said, *Um, maybe you fell on a twig?*) It wasn't so bad that I needed dialysis: They just put me on an IV drip. I spent the first two days on that, trying not to think about how many calories are in it.

Now I'm off the drip and on a *restricted carbohydrate diet,* which basically means lots of toast. Renal failure happens when there's too much salt and protein in your lungs, so the treatment is basically just to eat toast and porridge and drink water until things calm down. I asked for some peanut butter on my toast, and they told me it had too much protein in it. That's right: I actually asked for extra food, without anyone telling me I had to. *And they said no.*

They let me have jam instead, though.

For the first time in a whole year, I don't feel hungry. I just feel . . . normal, I guess. Except it's not at all normal to me. It's like when you're used to wearing a watch, and then you forget it one day and your wrist feels weird. You get used to stuff and only really notice when something changes.

I'm allowed to get up and walk around the ward, as long as there's someone with me, and I have enough energy to do it. I'm getting better. I can now concentrate on one thing long enough to read a book or have a conversation. Yesterday Dr. Singh said she thinks I could be out in a couple of days. I can probably go back to school next week. Lindsay and the nutritionist are coming to the ward later today, to help me figure out a plan. Which is, like, *GULP.*

It's easy enough to go along with everything while I'm in the hospital. I follow the rules; I don't really have a choice. Also, there are no mirrors, which definitely helps. But when I'm back at home, and have to make it work all by myself, and forget all the habits and tricks I've come up with over the past year . . . I don't know how I'll cope. But I don't exactly have a choice.

Either I learn how to eat, or I die.

"Hey, little bro."

As usual, I do my best to ignore him. I'm reading a book about Walter Rothschild, who's one of the most famous zoologists ever. It's pretty interesting. Once, he rode a zebra-drawn carriage to Buckingham Palace, to prove that zebras can be tamed.

"I brought you a present," Robin says cheerily, as if I've acknowledged him in some way already.

I make him wait another ten seconds, just because, then turn around. "Hi," I say. "Um, thanks for coming."

The light's starting to fade. I'm guessing it's like 5:00 or 6:00 p.m. Mum left at noon. She told me, *I need to pop into work for a bit, but I'll be back this evening. And your dad's coming first thing tomorrow.* My plan to be less of a burden on my family isn't going so well.

Robin shrugs and raises the coffee cup in his hand. "As you know, I'm mainly here for Suzanne."

"The girl in the coffee shop?" Robin talked about her last time he was here. In fact, he talked about little else.

"The very same."

"You know her name now," I say. "That's a start."

Robin puts a hand to his chest and closes his eyes. "Suzanne and I are taking things slowly. We don't want to rush into anything."

"Clearly," I say. "Anyway, what happened to Ffion?"

Robin bites his lip. "She, um, wanted to rush into something."

I frown. "So, what's my present?"

Robin gives the guy in the bed next to me a sideways glance. There are six beds in my room, and five of them are occupied right now, including mine. I realize that everyone is looking at Robin, curious to find out what he's brought me. He doesn't seem to be carrying anything.

"Er," he says. "Fancy a walk?"

Robin doesn't want to go to the café where Suzanne works. He says he doesn't want to seem too keen.

"It's probably a bit late for that," I tell him.

He doesn't respond. We walk the corridors in silence for a while.

"The day you came here . . . ," Robin says eventually. But he immediately peters out.

It was Robin who found me. It was the first thing Mum told me when I woke up. *We said you were missing, and he ran right off. Goodness knows how he knew where you were.* That's how I knew Robin hadn't said anything about the cache. He hasn't mentioned it to me so far, either. All he said about finding me was, *You've got to stop passing out on me, little bro. I know you're skinny, but carrying you around is a pain.*

"After we put you in an ambulance, I went back to find your cache."

For some reason, my throat goes dry, like someone's asked me to give a speech in front of a thousand people or told me they've got naked pictures of me that they're going to post on the Internet. I'm not sure why I'm nervous—after all, it was Robin who got me into the whole thing. And it's not like any of my diary entries were still in there. It had been empty for weeks.

"How come?" I croak.

"I figured that's where you were headed. And since you hadn't exactly been out and about much lately, I figured there might have been, y'know, a good reason."

I take a second to respond. "Yeah," I say. I'm looking at the floor, which is polished so bright I can almost see my face in it. Am I imagining it or do my cheeks look rounder? To be fair, compared to how I looked a week ago, even a supermodel would look like a guinea pig.

Or maybe that's just what I want to tell myself.

"Well, someone left you a note."

Robin holds his arm out. I go to take the thing he's holding and notice my hand is shaking. It's—guess what?—a blue note, folded up inside a little plastic bag, one of the ones you pinch at the top to make it airtight. And watertight. Does that mean she knows my cache got soaked, and I never got her last note? Does it mean she knew I wouldn't be able to get back there anytime soon?

Robin clears his throat and shifts his weight between his feet. "Is everything all right, Max?"

Robin doesn't usually call me by my actual name. I stare at him in a has-my-brother-gone-loopy way. "Um . . . you know we're in a hospital, right?"

He grins, but it almost looks like a grimace because he's frowning, too. Something's obviously on his mind. "No, I mean . . . with the cache. No one's bothering you or anything?"

He thinks I'm being bullied. He's upset and nervous because he thinks the cache is making me like this, making things worse, and it's all his fault.

"Nope," I say. "No one's bullying me."

"Are you sure?"

"I promise."

~

Lindsay says she is *delighted with my progress.* The nutritionist, Dr. Siskin, who isn't my usual nutritionist, agrees. The renal specialist, Dr. Singh, is here, too. The three musketeers. I feel pretty embarrassed that I'm taking up three doctors' time. We're in a consulting room off the main corridor of my ward. It's tiny: If I lie down on the floor, I'd touch both walls, like in Robin's flat. And I'm boxed in on three sides by people wearing white coats. It's pretty stressful.

Lindsay weighed me before we came in here. She wouldn't let me see the scales: She says we really need to focus on getting my weight up now, and she understands how difficult it is, yada yada. Given how happy she and Dr. Siskin are, it's not exactly rocket science: I've put on loads of weight.

I don't mind, though. Or at least, I don't mind as much as I would have a week or a month or even six months ago.

Anorexia kills. It's the first thing you find if

you google it: Anorexia is the most deadly mental health problem in the world, bar none. And kidney failure is the biggest cause of death. You still never think it's going to happen to you, though. Even when it's really bad, and you really want it to. When you're desperate for all of the pain to end. It's weird. You simultaneously think, *I'm never ever going to get better and I can't cope with another day of this* and *I'm never going to be one of the ones who actually DIES.* I swear, anorexia is mostly about finding a way to hold five thoughts that all contradict one another together in your head. I got really good at it. But near killing myself has changed things. A bit. So I'm trying my best to go along with the whole don't-tell-Max-how-much-he-weighs routine.

"So what happens next?" I ask.

Lindsay looks at Dr. Siskin, who nods.

"Well, Max, that's sort of up to you."

"What do you mean?"

"We're here to help you get better. Now, some people with anorexia prefer to do that while living with their families. But I know things with your family are tough at the moment."

I almost reply, *Only because of me,* but I stop myself,

because I know it would make me sound even more selfish, even though I don't mean it like that. *La-la-la, it's all about me!*

"What else can I do?"

"Everyone's recovery is different," Lindsay says. *And some people don't recover at all,* I think. I know why she does it, but it annoys me how Lindsay doesn't even acknowledge the alternative. It makes me feel like a child. "Some people find the best environment for them to recover in is . . . away from their home."

"A residential treatment facility," says Dr. Siskin.

"Like a hospital?"

"It's much more relaxed than a hospital," Lindsay says. She smiles. "More like a youth hostel."

Yeah, right, I think. "How long would I be there for?"

"It depends how you get on," Lindsay says. "We'll do an assessment every week. It could be a couple of weeks. It could be a little longer."

That means months. Or years.

"What do you think I should do?" I ask her.

I can see Lindsay biting her lip. She doesn't want to give me an answer. I turn to the others, to see if they will. But they all look at me with these dumb, patronizing grins. Professional grins that don't give you a clue what they're thinking.

I've spent the past year obsessing about being in control of everything. And over the past few days, I've had to give up some of that control. And it's felt . . . good. Better than it did before.

And now they're asking me to make a decision that could kill me, or save my life. I feel like screaming at them. *I don't want to be in control of this. Just tell me what to do.*

Please, just tell me what to do.

27

Last Christmas, I thought that was the hardest it could get. I was wrong. Today is harder. It's like climbing a mountain, and thinking you've nearly reached the top, then seeing the summit curve slowly away from you. There's still miles to go.

I weighed myself this morning. I couldn't help it. Mum and Dad hid the scales months ago, but I know where they are: in the airing cupboard, under the beach towels. I grabbed them and rushed into the bathroom before I could change my mind.

I've put on three pounds since we went on holiday.

At first, I was horrified. My stomach did a few somersaults, and I started wondering whether, if I tried to throw up, I could get rid of any of last night's dinner. *I'm disgusting. No girl will ever like me. My parents must be so ashamed of me.*

But I was prepared. I was ready to deal with this situation. *This is a good thing, this is a good thing,* I told myself over and over, doing my best to drown out the bad thoughts.

Now, I'm standing in front of the mirror, naked. And I can see things I've never seen before.

Fun fact: Anorexia literally changes the way you see things. There's this study they did, where they asked anorexics to judge the size of their bodies in the mirror. I'm not sure where I read about it. Anyway, it turns out that it's not just about wanting to be thin. We—by which I mean, anorexics—literally can't see how thin we are. When I take my clothes off and stand in front of the mirror, I see a different naked body from the one you'd see, if you were standing there, too. The limbs look thicker. The ribs don't stick out as much. Sometimes, even your own eyes lie to you.

Two weeks ago, when I looked in the mirror, all I saw was the curve of my belly. I'd pinch my skin and pull it away from my arm and think, *There must be fat under there.* As if *having skin* is proof that you're fat. But now it's different. I lean in close to look at my face, and I can see the shadows under my eyes where the flesh in my cheeks has melted away. I never noticed them before. When I step back, I see how far my ribs jut out now, like the bars on a xylophone, casting zebra shadows across my body. I see the veins like rivers on my hands and forearms, and think to myself, *Oh my God, I look like a piece of blue cheese.*

Okay, so it's not exactly news that I'm thin. I've known I'm thin all year. It's pretty obvious when the slightest breeze takes the warmth out of your body in seconds, or when you can't sit on a bench because it hurts your ass too much. But now I *feel* thin. Even though I've put on two pounds in a week. Even though Ana is telling me I'm a zeppelin. Now I know she's talking bollocks.

I stand in front of the mirror and say it out loud. To myself, to Ana, to the skeleton staring back at me. "Max, you're skinny."

I think for a second, then I add, "And today will be different."

〜

Ram and Evie aren't in my homeroom, but Stu is. I arrive before him and sit at a desk in the corner, as far away from everyone else as possible. No one says anything to me, although when Shinji walks in, he does that thing where he just tuts and rolls his eyes, like, *Insulting you really isn't worth my time, sorry,* which makes me feel super-great.

Lindsay and I have come up with three rules for me to follow. Rule One is, if I'm having a bad day, I go straight to Miss Madeley, the school nurse. Do not pass go, do not collect two hundred pounds. She's even given me her mobile number. I've known Miss Madeley since first year, when Stu wiped out playing football, and she came with us to the hospital. She's pretty nice.

Rule Two is, stick to the menu. Lindsay says it's important that I learn to manage my own eating—but for now, she wants to make sure I settle in smoothly. So she's literally written me a meal-by-meal menu, like she did for Christmas last year. (I've really moved on in the past ten months, hey?) Only this time, there's way more food for me to eat, and a strict schedule to stick to: *11 a.m.—one Go Ahead! Yoghurt Break; one banana. 1 p.m.—one ham sandwich (two slices of bread, one slice of ham, spread); one Mars bar (or equivalent chocolate bar); one apple.* It's a scary amount of food. But on the other hand, it's kind of nice not to have to think about it.

Because I'm an idiot, I've sat around the corner from the door, and Stu doesn't see me when he comes in. He's with a load of people from football. I guess they had practice this morning. He sits down with them at the front. I can feel my cheeks burning red-hot, as if I'd dropped my pants in front of the whole class. It's not like I've actually done anything embarrassing. Except for Shinji, no one's even noticed I'm there. But I feel like the biggest loser in the whole world. Like some desperate puppy, waiting for Stu to notice me.

I count to ten under my breath. This is Rule Three, count to ten. Lindsay says that if you can deal with something for ten seconds, nothing can touch you. Because once you get to the end of the ten seconds, you can always add another ten and another ten and so on. The whole of human history can be broken down into ten-second chunks. You're only ten seconds away from Darwin or the pharaohs or dinosaurs. I'm not that sure about Rule Three, mainly because it involves more counting, and obsessive counting hasn't exactly gone well for me recently. But I have to admit, once my ten seconds are up, I feel a bit less like jumping out of the window.

I still don't have the nerve to go up to Stu's group, though. At the end of attendance, I slink out hoping no one will notice me.

God, am I a loser or what?

Things don't get any better after registration. I look at my schedule, and realize my first double-period is PE. I've got all psyched up about finally facing everyone—but instead, I'll be spending the next hour and a half sitting quietly in Mrs. Braithwait's office.

This was actually my idea. I figured that, sooner or later, someone was going to find out about the whole running-during-PE thing. And if I just had to stand around while everyone else did PE . . . I mean, I may as well have the word FREAK tattooed on my forehead. I asked if I could go somewhere and do homework during PE lessons instead. I didn't know that that somewhere would be five feet away from the assistant principal.

I knock on Mrs. Braithwait's door at 9:01, and she says, "Enter," in this deep, booming voice, like the Wizard of Oz. Mrs. Braithwait is kind of old-school. She wears these bonkers tartan twin sets, and her hair looks like one giant Lego. It never moves. I'm not sure I've ever seen her smile, either. When you first meet her, she kind of seems like the schoolmistress in some Victorian novel. You can imagine her rapping orphans on their wrists with a ruler. I remember saying this when I came home from my first day at Deanwater. Robin told me I'd got her all wrong. *Okay, she doesn't smile much,* he said. *But she's always got your back. Trust me, Mrs. Braithwait is the coolest.* I never asked him what she did to get in his good books.

"Max," she says when I open the door. Not *Hi, Max* or *Oh, look, it's Max.* Just *Max,* a simple statement of fact. If a tiger had walked in, I'm pretty sure she would have just said, *Tiger.*

"Hello, miss," I say.

"You have something to be getting on with?"

"Er, I have a book, miss."

"Very well then."

And that's it. I sit down with my book—*The Life of a Cuckoo,* naturally—and read in silence for ninety minutes. To be honest, it feels a lot like being in the hospital.

~

I nearly chose the other option. The nuclear option. The red pill. Honestly, I was *this close.* When Lindsay first suggested it, it seemed like the perfect solution. I'd go into treatment and have people help me get better full-time. And Mum and Dad would have a break. Perfect, right? But after I'd finished talking to Lindsay and the other doctors, I began to wonder what exactly happens there.

Do you get to read the books you want to read?

Do you get to go outside if you want to?

Can I take my computer and a pair of binoculars?

I googled it.

Bad idea.

I don't know what being anorexic was like before they invented the Internet. I've only ever tried it *with* the Internet. I guess the upside is, you can find people to talk to if you want to. At least, you know other people are going through the same thing.

The trouble is, you don't really want to talk about it.

Also, the people you read about are never *actually* going through the same thing. Usually, they went through it years ago and have now decided they want to *tell their story*, and *help others with their suffering.* I know they're trying to help, but I end up hating them. *You're better. I'm not. Stop rubbing it in my face.*

Or you read horror stories. Forums full of anorexics whose main goal seems to be to egg on one another.

What's the best laxative to use? How can I get it without a credit card? Can I use it every day?

They're always girls, with names like Paige and Grace and Lyra. (Come to think of it, I'm pretty sure one of them was called Ana, but maybe that was a joke.) I kind of don't believe most of the things they say. But either way, I don't have anything in common with them. Everything they say makes me want to scream, *That's not what anorexia feels like. That's not how it is.*

The first thing I found when I started googling residential treatment was this blog by some girl called Jenna in Ohio, USA. There were thirteen entries, dating back almost three years. I scrolled halfway down the page and started reading.

June 16—Group Sessions :(

We have two group sessions every day, at 11 a.m. and 3 p.m., and they are the WORST THING EVER!! We all sit in a circle and listen to one another as we talk about how treatment's going, or at least that's what we're SUPPOSED to talk about. All people do is complain about the food and talk about how much they miss their boyfriends. I never know what to say. Becca makes stuff up. Yesterday, she told us that her boyfriend broke up with her—which definitely isn't true—and we all spent like 20 minutes trying to cheer her up. She's such a bitch.

I'm pretty mad because I got my first 4 in my Achievement Plan this week. 4 = Unsatisfactory. I got it because one of the assistants saw me giving pills to Becca. I tried to explain they were just Tylenol, but she wouldn't listen. You get worse punishments for doing stuff to other people than doing it to yourself because you're "enabling their disease"—which is such bullshit because it was Becca who gave me the pills in the first place!!

In five minutes, Jenna's blog put me off residential treatment. I read this thing in the newspaper about how once you go to prison you're screwed because you're surrounded by criminals all the time. Residential treatment sounds a lot like that.

Maybe it depends where you end up, but I'm worried the only thing I'd learn is how to be more anorexic.

And I really, really don't need any help with that.

~

"Max!"

I spin around. I'm kind of disorientated because I've stepped out of Mrs. Braithwait's Silent Victorian Time Warp, and it takes me a moment to get used to things like sound and color again. Stu sidles up to me with this huge grin on his face. "Nice of you to join us."

"Um, hey," I mumble.

"Hey."

I don't really know what to say next. I honestly, genuinely almost talk to him about the weather, like I'm Bill from the hospital, the eighty-five-year-old man with a garden plot. *It's been rather mild lately, hasn't it? Good for my petunias!* But at the last moment I spot his kit bag. "You have football this morning?"

"It is my burden," he says. Stu's kind of like Robin, in that he *thinks* he's funny. The difference is, he's right slightly more often. We carry on walking in the direction of the playground. "Hey, have you listened to the new Parawax album yet? It's pretty sweet."

And just like that, we're off. We're having a Normal Teenage Conversation. It may not seem like much, but over the summer, I kind of convinced myself that I'd never have another conversation like this again.

"Nope," I reply. I hate Parawax.

"Wanna listen?"

"Sure."

We spend break listening to music on Stu's tinny headphones (apparently, he's softened his policy on personal technology). When Ram joins us, he does exactly the same thing, i.e., totally ignores two pretty major facts: 1) I missed the first week of school for some reason; and 2) I look like Jack Skellington. I eat my banana and my Go Ahead! bar at 11:00 a.m., in accordance with Rule Two. I notice Ram doesn't ask me for either, which is weird. Has he finally clocked that I'm ill? Has he realized that I need all the food I can get? I get my answer when he whips out a slice of takeaway pizza and a Peperami. No, Ram has not come to a new understanding about the nature of anorexia nervosa. He's just been at his dad's and doesn't need me.

There's no sign of you-know-who. I want to ask

about her, but I don't know how. Maybe they've cut her out because she was too much of a weirdo. Or maybe *she's* cut *me* out.

Stu keeps changing the track. He plays thirty seconds of one song, and then goes, *Oh, wait, you've got to listen to this,* and starts another one. I have one earbud, and Ram has the other—because, when he does use technology in public, Stu's pretty great about sharing—so it's not like he can even hear it. But he still sings along in perfect sync.

When the bell goes, he asks me: "So, what do you think?"

"It's shit, Stu," I reply. I grin at him. "Sorry. See you at lunch?"

He looks pretty miffed, but nods.

"Cool," says Ram. "Max, we're in physics together for fourth period. Catch you later."

"Okay," I say. I lift my rucksack onto my shoulder and head off toward the languages building, thinking, *That was the best fifteen minutes I've had in months.*

~

Third period is German. Our school is a specialist language college, which means we take languages super-seriously. One of the rules is, for GCSE and A-level, the whole class is conducted in whatever the language is: French, Spanish, or German. You're literally not allowed to say a word of English. If your liver bursts and you can't explain what's happened in German, you've got to wait for the bell before anyone will call you an ambulance.

Okay, that probably isn't true. But you get the picture.

Anyway, when I walk into my new German class for the first time, I forget about this rule. I go to the front of the class and ask, "Miss, where do I sit?" There are like three empty seats, and one of them is mine. But I don't know which.

It doesn't go well.

"Ah, Max. Schön dich zu sehen," Mrs. Müller replies. Mrs. Müller isn't actually German. Her husband is. So she's ended up with a British cliché of a German name, the first one you'd come up with if you were trying to name a German person. Kind of funny for a German teacher.

"Uh," I say. "Danke?"

"Bitte fragen sie mich auf Deutsch, Max."

"Um . . ."

Everyone else has already sat down. They're watching this whole thing. So Mrs. Müller does that thing teachers do sometimes, when they decide your stupid question is a Teaching Opportunity, and bring the entire class into your conversation. Even if you really, really don't want that to happen.

Mrs. Müller turns to the class, and says, "Kann jemand helfen?"

I can guess that much. *Max is a charity case. For God's sake, someone please help him.*

And guess whose hand shoots into the air?

Yep.

"Wo sitze . . . mich?"

"'Wo sitze *ich*, Evie. Aber sehr gut. Max, bitte hinsetzen," says Mrs. Müller, pointing to the empty chair right next to Evie.

I shuffle down the classroom, trying not to notice that Evie's laughing at me. That everyone's laughing at me. In my head, I'm reciting a new personal motto: *I want to die I want to die I want to die.*

I start counting to ten. I feel like today, I'm going to need Rule Three a lot.

Once I've sat down, I risk a sideways glance.

Evie grins. But I can't tell whether she's grinning *at* me or *with* me.

I jam my hand in my pocket and trace the corners of the plastic bag with my fingers, to check it's still there. I don't know where I was imagining it would've gone in the past thirty seconds exactly. Or the thirty seconds before that. But apparently, I need to keep checking that the note is there.

I've still not opened it. I can't really explain why. Maybe it's because it's from before everything happened, and I'm scared that if I read it, it could suck me back into the past.

Or maybe it's because I don't want to know what it says.

I know that sounds stupid. But think about it. Right now, inside that plastic bag, there could be a check for a million pounds.

Or a magical incantation that you say three times, under a full moon, to cure anorexia.

Or a message from Evie, confessing her undying love.

As long as I don't know, it can be whatever I want it to be. Which means there's *hope*.

Like before I knew Mum and Dad were separating.

Like the moment before you step on the scales.

In my pocket, I have a little bit of hope. And I kind of need it right now.

"Psst."

I look across at Evie, and mouth, *What?*

She shrugs.

Great, thanks, Evie, I think. *That clears everything up. Thanks for telling me exactly how you feel about me in such a clear and unambiguous way.*

"Psst."

I roll my eyes this time. I'm trying to do a worksheet I definitely don't understand, on how you conjugate irregular verbs. In German, there's a rule for irregular verbs, which makes zero sense. Germans are weird.

What? I mouth again.

This time, Evie holds up her notebook. There's a message written on it. I have to peer at it, because her handwriting is so loopy. I lean forward, so Evie gets a really close-up view of my face as it turns scarlet.

Can I have lunch with you?

28

I have the same physics teacher as last year. Dr. Magnussen. He's pretty much the worst teacher in the world. He always sets us tons of homework—like, crazy amounts. Amounts we can't possibly do without handing in other homework late. Maybe he's different when he's teaching GCSE, but I kind of doubt it.

The first thing he says to me is, "Ah, you decided to come in this week, Mr. Howarth."

Gee, thanks, Dr. Magnussen. Thank you for drawing everyone's attention to the fact that I wasn't here last week. Naturally, I don't say anything, because I know it won't end well for me. I stroll over to the bench Ram's sitting at—he's waving at me like an air traffic controller—and count to ten twice on my way.

"What an ass," Ram whispered to me as I sit down, cocking his head in Dr. Magnussen's direction.

I laugh. "Totally."

We didn't really talk about it at break, so I ask Ram how his holidays were. Now that I'm also from a Broken Home, I'm kind of interested in how it works.

Ram shakes his head. "With Mum it was the usual stuff. We went to the beach or the hotel pool every day."

"*Every day?*" I say. I'm used to going on holidays where we look at three museums before breakfast. Garda was the most chilled-out holiday I've ever been on. Well, the first part was, anyway.

"Yup. And, uh, you know all about Portugal . . ." He trails off. I'm about to reply—*Um, do I?*—but before I can, he says, "Hey."

"Huh?" I say, and then immediately realize he wasn't talking to me. I wince.

"Hey," Evie says, sitting down on the other side of me. "How's tricks?"

"Not too bad, Evie, not too bad," Ram says. He slaps me on the back. "Glad to have this idiot back."

"Yeah," Evie replies. "I just hope he's kept up with his physics better than his German."

Wait. What?

While Evie and Ram are joking around, I'm sitting there with my mouth half open, like a goldfish watching porn. Because I have questions. For instance, are Evie and Ram best mates now? Has she been writing him notes like she's been writing me notes? What about Stu and Darren and Dr. Magnussen?

And was my German really *that* bad?

"Right, everybody," says Dr. Magnussen. "If you'd like to finish off your conversations . . . *thank you*."

Dr. Magnussen has this high, squeaky voice, like a chipmunk who's been sucking on a balloon. He kind of looks like a chipmunk, too. He has a beard but almost no hair on his head, which makes his face look really round. And when he's explaining things, he holds his hands up like paws. Seriously.

"Now, can anyone give us a quick recap on Newton's First Law of Motion, for the benefit of those that weren't here last Thursday?" He looks right at me as he says it. I'm wondering if he knows I wasn't here because *I was in a bloody hospital.*

No one answers. You could honestly hear a ball of cotton wool fall to the floor. Dr. Magnussen pinches the bridge of his nose.

"Anyone? You may remember I like to call it 'the lazy law'."

Nothing. Nada. Zilch.

"Very well, I'll pick on someone." He looks around, like a meerkat on watch duty, until he locks in on our bench. "Ram," he says. "Any idea?"

"No, sir," says Ram immediately, in a kind of sing-song voice. You can tell he hasn't really considered the question: it's just his default response. Like in a TV show, when a police officer asks a member of a gang question after question, and they just say *No comment* every time.

But Dr. Magnussen isn't easily put off.

"Come on, Mr. Ahmed. The lazy law: The clue's in the name. What happens to an object when no forces are acting on it?"

Ram puts his elbows on the desk and leans his head on his palms. "Nothing?"

Dr. Magnussen sighs. "I was hoping for a little more detail, but I guess that's basically right. Newton's First Law of Motion—everyone, listen up, please—Newton's First Law states that, unless an object is acted on by an *unbalanced force*, it will remain stationary, or continue moving at the same speed and in the same direction if it's already in motion. Is that clear?"

Everyone murmurs a yes. It's the least-enthusiastic yes I've ever heard. It's the kind of yes you'd get if you were on a spaceship that only had twenty minutes' oxygen left, and you started asking people whether they'd made their beds that morning.

"Very well then," Dr. Magnussen says. "Please turn to page thirty-six in your textbooks."

I risk a glance up at Evie. She's staring straight at me.

I start scribbling a note in the back of my exercise book. I can't tell if it's a good idea or not, so I do it quickly, before I change my mind.

Has your dad dumped Katya yet?

I push the book toward Evie. She leans over and reads it, and looks at me, then pushes it back, and stares down at her desk.

I guess that's a no.

No prizes for guessing what Dr. Magnussen moves on to after Newton's First Law. "The Second Law deals with unbalanced forces. If an unbalanced force acts upon an object, that object will *accelerate*. And we can say three things about that acceleration . . ."

He rabbits on like this for ages. I look down at my textbook and realize he's just reading it out—but the way he says it, you'd think he came up with Newton's Second Law himself.

"He *really* loves the sounds of his own voice," Ram says under his breath, and I have to concentrate pretty hard on stopping myself from bursting out laughing.

Once we've read the theory, Dr. Magnussen demos it with a tennis ball and a cricket ball. He hits them both along the front bench with a pool cue, so we see how the tennis ball moves faster.

Ram leans over to me and whispers, "Then how come heavy stuff *falls* faster?"

I know this one because I read a book about Galileo once. "It doesn't. If you drop those two balls from the top of a skyscraper, they fall at the same speed."

"Bullshit," says Ram.

That's what Galileo taught us, I think. But then I confuse myself. If acceleration is inversely proportional to mass, shouldn't the cricket ball drop more slowly? I whisper to Ram, "Wait, I'm not sure I've got it right."

"Max," booms Dr. Magnussen. I jump slightly.

"Sorry, sir, we were just—"

"Talking in the middle of my demonstration. I

know. Given that you're already behind everyone else, perhaps you'd like to pay attention?"

I count to ten.

Once Dr. Magnussen's stopped eyeballing us, Ram nudges me in the ribs. "What's up with Evie?"

She's still staring at the desk.

So I write another note.

You okay? Don't worry. Your dad's an idiot. He'll snap out of it soon!

She glances at what I've written, then looks up at me.

"Why are you doing this?" she says out loud.

I put a finger to my mouth because I know Dr. Magnussen is looking for any excuse to bite my head off.

What do you mean? I mouth to Evie.

"Leave me alone."

"MR. HOWARTH," Dr. Magnussen shouts. "Perhaps I didn't make myself clear before?"

Ram pipes up. "We were talking about Newton's Second Law, sir," he stammers.

"I see," Dr. Magnussen says. "You're getting Max up to speed, are you?"

I give Ram this just-drop-it look, but he either

doesn't get it or ignores me. "Actually, he was helping me. He told me about Galileo."

"Did he indeed? And Mr. Howarth knows a lot about Galileo, does he?"

Ram glances at me. His expression says, *I have no idea what I'm getting you into.* "I guess," he says. Then he adds, "He went to Italy this summer."

I'm thinking, *Now would be a good time for the ground to open up under Lab 2B.*

"Oh, well then, I'm *sure* he's an expert. Max, perhaps you'd like to come up and demonstrate for us."

"No thank you, sir," I say quickly.

"But I insist. Class, we have a special treat today. Our resident expert in classical mechanics is going to demonstrate Newton's Second Law."

The trouble with Rule Three is, you have to remember to count. And right now, I'm barely even remembering to breathe.

"Sir, I—"

"Come on, Max, up you get. We haven't got all day."

I have to use my arms to get up from the stool, because apparently my legs have decided to stop working. I start talking, "Well, as it says in the, uh—"

"At the front of the class, please," Dr. Magnussen says.

I stumble forward.

I can feel the blood draining out of my head. You know when you're in a swimming pool, fully underwater, and you stand up quickly, and all the water pours off of you? That's kind of how it feels. My vision starts to go cloudy.

"Sir, I don't feel well."

He laughs. He actually laughs out loud at me. And it's like in a gang film: When the boss laughs, everyone else knows it's time to laugh, too. The whole class is laughing at me.

I look back to my bench. Ram isn't laughing, at least. But Evie is.

I want to die I want to die I want to die.

"Max, we're all waiting. Get on with it." The way he says the last line sounds really menacing. There's this edge in his voice, like, *Or else.*

I lean against the front bench, because if I don't, I think I'm going to collapse.

"I don't know, sir."

"You don't know what?"

"I don't know anything."

I want to cry.

I want to die.

I want to kill him.

I want to kill Evie.

I want to set fire to the whole laboratory.

"But you think you can chat all the way through my class anyway?"

"No, sir."

"You think you can turn up a week late—"

And then I find out what happens when you forget to count to ten.

"SHUT UP, YOU BASTARD! SHUT UP SHUT UP SHUT UP!"

He doesn't flinch. This little smile spreads across his face, like, *Thanks for giving me what I wanted.* "Mrs. Richards's office," he says quietly. "Now."

I'm shaking. I take three big gulps of air, then walk to my bench, and scoop up my rucksack and books, avoiding Ram's eye. Avoiding everyone's eye. I want to leave the room calmly. I want to act like it's all over. Water off a duck's back.

But when I get to the door, I glance backward and see Evie. And I can't stop myself from slamming the door behind me.

~

Shit. Shit. SHIT.

I start counting. *One, two, three, four* . . . Then I stop myself, because what's the point of counting now? It's too late. It's like shutting the stable door after the horse has bolted, as Dad would say.

This was supposed to be the start of my new, healthy life. This was supposed to be the first step toward getting better.

And it lasted *three hours.*

SHIT.

I know I should go straight to Mrs. Richards's office, so I can explain what happened before she hears it from Dr. Magnussen, or from someone else. It doesn't exactly look good to wander off when you've been sent to the principal. *Not only did he shout and swear at me, he went for a leisurely stroll around the school when he was supposed to be on his way to your office.* But I don't have a choice. I need time to think.

Maybe the fact that I've been a straight-A student since I came to the school will count in my favor. Or maybe they'll think, *Wow, he* really *must be losing it.*

I walk away from the science corridor into the art department. It's quieter here. Art is at one end of the main school building, so there isn't any through traffic. There's a big square corridor that runs around a little courtyard. We've had art lessons out there before, in the spring, painting the tulips that are planted in beds on three sides. You're not really supposed to go into the courtyard the rest of the time. But hey, it's not like things can get any worse for me.

I push through the big glass door.

I can't stop picturing Evie. I only saw her for a second, but it's seared into my brain. She was laughing so much, her shoulders were shaking. Forty minutes ago, she asked me to lunch, and I pretty much started planning our future together. Now I wish she were dead.

I wish I were dead.

Then I remember the note.

I move my hand to my pocket, slowly, gingerly, like I'm not sure it's going to be there. But obviously it is. I pull it out of my pocket.

As soon as I see it, I know what I've got to do.

I jump up and race out of the courtyard, across

the corridor, through the double doors that lead to the recycling area. I pull the note out its plastic bag, because even in a crisis, you've got to separate your recycling. Dad's brought me up well. I lift the lid on the paper-only dumpster, and start counting to ten.

One, two, three...

But then I stop myself.

I can't help it.

I open the note and start reading.

~

"Lovely spot you've found here, mate." Ram sniffs, as if he were a hunter walking through a bluebell wood in spring. A long, theatrical sniff. "You really get that fresh dumpster-juice smell."

"Leave me alone," I tell him.

"I hope you're not about to throw that away," he says.

"Why do you even care?"

He pauses, like he's really thinking about it. "One, because I'm your mate. And, two, because I used some of Mum's best stationery to write that, which was a big risk to my personal well-being, let me tell you."

"Stop messing with me. I'm really not in the mood."

I still can't bring myself to look at him.

"I'm not messing with you."

"Yes, you are. I've had a bunch of these. They're all about Evie's broken family and her deadbeat dad and . . ."

And then it hits me.

It hits me like a freight train.

It hits me like the meteorite that snuffed out the dinosaurs.

Evie didn't write those notes.

It wasn't Evie whose dad promised her a super-cool holiday, all on their own, and then decided to bring his new girlfriend along with him. When Evie asked me to lunch, I could barely read her handwriting. Because I'd never seen it before.

I look up at him. "I thought the *E* was for Evie," I say.

Ram laughs. "Ehtiram Ahmed," he says, holding out his hand. "Pleased to meet you. Not sure if you remember me, but I've been your best friend for, um, like, ten years?"

"Shit," I say.

"I also go by Stallone05, if you hadn't guessed. I

thought you'd get the *Rambo* reference." He sniffs and pulls a face. "Okay, we *have* to move away from these bins. Follow me."

So I do. We head away from school, around the playing fields.

"If I'd known it was you . . . ," I start to say. Then I peter out. What *would* I have done if I'd known it was him?

Ram raises a hand. "If you'd known it was me, you wouldn't have said anything. And I would've freaked if you'd try to talk to me about it anyway. But I thought with the notes . . . I wanted you to know someone had your back, y'know? And I guess I wanted to know someone had my back, too."

Shit.

I don't know how to respond. This whole time, I was only thinking about myself.

Ram waves a hand, like, *Forget it.* "It was pretty cool watching you tear into Dr. Magnussen, you know."

"I'm going to get hell for it."

"Probably," Ram says. "But he was being a jerk. I'll back you up, and so will Evie."

"Yeah, right," I say. "She thought it was hilarious."

Ram shakes his head. "No, she didn't."

"You don't have to pretend, Ram. I saw her. She was laughing her head off." He's trying to cheer me up. He probably thinks I'm going to lose it again. "I don't even care."

Ram punches me on the arm. If it were Robin, I definitely would have dodged it. But I wasn't expecting this one.

"Ow."

"Listen to me. She wasn't laughing . . . wait, what did you say to her?"

"What?"

"You wrote her a message, right? In class. In your exercise book. I saw you. What did you say?"

"Oh, nothing." He raises his arm again, fist clenched. "Okay, okay, it was something about . . ." I trail off, because he's giving me this pained look, like, *Don't make me punch you again.* "Something about her dad. What's up?"

He doesn't punch me. Instead, he slaps himself on the forehead. "You mean *my* dad. No wonder she is so upset."

"She wasn't . . ." But then my brain catches up. Head bent over, shoulders shaking. She wasn't laughing.

She was crying.

"Shit," I say.

We sit down on the far side of the rugby fields, behind a little hill. You can tell it's a good hiding place because of all the cigarette butts. It's quiet—the hill blocks out most of the noise from the fields.

"Okay, there's something I've got to tell you. Remember after that terrible biology exam when Evie was talking about her parents?"

"Kind of."

"Remember anything weird?"

My brain churns for a while. "She calls her parents by their names."

"Right. Ben and Jacob. You know why?"

I shake my head.

"Evie's in a foster home. Her mum . . ." He scratches his neck uncomfortably. "Look, I probably shouldn't be the one to tell you this, but . . . Evie's mum walked out on her. Years ago. And then her dad, um . . ."

I think back to that day at the zoo, when I asked her why she took so many photos. *You don't know what's important until later*: That was her explanation.

"Her dad's dead," I say quietly.

Ram nods.

We sit there for ages. I try to count the cigarette butts on the grass, but I keep losing track. I punch the ground instead. "I can't believe how much I've screwed things up in one morning."

"It's kind of impressive," Ram admits. "Now, haven't you got somewhere to be?"

"Mrs. Richards is going to skin me alive."

"Probably. But at least you won't die alone."

I cock an eyebrow.

"After you left, um . . . Evie kind of lost it with Dr. Magnussen, too."

"You're kidding," I say.

Ram shows me his palm. "Scout's honor. You can ask her yourself in a sec. Hey, I guess you didn't read the second half of that yet." He's pointing to the note in my hand.

"Not yet," I admit.

He grins. "If you had, you probably would've figured it out."

"What do you mean?"

He pulls a face.

I hold his gaze for a minute. I've been trying to push Ram out of my life all year, because I thought he'd never understand. I mean, I've been doing that with everyone. But Ram and Stu probably got the worst of it. One minute, they had a proper friend who wanted to hang out with them and play video games and share food. And then, they had a ghost. Someone who was there, but not really there. Someone who was desperate for their attention and equally desperate to be ignored.

I turn the note over. Ram's actually laughing now.

I read it slowly, a grin spreading across my face. Then I take off my rucksack, open it, and pull out my lunchbox.

"Max, you don't have to," Ram says.

"It's cool," I say. "Really."

I've always followed the rules, since as early as I can remember. I've never been grounded or had detention. I've never stolen anything. But today, following the rules hasn't exactly worked out for me. I broke Rule One earlier, when I bit off Dr. Magnussen's head instead of going to see Miss Madeley. In fact, I'm kind of breaking Rule One right now, just by being here. And I've already broken Rule Three about fifty times. It was a dumb rule anyway, in my opinion, asking someone with anorexia to do even more counting.

Well, now I'm going to make it a hat trick.

I give Ram a serious look. "Are we doing this, or what? I assume you've got the usual?"

Ram grins, then nods. He slides his backpack off his shoulders, opens the zip, and pulls out his lunchbox, too.

I crack mine open and pull out the little foil package. "Two ham sandwiches," I say.

"Two cheese sandwiches," Ram replies, offering me his little parcel in return. He nods. "Pleasure doing business with you."

I nod back. "I guess I better go get my head bitten off."

"I *think* you mean, you better go on your hot date with Evie."

I laugh. "See you when I get out?"

"I'm guessing you'll know where to find us."

I put my lunchbox away, lift the bag onto my shoulder. "See you in a bit," I say.

"Wait a second," says Ram. He goes into his backpack again, and pulls out a Kit Kat.

"I think I have a Snickers?" I say nervously. To be honest, I don't really want to trade chocolate bars with him, too. Not because I'm going to freak out, or hopefully not. Just because, well, Snickers are way better than Kit Kats.

"Good for you," he says. "But this isn't a trade. This is a gift of love."

"Um, okay."

"It's a well-known fact, Max, that Kit Kats are the most romantic food in the world."

"O-kay," I say. I'm trying to decide if he's actually lost it.

"Split it with Evie," he says. "She loves Kit Kats."

For a moment, I wonder how he knows this. Then I remember how much attention he always pays to what everyone else is having for lunch. Ram could probably tell me the favorite chocolate bar of everyone in Deanwater High.

I take the Kit Kat from him. "Thanks, man."

"Don't mention it. And don't get used to it, either. I never give away food."

"I know. Tomorrow will be different, right?"

He snorts. "Exactly."

29

Robin insisted on making the spaghetti this year. That's right, Robin. *Robin.* The man who has been known to eat Pot Noodles dry because he can't be bothered boiling the kettle, and who once tried roasting a chicken in its plastic shrink-wrap. He's now been in the kitchen, alone, for two hours. We're all kind of nervous.

I don't know why, but spaghetti Bolognese is our traditional Christmas Eve dish. Every year, we eat spaghetti, go and listen to the sleigh bells, and then go to bed.

The only difference this year is, we're probably going to go to bed with food poisoning.

Mum gets up, for the fourth time, to ask Robin if he needs any help.

"I'm *fine,*" he tells her, and shoos her away from the

kitchen. He's said the same thing every time—but this time, the *I'm fine* had a definite edge. Less *I'm actually managing remarkably well thank you*, more *For God's sake, please don't come in here.*

This morning, I had my session with Lindsay, my first in a month. I've put on another two pounds, which means my BMI is now officially in the Normal range again. Lindsay's always pretty careful about how she reacts. She knows that, whatever my weight, I'm usually upset about it. Gained weight? The sky is about to fall in. Lost weight? I'm going to die. Stayed the same? What a waste of time. I feel sorry for her; she really can't win.

But today wasn't like that. Today, she could see how happy I was.

Okay, so I'm *right* at the bottom of Normal. It's a pretty big range. But it still feels good. According to my official NHS chart, my weight is now no longer a big, immediate risk to my health.

"How do you feel?" Lindsay asked me.

She's asked me that in every session we've had. And my go-to answer has always been: fine. I feel fine.

But I'm getting better at being honest. "Scared," I told her. "Scared to death."

And you know what I *don't* feel?

I don't feel fat.

I really thought I would. I told myself, *If you don't want to die, you're going to have to get used to feeling fat.*

I mean, maybe I will at some point. But so far, so good.

I texted Evie right after my session. Just the number: my new BMI. She replied in about eight seconds.

Cuckoo: You're kidding.

Me: Nope.

Cuckoo: OMG!

Me: Yep.

Cuckoo: THAT'S AMAZING. YOU'RE FRICKIN AMAZING, PACKHAM.

Cuckoo: P.S. Elephant juice! :D

Before you ask, yes, Evie's in my phone as Cuckoo, which definitely sounds like some lame pet name. But the thing is, she really *is* a cuckoo. Her mum abandoned her. She's kind of a loudmouth. She came out of nowhere in spring and makes a *lot* of noise. Okay, she hasn't killed all her foster-siblings yet. But I'm pretty sure it's only a matter a time.

I texted Stu and Ram, too. Stu still hasn't replied, probably because of the whole no-phones-in-the-house rule. Also, he told us he was going to be on a *major Star Trek marathon* on Christmas Eve. But Ram replied straightaway, too: Good. Does that mean I can start stealing your food again?

~

Robin comes into the lounge. He's wearing a white apron, and it honestly looks as though he'd slaughtered a cow in it. It's like a scene from a horror movie.

"Dinner is served," he says.

"Whether we're ready for it or not," Dad replies.

Robin raises the dish towel he has in his hand threateningly. "Watch it, Pops," he says.

Dad's been around more lately. He came for tea twice this week. He even stays over sometimes. (Tonight, Dad and Robin are going to arm wrestle to see who gets my old room. The loser has to sleep on the sofa downstairs.) Don't get me wrong: Mum and Dad are definitely still off. But, to be honest, they seem happier around each other now than they have for years.

We go through and sit at the table. Robin's already laid out our plates and cutlery. I asked him if we could serve ourselves. I still find eating a portion that someone else has dished out kind of tricky.

Robin brings over a big pan of Bolognese while Mum pours us all wine. Even me. *I drink wine now.*

"Wow," I say, when Robin puts the pan down on the table. "That smells . . . *good.*"

"*Really* good," says Dad.

"You don't have to sound quite so surprised," Robin grumbles.

"It looks lovely, Robin," says Mum. "Thank you."

And it is. Spag bol isn't something I've eaten a lot of lately: difficult-to-measure portions plus loads of different ingredients plus a ton of carbs equals an anorexic's worst nightmare. Okay, maybe I'm not the best judge. But the sauce is nice and meaty. The pasta's got that little bit of bite it should have. He's even made his own garlic bread, by cutting up some baguette and rubbing garlic and herbs on it, then grilling it.

It's really, really good.

I raise an eyebrow at my brother. "Turns out you can cook, Robin. Who knew?"

"Thanks, little bro," Robin says. He gives me this

weird look, then reaches for his wineglass. "Now, I'd like to propose a toast."

"To Santa Claus!" says Mum.

"To the Ghost of Christmas Past!" says Dad.

Robin looks at me and shakes his head. "Honestly, with these two around, it's a miracle we both turned out so well."

Mum sniggers.

"No, Mother and Father," Robin continues, giving them both a disappointed look. "I think Santa gets enough praise for doing one evening's work a year, frankly. I'd like to propose a toast to the bravest person I've ever met."

I'm expecting Dad to chip in again, and say something like, *Oh, you mean Rudolph.* But he doesn't. He's beaming at me. And then I realize they all are: Mum, Dad, and Robin are all grinning at me like Cheshire Cats.

"Wait, what's going on?" I say.

Robin raises his glass, and Mum and Dad do the same. "You kicked this year's ass, little bro."

~

"Right, who wants to see if they can hear the sleigh bells?"

I look up at Mum. She's wearing a Santa hat, and a sweater that says I WISH IT COULD BE CHRISTMAS EVERY DAY across it in huge letters, and a smile as wide as Siberia. I realize the last time I saw her this happy was last Christmas, before everything got really bad.

"Nope," says Robin cheerily, without looking up from the *Radio Times* he's been reading for twenty minutes.

"Come on, Robin," says Mum. "It's almost midnight." She disappears into the hallway.

"Why do we do this, exactly?" Robin says, to no one in particular.

Dad comes up behind him and grabs the magazine, whips it away in one smooth movement. "Tradition," he says.

"That's not a reason."

"How about *Because your mum and dad asked you to* then?"

Robin shrugs.

"Cheeky sod," mutters Dad. He looks across at me.

I'm already putting my coat on. Another year, I might side with my brother. But not this year. "Why can't your brother be more like you, eh?"

It hits me like a sledgehammer. I know it's a joke, but it's not a joke Dad could have made at any other point this year. The idea of being more like me being a *good* thing would've seemed too ridiculous.

"Beats me," I say.

Robin gives me this *how-could-you* look.

Mum comes back into the room with Santa hats for the rest of us. And a huge plate of mince pies.

I hate wearing hats: My hair is so fine, I end up looking like I've been electrocuted when I wear one. But it's Christmas, right?

"Thanks, Mum," I say.

I pull the hat on, eventually; it's so tight I'm pretty sure it's cutting off the blood supply to my brain or something.

"Mince pie?"

She offers me the tray. And I'm about to take one— really—when Dad's phone beeps.

"It's midnight!" Mum squeals. She puts the tray down on the coffee table. "Come on!" she says, frantic. She unlocks the patio door, grabs Dad's hand, and marches out into the cold.

"She's insane," Robin mutters.

"Sultan!" I shout. I beeline toward the coffee table, but it's too late. Our dog may not walk so fast anymore, but he still eats at a thousand mph. He's already on his second mince pie by the time I get there—and naturally, he's managed to slobber all over the rest.

"Whoops," Robin says.

"Mum's gonna be pissed," I say, hoisting the plate away from Sultan. Unperturbed, he switches to hoovering up the crumbs. His tail thwacks the sofa over and over.

Robin shrugs. "She's already made three batches. It's like therapy or something for her. Personally, my cooking career is over."

I take the plate through to the kitchen and put it down on the side. I can't quite bring myself to throw it in the bin. I'm still not that great with food waste. Maybe we can throw away the mincemeat—I'm pretty sure dogs aren't supposed to eat mincemeat—and give Sultan the pastry.

I go back through to the lounge. Sultan's finished

clearing up; he's now slumped in front of the sofa, looking pretty content.

"We should go join them," I say. "They must be freezing their asses off."

Robin holds up a hand, like, *Wait*.

"What?" I ask.

He points at the tree. Specifically, at the presents under the tree.

"When we come back in, I'm going to show you which is yours. It's technically Christmas already, right?"

"Technically," I agree.

He puts an arm around my shoulder and guides me toward the door. "I think you're going to like this one, little bro."

December 24
Dear Ana,

Lindsay told me about her eating disorder the
first time I met her. She had been bulimic for
eight years. At the time she told me, I was fourteen. I remember doing the sums in my head.
Divide 14 by 8, times 100 = 57.1. Lindsay was bulimic
for the equivalent of 60 percent of my life.

It felt like forever.

She said something else, too. Something that
haunted me. "You learn to live a normal life
around your eating disorder." I'm probably not
remembering it exactly right, but it was along
those lines.

I thought she meant that I'd never recover.
I figured she was trying to stop me getting my
hopes up. "Max, sorry, but there's no miracle cure.
You'll always be this way. You just need to deal
with it." I could barely breathe after she said it.
Scratch the 60 percent: I was going to be ill for
the next 100 percent of my life.

I brought it up again this morning. And it turns
out I kind of got the wrong end of the stick.

"I'm cured. Of course I am," she said. "What I
meant was, having a normal life is part of what

fixes you. When you have an eating disorder, you withdraw from the world. And that makes everything worse."

It all sort of clicked when she said that.

Lindsay was ill for 60 percent of my life so far. But for the other 40 percent, she was okay. She was just Lindsay.

Funny how that number keeps coming up—60 percent. Mr. Edwards told us that humans are 60 percent water, and afterward, I was obsessed with the fact. In my head, human beings became these giant wet amoebas, rolling around the surface of the globe.

But I was forgetting the other 40 percent. The 40 percent of me that isn't water. The part that makes me, me.

It's just like that soup, the one in the story that isn't really made from a stone. There's no magic to it. A stone is just a stone. Water is just water. To make a human, you need carbohydrates and fats and proteins and vitamins. You need roast potatoes. You need Mars bars. You need prawn crackers and cheese sandwiches and Kit Kats. And where do they come from?

I always thought the moral of that story was that people are gullible. But this year—the year I didn't eat—it's changed my mind. The moral of the story is that, if you ask for help, people will help you. Not definitely. Not always. But most of the time.

And here's the important bit. The bit I got really, really wrong. Those people who are trying to help you? Those people who end up saving your life?

They don't need to understand everything.

No one will ever 100 percent understand you. They probably won't even 40 percent understand you. I know that's what teenagers say in TV shows, and maybe sometimes in real life, too. "You don't understand me!" Well, anorexics are kind of like ultra-teenagers, I guess. We're extra-super-double sure that no one understands us. Not even, like, Kurt Cobain. And you know what? I think we're right. As Robin puts it, being a teenager blows, and the older you get, the more you forget how much it blows.

But the thing is, it doesn't matter. Someone doesn't need to understand you to save your life. They just need to care.

It can be your biology teacher or your ex-bulimic psychologist. Your mum, your dad, your brother, or your dog. It can be a PE teacher you always thought hated you or a girl you want to talk to.

It can be a mysterious stranger who leaves you anonymous notes.

or it can be your best friend.

I'm not sure why I'm telling you this, Ana. we've already established you don't exist. Actually, that's a good point. I'm talking to myself again. I'm gonna text Ram instead. He's probably already opened his presents by now.

AUTHOR'S NOTE

"What does it feel like?"

That's the question I kept asking myself as I was writing this book. It's a question without a good answer, because an eating disorder feels like a million different things. Sometimes it's unbearable, and sometimes it's barely there. Sometimes, you never want to see anyone ever again; other times, you would do anything—absolutely anything—just to have someone to talk to. It's maddening. It's silly. It's boring.

It's complicated.

Max is fourteen when he becomes anorexic. Me, I was twelve. It's taken me almost two decades to organize my thoughts, to try to come up with a better answer to that question than "it really, really, really sucks." This book is that answer. It's not a perfect answer, but it's probably the best one I've ever given. I hope it will help some people who are going through it, and the people around them.

Of course, Max's story isn't anyone else's. It isn't

even mine. Every eating disorder is different, which means no one can fully understand what you're going through. Not even someone who's been through it.

But that doesn't mean they can't help.

This is the mistake I made. This is the mistake everyone who's ever had an eating disorder seems to make. We assume that we're beyond help. We assume that all the advice and support out there is for other people. We tell ourselves, *This doesn't apply to me. It's for someone thinner. It's for someone who hasn't been ill as long as me. It's for an outpatient. It's something that only affects girls and women, not boys and men.*

And that's all wrong. As Max puts it, "Someone doesn't need to understand you to save your life. They just need to care."

So if you're living with an eating disorder, know this: I don't 100 percent understand what you're going through. No one does. Even if you have an identical twin who also develops an eating disorder on the same day you do—they still can't see inside your head. But let's say, for instance, that I understand 10 percent. Even 5 percent. Let's say you read this book and one or two lines hit home. Let's say your mum gives you a hug when you really need a hug, or a teacher stops you after class to ask if you're okay. What you should take from that is this: There are people out there who really care about you, who want to help. They might not know exactly how to and they might not even know what it is they're trying to help with. But still, they want to be there for you. And if you can find a way to let them, things will get a whole lot better.

One time back when I was ill, my doctor said the strangest thing to me. She said, "Once you've recovered, you won't think about food any more than the average person." It sounded crazy. I could just about get my head around the idea of recovery, but I assumed it would be like turning a stereo down low. The music would still be playing, and I'd always have to worry about it to some degree.

For some people, it *is* like that. But for every one of them, there's someone else who recovers completely. Someone whose biggest food worries, once they've switched the music off, are whether the milk in the fridge has gone bad, and what time the pizza place on the corner closes.

An eating disorder is not an intrinsic part of who you are. It's just something you live with for a while—a year, a decade, or even longer. At some point, with the right combination of love, luck, and support, you can turn the music off. You can go back to being you.

It may sound crazy, but it's true.

ACKNOWLEDGMENTS

Like an eating disorder, writing a book is something you feel like you're navigating on your own. Then you look back and see just how many people helped you through it. Family, friends, health care professionals, editors—and also strangers. Shop assistants. People on the bus. Those who happen to throw a few kind words your way at just the right time, giving you a little bit of strength, a little boost, exactly when you needed it.

I won't be able to thank all of these people, unfortunately. But here are a few who really, really deserve a mention.

Thank you to my agent, Alice Sutherland-Hawes, and everyone else at Madeleine Milburn Literary Agency, for believing in this book first, and most fiercely. Thank you to Sonali Fry, Dave Barrett, Gayley Avery, Nadia Almahdi, and Lauren Carr, and the whole team at Yellow Jacket, who took this strange and very British book and remade it for America while still keeping it strange and fairly

British. (Sonali: I'm delighted to be the person who taught you what an Arctic roll is!)

Thank you to Sophie Beer and Rob Wall, for a cover that features no apples, no rib cages, no measuring tape, and makes this book feel every bit as optimistic and powerful as I wanted it to.

Thank you to the various irritatingly talented writers who helped me pull this book into shape. To Frances Merivale, Jayne Watson, Daniel Culpan, Jon Teckman, Sara Sarre, and Eleanor Maxfield, for your early comments; to Savannah Brown and Mariah Huehner, for your massively helpful sensitivity reads; to my colleagues, for your endless patience.

Thank you to the people who were there when I was where Max was. To Mr. Tatlock, who let me hang out in his office during PE, and the rest of the staff at Wilmslow High School. To everyone at the Macclesfield Eating Disorder Service—and, more generally, to the National Health Service—for saving my life without fuss or fee, as they have saved so many others.

Everyone who works in mental health care, in whatever capacity, is a saint. To everyone who is there for someone with an eating disorder, who reaches out a hand that they know full well will probably be bitten—from the bottom of my heart, thank you.

Finally, thank you to my family. To Angie and Meurig, the best siblings I could hope for. To my wife, Liv, who did more to make this book happen than she'd ever be willing to admit. Most of all, thank you to my parents. You put up with everything I threw at you without complaint. I still can't get my head around that.

RESOURCES

National Association of Anorexia Nervosa and Associated Disorders
A nonprofit organization working in the areas of support, awareness, advocacy, referral, education, and prevention. Find support and group treatment, hear recovery stories, learn about grocery buddies, and request a recovery mentor.
www.anad.org/
www.anad.org/our-services/treatment-directory/
Helpline: 630-577-1330

The National Association for Males with Eating Disorders
Established in 2006 by Christopher Clark, M.A., N.A.M.E.D. is the only organization in the U.S. exclusively dedicated to representing and providing support to males with eating disorders.
https://namedinc.org/

National Eating Disorders Association
www.nationaleatingdisorders.org/help-support
Helpline (confidential and free): 1-800-931-2237

APR - - 2019.